FLAWED

RILEY EDWARDS

FLAWED
TRIPLE CANOPY
BOOK 2

RILEY EDWARDS

Cover design: Lori Jackson Designs

Cover Model: Michael Scanlon

Written by: Riley Edwards

Published by: Riley Edwards/Rebels Romance

Edited by: Rebecca Hodgkins

Proofreader: Julie Deaton, Rebecca Kendall

FLAWED

ISBN Print: 978-1-951567-13-2

First edition: December 1, 2020

To my family - my team – my tribe.
This is for you.

1

"Addy, I am not doing yoga," Trey griped.

"Starting next week, we're adding yoga," I returned.

"That's not happening."

I rolled my eyes to the ceiling and counted to five.

I should've counted to twenty *and* prayed for divine intervention.

Trey Durum had worked my last nerve and he'd only been on the mat for ten minutes out of his sixty-minute physical therapy session.

I gave up on the yoga argument and not-so-nicely ordered, "Stop talking and tighten your glutes and straighten your leg."

"Woman, I'm clenching my ass so tight I could crack a peanut."

"Not good enough. Think walnut and keep your leg straight."

I did my best to ignore Trey's growl of frustration, something that was getting harder and harder to do as the months slid by. A sound that sent shivers down my spine and made me curious if he made that noise while he was doing other things...naughty things. *Things* that I couldn't begin to imagine because a man like Trey was so far out of my league it wasn't even funny. My sexual experience paled in comparison to his and consisted of two partners and two positions—top and bottom.

"You're the devil," he groaned. "You have everyone snowed. They all think Adalynn Walker is a sweet angel."

"I am an angel," I retorted.

And that was the unfortunate truth. The reason why a man like Trey would never look twice at me. Why I was in my mid-twenties and I'd never had an orgasm, not even self-induced. I was the pathetic, shy twin. I was the little sister to three beautiful, outgoing, loud sisters. It was funny how Hadley and I were identical, yet she turned heads and I never had. When we walked into a room, I received a cursory glance, people did a double-take only because there were two of us, but it was Hadley everyone gravitated to.

Being the good one in the family had its perks. My dad was hugely protective—over-the-top insane with it. In other words, overbearing in a loving way, but he lorded over my sisters. I flew under his radar, so the few times I had broken the rules I hadn't been caught. But that also meant my life was boring with a capital B and two exclamation points to punctuate just how boring I was.

"And I am sweet to people I like," I added.

That wasn't the truth, I was pretty much sweet to everyone, even people who were jerks. There was enough negativity in the world without me adding to it.

"So what you're saying is you don't like me."

"Has anyone ever told you, you whine a lot?" I inquired. "Slowly lower your hips back to the mat and keep your—"

"Ass cheeks tight. I know."

"Glutes."

"You gotta problem with me saying ass cheeks, Addy?"

Yes. *Yes*, I did.

I had a huge issue keeping my mind where it

needed to be. Trey was my patient. I was his physical therapist. I didn't need to be thinking about his ass cheeks any more than I already did. I needed to be concentrating on rehabbing his leg, not falling in lust with a man who irritated the holy crap out of me. I didn't need to be fantasizing about what his muscular *ass* would feel like under my hands.

Glutes—not ass cheeks.

Was my face red? It felt red. No, it felt hot. *Gah.* I needed to stop thinking about his ass cheeks.

What the heck was wrong with me?

What exercise were we on? Gluteal. Yes, I needed him to finish the set and get him off the mat before I crawled on top of him like a crazy person in need of a happy ending.

"Hello? Earth to Addy."

"I'm not one of your bimbos," I snapped.

"Come again?"

"I said, I'm not one of your bimbos, Trey. You can drop the flirtatious grins and overdone charm."

His eyes narrowed to slits. He settled his butt on the mat and bent both of his legs so his feet were planted on the foam before he rolled up to a sitting position. I was on my knees next to him so the change brought us face-to-face.

"Tell me, Adalynn, when have I ever treated you like a bimbo?"

I couldn't think of a single situation where he had, so I remained silent.

"That's what I thought," he unhappily retorted.

"I was out of line," I admitted. "Sorry."

"What gives?"

"Gives?"

"Yeah, Addy. What the fuck?"

"What the frick, what?"

"Known you awhile now. Sweet as sugar to everyone but me. I come around and suddenly you have a stick up your ass and a dirty look on your face. I've thought on it and I can't for the life of me figure out what I could've done to make you hate me so much."

"I don't hate you."

"Coulda fooled me. Again, you got a smile for everyone but me. I see you with your other patients, you're smiling. Me, you're a DI."

I absolutely did not hate Trey. He annoyed me. He irritated me. He blew off his PT sessions, which pissed me off, but I didn't hate him. It was the opposite, I cared too much about him. If anyone else I worked with gave up on themselves the way Trey did,

I'd expend half the energy I did trying to get Trey on the right track. I wouldn't be annoyed, irritated, or pissed. I'd feel bad for them. I'd try to encourage them and help, but I wouldn't lie in bed at night and worry. I wouldn't let it bother me to the point of obsession.

"I don't hate you. But I do hate that you're not taking your rehab seriously and that's the difference between you and my other patients. It's frustrating when you allow your impatience to hinder your progress."

"Have you ever stopped to think that maybe it's frustrating to me that my body no longer works the way it used to? That it has nothing to do with patience and everything to do with the fact I will never be what I was."

I *had* thought about that. And as much as I could empathize with him, I still had full range of motion and use of my limbs, therefore I had no idea what it truly felt like not to.

Was I being too hard on him?

Heck no. He was a Navy SEAL for crying out loud, he'd been through tougher training than any PT exercises I could give him.

"Trey," I whispered. "I know I've been hard on you. But I know you're strong. You're a SEAL—"

"No, I'm not. I'm not shit, not anymore."

His icy stare chilled me to the bone and his anger flared.

There was the crux of Trey's issues. Not the first time I'd seen the signs, not even the first time he'd voiced them, yet I still couldn't find a way to help him. And that was the root of my problem. I needed to find a way to break through. To show him he had so much to be grateful for.

"I know you can do better if you stop thinking about what you no longer have and start being grateful for what you do have. You still have both your legs—"

"Great, I have both my legs," he snapped sarcastically, rolled to his hip, and started to get up.

My hand wrapped around his bicep, and the instant it did, Trey's face blanked. *What in the world?*

"I didn't—"

"You cannot begin to fathom what it means to lose yourself, so save your bullshit for some idiot that'll buy it."

"There's your problem. That's why you fail. You've talked yourself into believing you've lost something. You've made up your mind—"

"Right," he huffed out a humorless laugh. His beautiful green eyes glittered with anger and I braced for his ire. And boy, did he give it. "You, perfect Adalynn, don't know the first goddamn thing about losing. You and your perfect family, your perfect life, your perfect fucking parents." He jabbed a finger my way. "You don't get to tell me jackshit about what my problem is when you've never known anything but fucking perfect your whole coddled life."

He got to his feet and stared down at me and my heart lurched at the blatant, unmasked pain. There was way more going on with Trey than his bum leg. More than no longer being a SEAL. Something dark and ugly had crawled inside of him and I realized I would never break through. Not because I didn't want to, but because he'd never let me.

I got to my feet and mustered up all the courage I could find and said, "I think you need to find a new therapist."

I instantly regretted saying those words but it was the right thing to do. He needed more, better, someone with more experience.

"I think you're right."

With his carefully blank stare, he shook his head and turned. Three steps later he stopped, craned his neck, and looked back at me.

"So much for never giving up."

My heart seized and my temper flared.

"You can lie to yourself but we both know it's not me giving up, it's you."

"Funny, Adalynn—"

"There's not a damn thing funny about you giving up," I cut him off. "You wanna act like a jerk and turn this around on me, tell me all about my perfect life when you don't know crap about me, that's on you. But the truth is, you quit. You gave up. You're allowing whatever is inside of you, eating at you to win. So don't blame me, go home and look in the mirror."

"I would if I could stand the sight of myself."

With that parting shot, Trey walked across the empty gym and left me hollowed out.

Crap.

Logically, I knew Trey had to want to help himself, I knew I couldn't force him, I knew it had to be done on his time. But what my brain knew and what my heart felt were two different things.

I had totally failed him.

2

"Hey there, you want company?" The soft purr coming from the barstool next to me grated on my last nerve.

The woman was on my *good side*—never thought that would be something I ever thought about, nor had I ever considered which side of my face a woman saw first. The truth was, whichever side a woman approached from she'd always liked what she saw. But not now, and the woman standing next to me hadn't seen the shrapnel scars that marked my other cheek, temple, and neck.

The bitch was in for a rude surprise when I turned to fully face her.

"Sure, honey, what'd you have in mind?"

Three...two...one...and there it was—the flinch,

followed by the eye flare, and finally the poor attempt of a cover-up.

Oh, how things had changed. There had been a time when there was no flinch. There'd been blatant interest, the eye flare was open hunger, and women had never attempted to cover up shit. They liked me knowing they were available and up for a good time.

Now, I still got the lame pick-up lines, followed by this bullshit. I hadn't figured out which way I hated more. Both were annoying as fuck. There was nothing that turned me off faster than an aggressive woman. I was a man who enjoyed the chase however that chase came to be.

"Um..."

I took in the woman next to me—decent-looking, nice eyes, flawless pale skin, huge tits on display, tight jeans, and blonde hair. I didn't do blondes, they were high drama. I also avoided women who sought attention by showing skin. A man likes to be surprised, he enjoys the journey of uncovering the beauty of a woman's body.

The woman next to me left nothing to discover. It was in your face in hopes you'd like what you saw and want to take her for a test drive.

I'd had enough women in my bed to tell the difference between one I'd buy a drink and one I'd buy breakfast. The two were vastly different. Then there were the ones you did all you could to extradite yourself from their presence because they screamed desperate.

This woman screamed desperate, but not desperate enough to overlook my scars.

I should've been more grateful than I was that most women now left me to drink away my misery in peace. But it was hard to be grateful when every time a woman stared at my face I was reminded of how shallow people are.

It was on that thought, I faced forward, snagged my beer off the bar, and took a long pull. What I really wanted was a bottle of whiskey to chase away the bitterness of my argument with Adalynn. Actually, what I needed to do was stop thinking about the woman altogether.

But guilt churned in my gut.

God, I was an asshole.

"Well, do you?"

I slowly turned my head as the woman next to me stepped closer, so close her cheap pump-bottle perfume assaulted me and I choked back a cough. Christ, was that FDS? It was on the tip of my tongue to ask her when she pressed her tits against my shoulder. And being the asshole I was I tried to find it; I dug down deep and let my imagination run wild, tried my best to picture what those tits would look like bared to me. But blonde hair morphed into dark brown and once again my cock revolted and wouldn't even twitch.

Fucking Adalynn Walker had ruined me.

It had been months since I'd been laid and it had nothing to do with the marks on my face and everything to do with my dick no longer working when there was a real-life woman in front of me. It worked just fine when I was alone in my house and visions of Addy's pretty face came to mind. It was up and ready when I remembered the way she smiled at me when I first met her. I was beginning to think there was something physiologically wrong with me that the only way I could get an erection was when I thought about a woman who hated me.

"I'll pass."

"Seriously?" she whined.

"I've got plans," I lied.

"Seems to me that your plan's sitting here alone drinking," she rightly retorted.

"Like I said, I've got plans."

"Suit yourself." The woman shrugged and walked off.

There was something seriously fucking wrong

with me and I was beginning to think I'd hit my head harder than the doctors thought. That's the thing about being in close proximity to a bomb when it detonates—it destroys everything in the blast radius. My buddy Luke was nearly blind in his left eye, less than perfect vision in his right. Both of our careers in the Navy, gone. I was left with scars, almost lost my leg, and with welted, puckered skin across my back. I suppose I got lucky and the burns could've disfigured my face. But mostly I was left with disapproval and disappointment. The pride I used to see on my father's face had turned into censure. He didn't bother to hide his disgust when he looked at me. My younger brother the same. What used to be a healthy sibling rivalry had turned into something ugly and bitter.

"Damn, brother, that's what, the third one this week?" Matt said as he slid onto the stool next to me. "You're losing your touch."

I was losing something, all right, but it wasn't my touch—it was my goddamned mind.

"What are you doing here?" I glanced over at my friend.

"Came in to check on you."

"How the hell did you know I was here?"

"Went by your place, you weren't there, knew

you were here," Matt informed me, then went on, "Now, what's up with turning into Carter and going celibate all of a sudden?"

Carter Lenox was a teammate and close friend. He wasn't actually celibate, we'd just never seen him with a woman while we served in the Navy together. It wasn't until he left the teams we all found out he had a woman back home and he'd been in love with her since he was a kid. They were now married with a daughter.

I couldn't begin to imagine what it would be like to love someone so completely, all other women faded into the background. Hell, for Carter they didn't fade, they ceased to exist. I'd never even seen him eye one up, it was like his world revolved around Delaney. And the lucky son of a bitch had found a woman who returned that loyalty and love in spades.

"Exaggerate much?"

"Been out with you three times in the last seven days. Three times I've watched you send women on their way. Now, I admit, that's not new, but thinking on it, I haven't seen you take one home since we moved to Georgia."

I internally winced at his statement. It had been a long time and maybe that was part of why I couldn't stop thinking about Addy.

"Is there a reason you're concerned about who I'm fucking?"

"*Not* fucking," he corrected.

I drained the dregs of my beer and jerked my chin to the passing bartender.

"Another?"

"Jack and make it a double," I returned.

"That's telling," Matt mumbled.

I clenched my jaw and wondered how in the hell my life had come to this. There had been a time when no one commented on my drinking habits, no one kept track of where I chose to stick my dick, and no one cared about either.

"Why are you here?"

"Told you, I wanted to check on you."

"What—"

"You had PT today," he told me something I very well knew. "Also know you've been ditching it more than you've been going and Addy's losing her patience with you. The way I see it, one of these days shit's gonna finally blow."

He wasn't wrong. I had been dodging PT. But more, I'd been avoiding Adalynn.

"Then it's a good thing you no longer have to worry."

"Why's that?"

"She kicked me to the curb."

"You're full of shit."

"No, I'm not. She told me I needed to find another therapist."

The effort it took not to rub the ache in my chest was ridiculous. Part of why I was at the bar drowning my sorrows. I couldn't get the hurt that had flashed in her eyes out of my mind. I couldn't stop thinking about the way she'd looked at me when I acted like a dick. It was no wonder the woman hated me. Even me bringing it up to her and asking her why was an asshole thing to do.

I *knew* why.

I just didn't know why I couldn't stop myself from lashing out. When she turned those pretty green eyes my way, something inside of me cracked. Every damn time since the moment I first saw her. Adalynn was the last person I wanted to feel sorry for me. I didn't want her pity, I didn't want her to see me as a patient, I didn't want her to see how fucking broken I was. I wanted her to see me as a man. Like I used to be, strong and capable. Not this sad excuse.

The truth was I just plain wanted her with an unhealthy obsession that was beginning to seriously fucking worry me. She was all I thought about. Night and day. Day and night. And the worst damn part was I knew—she was the one woman in the world I wanted for a lifetime, the woman who would challenge me and complete me the way no one else ever would.

And I was a washed-up has-been.

Flawed. Broken. Wrecked.

I felt Matt's eyes boring into my skull. I didn't need to turn to know he was scowling at me. Further, I didn't need a lecture.

"Not in the mood to hear how I fucked up," I warned.

"How *did* you fuck up?"

"Don't want to talk about that either."

"One day, you're gonna have to sort your head. You have to let go—"

"I do, really, Matt? What exactly do I have to let go of?"

I heard the legs of the stool scrape on the floor before I felt Matt lean close.

"Everything," he grunted. "You've been so busy feeling sorry for yourself you missed it. So let me clue you the fuck in. You're not the only one struggling with the change. But you're the only one trying to hold on to the old days with an iron fist. You're the only one glorifying what we did, where we went, and the sacrifices we made. Not saying I regret a minute of it. I wouldn't change it and I'd do it again. But, brother, it fucking sucked, and if you'd pull your head out you'd remember. You've never been about ego, you've never been about being a *SEAL*—you were a team guy, a team player, and team leader. Now you're acting like a fucking *SEAL*, and, Trey, that shit ain't you. That's your dad and brother getting in your head. That's their bullshit, *you* did your time. *You* did it with honor. *You* served your country, not them. You. It's your life, not theirs, and if they're so fucking torn up they lost their bragging rights, that's their problem.

"But you're taking that on when you should be fucking grateful you have an opportunity to start over. You and I both could name at least a dozen men, good men, brothers, fathers, and sons who weren't so fucking lucky. Think about that as you sit here having your one-man pity party. Think about those mothers, wives, children, siblings, who wish their men came home with a few scars instead of in a pine box."

Matt stepped away but he wasn't done. "One last thing to think about—if we hadn't gone on that mission, where would Liberty be? Your face would be as pretty as ever, your back clean of burns, your dad still up-your-ass happy, you'd still be in the Navy, but that woman would be dead."

When Matt was done hurling insults, he turned and strolled out of the bar.

Fuck. Fuck. Fuck!

I sat in silence and drained my Jack. I did this thinking I was a selfish prick full of ego and self-pity.

Now you're acting like a fucking SEAL.

I damn well was and it fucking sucked having to admit to yourself you'd turned into someone you didn't like very much. All of my years on the teams I'd never acted like a douchebag SEAL, I was a member of a team. There was a distinct difference between the two. SEALs loved to brag they were a SEAL. A Team Guy was all about the team, the job, the mission, the important work they did—there was no ego involved.

Now I was crying in my soup and moping around because...why? I wasn't a SEAL anymore? Because my dad was a fucking jackass and had made me feel worthless? Or was it because I no longer had a purpose?

I tossed cash on the bar, got up, and glanced across the room at the blonde. Her back was to me, her ass encased in tight jeans, and I gave it two beats —taking her in, trying to find some sort of interest.

Nothing.

Not a damn twinge.

Blonde turned into shiny dark brown and I knew I was more fucked than I was ready to admit.

Goddamn, Adalynn Walker.

3

"What happened with Trey?" my sister Hadley asked over the phone.

My step faltered and my purse slid down my arm. I shifted, caught the strap in the crook of my elbow, and fumbled the high-density foam roller, recovering the cylinder before I dropped it. I did all of that as I balanced my phone between my shoulder and my ear.

I did *not* want to talk to Hadley about Trey. Actually, I didn't want to talk about Trey to anyone. It had been nearly a week since our blow-out, and in those six days, all I'd thought about was him. Would he find another therapist? Would he continue his PT? Was he okay? Why did I care? Why couldn't I get his wounded, vulnerable expression out of my mind? Did I give up on him? And again, why in the heck did I care?

"I'm late, Hadley, I don't have time to get into this."

"You're not late. You're never late. It's five after ten which means your first session doesn't start until eleven."

Of course she'd know that; I was Addy Walker, the predictable one. The boring one. The one who lived by a carefully timed schedule.

"It's five after ten, which means I'm five minutes late," I told her and stopped ten feet away from the double, sliding glass doors of the veterans' affairs building I worked at two days a week.

"Addy," she snapped, frustrated.

"Hadley," I returned just as irritated.

This was the point in our conversation that, had we been face-to-face and not on the phone, my twin would've initiated a staredown. Instead, silence befell but that didn't mean I couldn't picture her pinched lips and creased forehead. A disapproving look she'd perfected over the years. A look she gave me when I declined to go out with her and her friends for a night of shenanigans. It was a variation of the one she gave me when I did agree to go out yet turned down invitations to dance with random guys who approached our table.

Hadley was the fun one. I was the shy, cautious, lame twin.

"Can we please not talk about this?" I broke the silence when it became evident Hadley had nothing better to do than wait me out.

"I'll drop it if you promise to call me later and tell me."

"That's not dropping it, that's postponing it."

"Fine," she huffed. "I'll postpone the conversation if you promise to call me on your way home and tell me what happened. Trey's miserable and being bitchy to the guys at work and he won't even look at me. I know *I* didn't do anything to him, which makes me think he doesn't want to see me because when he does he sees you."

I didn't need to know that.

I also had to get into the gym and set up for my class.

"What Trey is going through has nothing to do with me. Besides, I haven't seen him since last Thursday."

"Thursday? It's Wednesday. Is he ditching PT again? I thought you saw him—"

"I told him he needed to find a new therapist."

"You did what?" Hadley screeched, and I wished my arms weren't full so I could've pulled my phone away from my ear. Unfortunately, I didn't have that option so I almost went deaf when she continued on in a high-pitched squeal, "Why would you do that, Adalynn?"

"Like you said, he blows off his sessions more than he shows. Obviously, he doesn't take his PT seriously. He needs to find someone who can motivate him. We're not a good fit."

"You're a perfect fit," she argued.

"Don't go there, Hads. He and I don't mix well. He doesn't respect me or my time. A man like him needs to be pushed, and let's just say he made it clear I was not the right person for the job."

"What'd he say?"

"I don't have time to talk about it. Heck, I don't want to talk about it. He'll find someone new. In the meantime, the guys will have to suck it up and deal with him. I'm sorry he's avoiding you, but that's not my problem either."

"Are you okay?"

"Hadley! I have to go."

"Fine. Call me when you're done."

"I'm busy."

"Liar, liar pants on fire."

I rolled my eyes at my sister's juvenile response, then looked back at the doors to the VA. I was indeed late and I had to get my immature sister off the phone.

"You're so annoying."

"I know. But you love me. Talk to you later."

Hadley disconnected, I juggled the load in my arms, and grabbed my phone off my shoulder. I was in the midst of trying to adjust my purse while simultaneously thinking about what in the world I had in my bag that was so heavy, when I heard my name called and scanned the courtyard for a familiar face. Not seeing one, I figured I was hearing things and started for the door when I heard my name again, this time louder, closer, and I glanced over my shoulder to find a man in uniform ambling my way.

"Addy?" he inquired and stopped a few feet away.

Out of habit, my eyes hit the soldier's front closure of his jacket to check rank—three chevrons—a sergeant. Then my gaze traveled to his name tape and I froze.

Belview.

Jake Belview.

"Jake?"

"I thought that was you," he returned.

I really, *really* wished I hadn't taken my sister's call. If I hadn't, I would've been in the tiny office I shared with three other PTs and not standing in front of my ex-boyfriend.

"It's me," I lamely returned, not knowing what else to say to the guy who broke my heart.

Jake glanced at the foam roller, likely took in my workout clothes, and smiled.

"You did it."

I didn't need him to elaborate. When we were together, I'd told him all about how I'd wanted to become a physical therapist. Further, he knew my desire to help wounded vets.

"I did." I tried and failed to return his smile.

His grin faded and his expression turned guarded.

"Addy, listen—"

Oh, no, I wasn't listening to anything he had to say. He'd said enough when he dumped me before he left for deployment. Something I didn't want. I grew up an army brat. I understood the hardships and I'd been willing to stick it out. Jake on the other hand was adamant it wouldn't work. His rejection hurt and had shaped how I viewed relationships.

So, heck no, I didn't want to listen. I wanted to get to work.

"Whatever you're gonna say is unnecessary. It was a long time ago."

Yet in the years Jake had been gone, I hadn't recovered. Not that I still had feelings for him—I was way over *him.* But I'd never gotten over the sting of him callously tossing me aside.

"Honey, the way you're looking at me says otherwise. I think there's a lot to say."

"I'm late for a session, Jake."

"Let me buy you lunch when you're done."

"I don't—"

"Just lunch, Addy. Please. I owe you an apology and an explanation."

"You really don't."

"There's not much I regret, but leaving you the way I did is at the top of that list. I'm asking you to please let me buy you lunch. It would mean a lot to me if I could explain what was going on."

It was obvious Jake wasn't going to let lunch go, and now I was seriously late. On that thought, I gave in.

"My session's over at noon."

Jake gave me a small smile and said, "I'll be in the lobby."

"Okay," I agreed.

I didn't bother returning Jake's half-hearted grin,

I didn't bid him a farewell or nice seeing you. I wasn't trying to be rude, but seeing my ex wasn't a pleasant surprise and he had to know that.

I rushed through the maze of hallways until I reached the far corner of the building and pushed into the physical therapy room. There were men and women on various exercise machines, some were stretching on the mat, others were being spotted by trainers. I glanced around and didn't see anyone from my class so I went into the office and dropped my stuff on the desk I used. The desk wasn't mine, I shared it with three others, but luckily I was alone in the office. With twenty minutes to spare, I plopped down in the chair and exhaled.

It would take a lot more than yoga and meditation today to clear my mind.

Thoughts of Trey and Jake battled for supremacy in my head. Two men, neither of them welcomed thoughts. Both of them had hurt me. But it was Trey who cut deeper.

You've never known anything but fucking perfect your whole coddled life.

Trey was right, I had been coddled. But not in a bad way—I'd been loved and protected and I wouldn't feel guilty about that. I had a great family. I had parents who were involved, present, and understanding. I had aunts and uncles who were the same. I had cousins and siblings who all bickered and argued but loved fiercely.

But my life hadn't been perfect. Far from it. My family knew pain, we knew hardship. However, when we hit trouble we stuck together and fought our way through.

Walkers didn't quit.

Yet, I had. I quit Trey when he needed help.

My dad would be disappointed in me. Heck, I was disappointed in myself.

AFTER TEACHING AN HOUR-LONG YOGA SESSION, I was in no more of a mood to have lunch with Jake than I was before class. I'd tried my best to relax into the poses and find my center. Nothing worked, I couldn't stop thinking about Trey and what Hadley told me. I'd been hasty and had reacted poorly to Trey's insults. I should've called it a day, called my dad, and sought guidance. Or alternately, I could've reached out to any of my uncles or to one of the VA counselors. Instead, I allowed him to hurt my feelings, then I'd dismissed him.

Now I had to endure lunch with Jake and listen to him dredge up a past I didn't want to remember.

I saw Jake before he saw me and it gave me the opportunity I hadn't had when he'd surprised me earlier. He'd changed a lot in the years since I'd seen him last. He'd lost all of his boyish good looks, and now he stood straighter, taller, alert. It was an assumption of course, and perhaps an unfair judgment, but taking in the hard set of his jaw I'd guess he's lost more than his boyish good looks—he'd lost something more important.

As if sensing my approach, his gaze cut to me, and right before my eyes Jake stowed the angry blank stare and smiled.

Yeah, he lost something big. And I didn't like how easy it was for him to mask his emotions.

Crap. I didn't want to have lunch with him.

"Addy. I wasn't sure if you'd stand me up."

I wish I had it in me to be rude.

"Sorry to keep you waiting, I needed to sign off on some paperwork."

And I needed time to push Trey out of my head.

"No worries. I'm here the rest of the day. Sprouts okay?"

Sprouts was a café across the street.

"Perfect. Do you want to walk?"

Something flashed across his face but it was so quick I couldn't read it.

"If you don't—"

"Walking's fine." He nodded to the door. I hitched my bag higher on my shoulder and Jake frowned. "Do you want me to carry that?"

"My purse?"

"It looks heavy."

Maybe I'd been quick to judge; it seemed there was still a bit of the old Jake left in him.

"It's fine. Besides, you're in uniform and if I remember correctly it's against regs for you to carry my purse."

"Jefferson was an ass," he remarked, referring to Command Master Sergeant Jefferson who had reamed Jake's behind for being in his dress uniform and carry my purse, backpack, and laptop.

"He totally was." I smiled at the memory.

"There you are," Jake whispered.

"What?"

"I'd forgotten how beautiful you are when you smile." My shoulders tensed at his compliment, but before I could respond, he continued, "Let's get out of here."

We filled the short walk across the street with small talk—how much the area had changed since he'd been stationed there. Me graduating from college and moving out of my parents' house. He was surprised to hear that Hadley and I had opted to live separately but he understood why, and he would because when we were together we'd talked about how I'd always felt over-shadowed by my twin. Not that Hadley did it on purpose or with malice but the differences in our personalities leaned toward her being in the spotlight and me fading into the background.

By the time we made it to Sprouts, I was feeling guilty for wanting to bag on lunch. There was more to Jake than the last week of our relationship. He'd been a good listener, he was kind, and he'd gone to great lengths to be gentle with me.

When he pulled out my chair, my attitude softened, and when he took the seat across from me and ran his fingers through his hair complaining about "hat hair" I was reminded how good-looking he was. I'd been right, there was no boy left in him. Jake was all man.

"What are you doing at the VA?" I inquired and started to look down but paused when I saw the same twitch in his cheek I had back in the lobby. But being the seasoned military professional, a beat later it was gone and I was questioning if I'd even seen it.

"My unit's just getting back from deployment. Routine debrief and psych evals."

His tone left no room for further questions. Though I had plenty.

I looked to his right sleeve and noted the American flag patch but no special forces, sapper, airborne, or ranger tabs. Then I looked above the U.S. ARMY tape stitched on his left breast and there was no occupation patch. Nothing on his uniform gave away his MOS. The only thing I knew was he was a sergeant.

"Do you enjoy working at the VA?" he asked.

"I do. I only work there two days a week. I also work at a sports rehab center. But I like working with our warriors more than the rehab center. They tend to whine less."

Unless their name is Trey. Then they complained and whined more than the athlete who pulled a muscle.

My attempt at levity fell short but Jake still chuckled.

There was an uncomfortable silence as we looked over the menu. By the time the waiter came to take our order, I was rethinking lunch.

Something about Jake was off. There was some indication the guy I'd once been in love with was still there but he was now encased in steel. But that wasn't what was off, it was something more than that. Something simmering below the surface.

"You wanted to talk," I prompted.

"Adalynn Walker, never one to procrastinate," Jake said, his voice dripping with sarcasm.

That was me. I lived by the motto "cinch by the inch, trial by the mile" therefore I didn't dally when something needed to get done or be said. I didn't like things stacking up and weighing me down. So far, the way I lived my life had served me well, but his tone told me he didn't like it.

There was nothing to say to his comment so I remained quiet and waited him out.

"Addy," he started and sighed. "I'm sorry. I didn't mean to offend you."

"You didn't," I lied.

"Honey, you know you have a shit poker face. I'm just nervous and don't know how to start."

Well, at least he's being honest.

"Why don't you start with why you wanted to have lunch with me?"

A beat of silence stretched to darn near a minute before he finally spoke.

"I don't like how I left."

Neither did I, but we couldn't rewind time. "There's—"

"I knew my deployment was going to be longer than six months and I couldn't tell you that. I knew I'd have no communication with anyone back home and I couldn't tell you that either. I didn't want you waiting for me thinking I'd ghosted you. I was stuck. Either I had to let you go or leave and let you think I was ignoring you."

"Why couldn't you tell me?"

"Addy, you know why."

I did know why, my dad and uncles had all been in the Army. There had been times when my dad had left in the middle of the night to whereabouts unknown for an undisclosed period of time. But my dad was Special Forces. Jake was in the regular Army. The two were vastly different. He could've told me, he simply chose not to, but I wasn't going to press it. There was no purpose; we'd been broken up for a long time and there was no reason to rehash the past.

"I wasn't regular Army, then or now," he said as if he pulled my thoughts from my mind.

"What?"

"I wasn't infantry, Addy."

My irritation spiked and I leaned forward. "You lied to me?"

"I lied to everyone. My family still doesn't know what I do."

"What *do* you do?"

"Can't tell you that."

Irritation turned to anger and I took a breath to clear my thoughts. Then I took another and another but it didn't work. I was pissed.

"Then why'd you bring it up? Why am I even here? So you can tell me you lied to me? Great. Thanks for the info."

"I wanted to explain why I broke up with you. I didn't *want* to. I didn't *want* to leave you. I was in love with you. I thought about you every day I was gone. And when I finally made it home, there were so many times I wanted to reach out. But I knew the same thing would happen. We'd connect, then I'd have to leave and the cycle would start all over."

"You do remember who my dad is, right? You do know I am well acquainted with how the Army works —both regular and Special Forces. So don't give me that crap. I grew up in a military family. One I am proud of and respect. I am fully aware of operational security and when I was with you, I was willing to stand by your side and wait. You wouldn't've had to tell me how long you were going to be gone, you wouldn't've had to tell me where you were going. All you would've had to say was 'Addy, I'm going dark and I'll be home when I can' and I would've known what that meant and I wouldn't have asked a damn question and you know it."

Jake's face had changed during my soliloquy. He'd gone from pale to red and finally to furious.

"I wasn't supposed to come home."

I froze and tried to process his statement. Surely he wasn't saying what I thought he was saying. The Army didn't send units out on suicide missions. Dangerous, yes. Risky, absolutely. But certain death —no way.

"Jake—"

"If I'd thought for one second I'd be coming home I would've found a way to keep you. But I didn't. Another reason I had to let you go. I didn't want our reunion to be held at a cemetery with me in a pine box hosted by the U.S. government." Then his face screwed up into a nasty scowl and he finished with, "And trust me, I haven't forgotten who your father is."

Hold on a minute.

"What's that mean?"

"It means Jasper Walker's a hard man to follow. Especially if he blocks the way."

What in the world is he talking about?

"Now, what does *that* mean?"

"It means just that. No man will ever be as perfect as him. No man will live up to Jasper Walker. In your eyes, no man will ever love you like he does. And in his eyes, he thinks he knows what's best for *everybody*."

Hell no. Fuck no.

"That's bullshit. I never compared you to my father—"

"You compared me to him every day!" he roared and I jumped. "And when you weren't, everyone else was. The great Jasper fucking Walker."

The chair legs sounded as they scraped on the floor. I felt my chair being pulled back but I didn't take my eyes off Jake. Not even when I lost his gaze and it went over my shoulder.

It wasn't shock that kept me tethered to him. It was fear.

Jake Belview was a man undone.

4

I'd been sitting across the café for fifteen minutes when it happened. At first, I'd thought it was my shitty luck I'd see Addy out on a date. It had taken extreme effort not to stare at the couple. But out of the corner of my eye, I could see her. Hell, if I was being truthful, I felt her discomfort from across the room. But it wasn't until she leaned forward and scowled that I put my sandwich down and pushed my plate aside.

Something was not right.

And a few minutes later, I was proved correct when the guy sitting opposite her slammed his fists on the table and yelled at her. His words rumbled throughout the small restaurant but I couldn't make them out over my fury.

I was out of the booth and behind Addy before she could get out of her seat. Then she was behind me clutching onto my hips. The asshole who'd yelled at her knocked his chair over in his haste to stand.

"I suggest you move—"

"Do not speak," I cut him off. "Addy, baby, you okay?" I felt Addy nod against my back but I didn't take my eyes off the dickhead in front of me. So I witnessed the man turn from hostile to homicidal.

"Sir, I'm going to have to ask you to leave," the manager tentatively said, obviously reading the situation correctly and having no desire to wade in, but his job necessitated him to.

"We're not done talking, Adalynn," the dickhead said.

"Actually, you are done," I corrected.

"You have no idea who I am," Dickhead snarled.

My gaze dropped to his name tab then to his rank insignia.

Sergeant Belview.

The name meant nothing to me.

"I don't need to know who you are to tell you if you come near Addy again you'll be spending the last years of your life breathin' from a tube."

"Big threat coming from a pretty boy."

"Sir. I'm gonna have to call the police—"

The manager's words died quick, fast, and in a hurry when Belview turned and scowled.

"I heard you the first time," Dickhead snapped. He turned back to me but what he was really trying to do was get a look at Addy. Luckily, her small frame wasn't visible. "We're not done, Addy."

Fuck this.

My forward motion was halted when Addy's hands slid from my hips and went around my waist and she pressed her chest to my back and held on for dear life. Dickhead didn't miss her gesture nor did he hide his revulsion.

"I see, you prefer some scarred-up punk to a real man. Thought you were worth it. But you and your daddy issues aren't worth shit. Never were. Best thing I did was getting shot of you."

Addy squeezed my middle in a silent plea for me not to reply. It was needless, I was smart enough to ignore the pissant and wait for him to burn himself out. As long as Addy wasn't in physical danger, the idiot could shout the place down and make himself look like a fool.

I also wasn't dumb enough to make my move in front of witnesses. No, that'd come later after I figured out who this jackass was and why he thought he had brass balls.

"Sucker," he muttered and jogged away.

The manager righted the chair and asked us to leave as well. It wasn't worth explaining that neither of us had done anything wrong. I simply pulled out my wallet, dropped a few twenties on the table, and tucked Addy to my side as we made our way through the café.

When we hit the sidewalk I scanned the area, grateful there wasn't a crush of people so it was easy to see the guy was gone.

"Where are you parked?"

"The VA."

"I'll walk you—"

"No!"

"Addy, you're not walking to your car alone."

"Jake's at the VA."

"Jake?"

"The guy. His name is Jake. He's at the VA. Or he had an appointment there, so he's probably parked over there."

Sergeant Jake Belview.

"All right, we'll go to my truck."

Addy nodded, and without argument, stayed tucked close.

My jaw clenched at her easy acceptance. This was not Adalynn Walker. She didn't silently follow orders, especially not from me. She certainly would never allow me to hold her.

Motherfucker.

There was a massive difference between shy and spineless. Addy was shy but she was no doormat.

Unless she's shit scared.

There were a plethora of reasons why I wanted to throat punch Jake. Scaring Addy was at the top of that list. Shouting at her and insulting her only a notch down—a small, minute notch.

We got to my truck, I beeped the locks, helped her in the passenger side, and rounded the tailgate. It wasn't until my ass was planted in my seat that I finally asked, "Who was that guy?"

Addy's head turned to the side window. Having her in profile, I saw one side of her mouth tip down before she pinched her lips.

I'd seen Addy smile, I'd seen her frown, I'd seen her happy, and I'd seen her pissed at me. But I'd never seen her unsure and scared.

Fucking dick.

"Babe, look at me."

She shook her head and answered, "My ex."

What she didn't do was look at me. She also didn't elaborate.

I thought back over the months I'd known her.

No one had mentioned she had a man and she'd certainly never mentioned him.

"How long has he been giving you trouble?"

I couldn't imagine Jasper, her brother, or one of her many male cousins not handling the jackass, which meant she'd kept the ex from her family. That was unlike Addy—she was open, she shared, she was close to all of them.

"I haven't seen Jake in years."

That made more sense, but she still wasn't giving me anything.

"Baby, I don't wanna sit here and pull every detail from you. Explain to me what just happened."

"So don't."

"Come again?"

"So don't sit here and try to get the details."

"Addy—"

"Don't, Trey. Don't pretend you care. I appreciate you coming over to the table but let's leave it at that."

"You think I don't care?"

"I know you don't."

What the fuck? My neck got tight as I stared at her staring out the window. Again, what the fuck? Why would she think I didn't care some dick was harassing her?

"You don't know shit."

I instantly regretted my biting tone when her head whipped to the side and she squinted her pretty green eyes.

"Really, I don't? I know you think I'm coddled. You think I lead a perfect life. I know you avoid me, you don't take me seriously, you don't like me, you—"

"I never said I didn't like you and I never said I didn't care about you," I interrupted.

But I'd said some pretty screwed-up things to her and she remembered. Of course she would, I'd behaved like an ass and hurt her feelings.

"You have a funny way of showing someone you like them."

Goddammit!

"Did you ever think maybe I wasn't avoiding *you*? I was avoiding PT."

"You made it clear you didn't think you needed to continue PT."

"No, Adalynn, I made it clear I was a prick who had his head up his ass. I avoided PT because I didn't want to *work* with you, not because I didn't need it. And not because I didn't want to see you."

Her face fell, and to my absolute horror, tears pooled in her eyes.

"I see—"

"No, baby, you don't, and I'm not explaining it right because I'm still being a prick." After the afternoon she'd had, the shit that fuckwad had served her she hadn't shed a tear, yet my stupid ass had made her cry.

With that in mind, I took a breath and gave her the truth. "I avoided PT with you because I didn't want you to see how screwed-up I am. I wanted you to see me a different way—not as a patient, not my injury, not my scars."

"I don't understand."

She wouldn't because she didn't go to bed thinking about me the way I did her. She had no clue I didn't want to spend time with her in the gym on a mat. I wanted her in my room on my bed. I wanted her under me, not overseeing my recovery.

"I know you don't, Addy. I didn't mean to hurt your feelings. As you pointed out, I'm struggling with remembering what I have. I've been so caught up in what I lost I allowed it to shade the many things I have to be grateful for. It's an uncomfortable realization when the light bulb clicks on and you see you've turned into a person you don't like. I'm sorry I said that shit to you. It was uncool of me to take my frustration out on you. But I want you to know, I respect you, I respect the work you do, you're good at it, and me ditching our sessions was about my ego, not your ability."

"Have you found someone new?"

"No."

"You need to," she murmured. "You've worked hard. It would be a shame to waste your efforts."

My hands shook with the desire to touch her. She was so close, it would be easy to reach across and unclasp her hands and take them in mine. It'd be just as easy to hook her around the neck and pull her closer and take her mouth. Either option would be good, but one would be phenomenal.

"Do you get what I'm saying to you?"

She nodded in the affirmative, but considering she hadn't jumped out of my truck and run a mile, I doubted she truly understood what I was saying. If she knew how I felt and the filthy things I'd dreamt of doing to her, she'd flee.

"Then you get I care. What happened back there was whacked in a way that's not just fucked because he said some seriously stupid shit, but in a way, that means he's dangerous. Straight up, Addy, there's something wrong with that guy and I didn't like the way he was looking at you."

Her eyes drifted shut and she exhaled before she reopened them. Sadness shone.

"A long time ago, Jake broke up with me."

That alone was proof positive this Jake guy was a complete moron. Adalynn Walker was not a woman you broke up with. She was the type of woman you tied yourself in knots to make happy.

"Why'd he break up with you?"

"He was leaving on deployment." Addy stopped and lowered her eyes. I sensed she had more to say so I stayed quiet and waited her out. A few beats later she said, "At the time, I didn't understand. I thought everything was good, so when he broke up with me, it hurt. I didn't see what the big deal was about him going on deployment. I mean, I come from a military family. When Jake and I got together, I knew it was a possibility and I didn't care. I was willing to wait for him. He was of a different mind so he made it clear we were over."

I didn't like the way that sounded and fought to keep my body relaxed. Addy was freaked out enough, the last thing she needed was witnessing me losing my shit.

"How'd he make that clear?"

Her gaze shifted to the side and she quietly answered, "Two days after he broke up with me, I went by his barracks. He was leaving the next day. I thought I had one more shot at getting him back. But *he* didn't answer."

The "he" was emphasized in a way that told me someone had answered.

"Who did?"

Addy shrugged but the hurt that raced across her face nullified her nonchalance.

"Some blonde wrapped up in a sheet. I was still standing at the door speechless when Jake came out of the bathroom wearing nothing but a towel. He looked at me, glanced at the woman then smiled. I was still too stunned to move. Jake however was not, he came to the door and asked me what I'd expected. When I didn't answer, he explained he was leaving the next day and hadn't had a decent fuck in months. That's when I came unstuck and left."

Jesus Christ, the asshole was stupider than I'd thought.

"Adalynn—"

"I forgot that part," she whispered.

"What part?"

"The part where I gave him my virginity and he threw it in my face. The part where he humiliated me. Today when I saw him, I was so surprised, I didn't remember. I'd shoved it down deep so I'd forget. When I agreed to go to lunch with him, I didn't remember how I felt standing there mortified and hurt."

Irrational jealousy reared and my chest tightened. Addy had given that asshole her virginity. What the fuck was wrong with that douchebag?

"Baby, listen to me—"

"He was right, he hadn't had a decent fuck in months."

There were so many things wrong with what she'd said—most importantly was her thinking he was right about *anything*. Next up was her cursing. Addy very rarely cussed, and hearing her say fuck in reference to sex made my stomach roil. A man didn't fuck Addy, he made love to her. It might not be sweet and gentle but in no way would it be fucking.

"He was not right about anything."

Something ugly filled the cab of my truck and it was coming from Addy. The sadness in her eyes had evaporated but something worse took its place —shame.

What the fuck?

"Baby—"

"He *was* right. It was bad. I was bad. I didn't know what I was doing and it was awkward. I was a fumbling twenty-year-old virgin for God's sake. It was pathetic and embarrassing."

"Addy—"

"And you wanna know how I know he was right?" she asked, and my gut clenched tighter. Before I could tell her I absolutely did not want to hear more, she answered her own question. "I couldn't even have an orgasm."

Jesus.

I didn't want to hear this.

"And, that's not all. It was the same exact way with the second guy, only worse. It was horrible. Beyond awkward and embarrassing."

I'd heard enough.

"Adalynn—"

"So after that, why bother trying again? It's obviously me. I'm shit in bed and—"

Yeah, I'd heard enough about her being with other men. Jealousy didn't cover the emotion that was coursing through my muscles.

"Enough," I ground out and Addy jerked in her seat. "Straight up, Adalynn, neither of those idiots knew what the fuck they were doing."

"You can't know that."

"Yeah, Addy, I can and I do. They were shit in bed, not you."

"You're wrong," she muttered.

I lost the battle. I'd fought hard, but I'd lost the

last thread of my control. My hand shot out, hooked Addy around the back of her neck, and I pulled her toward me as I shifted closer. I didn't stop until our mouths were touching. It took a moment for the shock to wear off and some of the stiffness to ease. When it did, I made another decision, although at the time I didn't understand the enormity of my next move. I took advantage of her surprise and licked the seam of her lips. Her mouth opened, my tongue slid inside, and she purred.

It was the mew that vibrated against my tongue that spurred me on. It was the innocence of the sound that clinched the deal.

Addy tasted great. Smelled great. Felt great.

All of it so fucking good. I slanted my head and took the kiss deeper. She purred again and this time, her hands moved and shoved under my tee. My hand slid up into her hair. Soft. So damn soft. I let my fingers glide through the strands before I gathered a fistful and tilted her head where I wanted it. It'd been so caught up in the way her tongue felt against mine it hadn't dawned on me, she didn't have the first clue what she was doing.

Real. Unpracticed. Inexperienced.

Once she'd relaxed, she let me take over.

Jesus. Perfect.

I wanted more so I took it. And she gave—her sweet, sexy sounds filled my senses, her hands roaming my chest fueled my need, but it was the way she openly gave that ratcheted up my desire. Unable to take the kiss where I wanted it to go, I slowed the kiss and she whimpered.

Christ.

Hot.

I let our tongues linger, slow and soft until I broke the connection and kissed the corner of her mouth.

Addy's eyes came open—dazed and languid. I released her hair but only so I could cup her cheek.

"Proof," I whispered.

"Huh?"

"Baby. That kiss."

"What about it?"

"Proof you're wrong."

She tried to pull away but I'd been ready and held her where I wanted. Face-to-face, so she couldn't miss what I had to say.

"Adalynn, there's no disputing you're gorgeous. You see yourself in the mirror so you gotta know you're beautiful. What happened with those other guys wasn't your fault, not by a long shot. Either they had no clue how to handle a woman or they didn't bother to try. Two seconds into that kiss, you melted into me and it became seriously fucking hot."

"Don't patronize me."

Christ. If I wasn't ready to come in my pants, I would've hunted Jake the dickhead down and bashed his skull in for making Addy unsure.

I snagged one of Addy's hands, pulled it out of my shirt, and lowered it to my crotch.

"Does that feel like I'm being patronizing?" I asked and cupped my hand over hers. "I'm not blowing sunshine when I tell you, you can fuckin' kiss, Addy. Not only that, but I can't remember the last time I was ready to come in my jeans from a kiss."

"Trey—"

"You ready for the truth?"

She nodded. Again, it was doubtful Addy was ready to hear anything I had to say. But after that kiss, everything had changed.

"If we weren't in my truck in a parking lot, I'd further prove to you how sexy you are, and you can believe when you're in my bed you will have no problem orgasming." Her hand resting on my hard cock flexed and I froze. "And, Adalynn, you will be in my bed."

"I don't think that's a good idea," she said, but didn't loosen the grip she had on my erection.

"Then it's a good thing when I get you there, you won't be able to think. Once I have my hands and mouth on you, all you'll care about is how good I make you feel. How sexy you are and how I respond to you. Contrary to what women think, a man's cock doesn't get hard unless he's seriously into what he's doing. At least mine doesn't. And as you can feel, my cock's hard, baby, and *you* did that. As I said, we weren't in my truck, my hand would be down your pants, and I would put forth a good amount of effort and time to make sure what you were getting got you off."

Her response told me everything I needed to know. Her hand on my cock moved, but not to pull away—to rub. Her hand on my chest moved, too, and glided down toward the button of my jeans.

"Trey." She whispered my name and I took it in.

The breathy sound full of need.

Hot.

But I needed to shut this shit down before I finger-fucked her in a parking lot while she jerked me off.

I caught her hand and shook my head. Addy

blinked and I knew she was coming out of her lust-filled haze.

"I said my *bed*, baby."

"Right."

It wasn't her retort that concerned me, it was the way she'd gone stiff.

"Listen to me carefully. I am not turning down your offer to get your hand down my pants. I'm simply telling you I have more respect for you than to allow this to continue in public."

Shit. I was losing her to the bullshit those two other asswipes had planted in her head.

"Don't close down on me."

"I'm not," she said, but her hand slid away from my cock and I lost her hand on my chest.

"Ad—"

"This isn't a good idea."

I didn't bother responding, not verbally anyway.

This time when I lowered my mouth to hers, I didn't have to coax her to open. And I didn't have to direct it or deepen the kiss. Adalynn did that herself, proving irrevocably it was a really great fucking idea.

5

I did not call my sister when I got home. I did not start my laundry as I had planned. I also didn't pay my bills, which was on my to-do list. I did, however, text Hadley so she'd stop blowing up my phone. And I did think about the fact that there had been a time when Hadley had hated her cell and very rarely carried it with her or answered. For a nanosecond, I wished she'd go back to that. Then I remembered the reasons why she now had her cell surgically attached to her person. Not literally of course, but Brady had drilled it into her, and getting kidnapped had hammered home how important keeping her cell close was.

But right then, I didn't want to talk about Trey. I didn't want to think about how awkward I'd behaved after Trey kissed me and how I'd stared at him for so long he'd had to call my name twice to break the spell. I really didn't want to contemplate the quick but silent drive back to the VA. And I really, *really* didn't want to remember how I'd jumped out of his truck when he'd stopped next to my car. I practically ran the five feet to the driver's side door and threw myself into my car.

God. I must've looked ridiculous. I hadn't even said goodbye.

How embarrassing.

So, right then, I didn't want to talk to my sister or think about how big of an idiot I was.

I wanted to do something else.

I was headed back to my bedroom so I could alleviate the ache Trey had created, when there was a knock on my door.

I was going to strangle my nosy sister.

I stomped to the front door annoyed beyond belief. Then I stopped and smiled.

So, this was what it felt like? Never had I been so worked up I felt like I was going to scream in frustration if I didn't take care of it. Never had I felt the urge to touch or be touched in a parked truck. We'd been in public, for God's sake. But I had been ready to...I still wasn't sure what I'd been willing to do but

I'd been so caught up in the moment it felt like I was going to die if I didn't get my hands on Trey's dick.

There was another knock at the door and I wanted to laugh. I was actually pissed I was being interrupted. I finished my short walk to the door and checked the peephole—one could never be too careful even when their panties were wet and they were on a mission of masturbation.

What in the world?

"What's wrong?" I asked when I opened the door to a scowling Trey.

His hand came up, landed on my chest, and he gave me a gentle shove back. When he was inside, he slammed the door, locked it, then stared at me.

"What's..." That was all I got out before Trey advanced. I retreated and he moved with me.

"You've got two seconds to tell me to leave."

"What?"

"Two seconds to stop this, Adalynn. You want me to leave, you say the word and I'll walk out the door. You don't, baby, you'll be naked in your bed, I'll be naked, and my face is gonna be between your legs."

"Trey."

"One second. No joke. In one second, I'm getting you out of those clothes, then I'm getting you off."

Suddenly my mission of masturbation didn't sound as satisfying as it did a few minutes ago.

"Time's up, baby."

This time when he advanced, I didn't move. Somewhere in the back of my mind, I was doing cartwheels, but nervousness took over. Trey saw it, so when his arm wrapped around me he held my gaze. And when his other hand came up, his thumb gently brushed my jaw but didn't stop until his fingers were in my hair. He kept looking into my eyes.

"Relax."

I nodded even though I wasn't sure if I'd be able to.

"Trust me to take care of you."

Trey being able to take care of me sexually wasn't in question. My ability to return the favor was what worried me.

"I see I didn't make myself clear. Thought I did, but I didn't. Not sure I can be any clearer but I'll try. For months, I've wanted you. For months, I've laid in my bed and fisted my cock thinking about you. Which means I've imagined us together in a variety of ways. But, baby, that kiss was far better than any fantasy."

Holy crap.

Holy, *holy* crap.

"Knowing that makes me more nervous," I told him honestly. "And talking about it makes me nervous because I feel like I'm ruining the moment."

His hand went to my butt, and at the same time, he pressed his hips forward. and his erection could not be missed.

"Does that feel like the moment's being ruined?"

"No."

"All I need you to do is trust me to take us both where I want us to go. You don't like something I'm doing, you tell me and I'll switch it up. You want more of something, you tell me and I'll give it to you. Can you do that for me?"

I wouldn't have to do anything but trust him. Surely I could do that.

"Kiss—" I didn't get the 'me' out.

His mouth slammed down onto mine, and just like in his truck, I was swept away. All thoughts vanished. All but him and me and the way he tasted and felt. His tongue tangled with mine and something crazy happened—his hand in my hair tightened. Intuitively, I knew that was the moment he'd taken over.

Yes, this was what I needed, Trey in control. And boy did he take control—or more to the point, he took us straight to hyper-speed. He broke the kiss, scooped me up, and moved straight to my bedroom. Later when I had my wits about me, I'd wonder how he knew which room was mine.

Then I was on my feet next to the bed, my shirt was off, my pants were next, then my undies. His clothes vanished just as quickly as mine had, and before I could get a good look at all the beauty God had seen fit to grant Trey, I was on my bed. After that, I wasn't thinking about a darn thing because Trey's mouth was between my legs.

"Oh. My. God," I half-panted, half-shouted.

Part of my response was to the shock of where his mouth went. The other part was because his hands on my inner thighs holding me open was so hot, I was going to lose my mind. His fingers dug into my flesh, his tongue licked and sucked until I was no longer in danger of losing my mind—it was just gone.

"Keep 'em open," Trey growled.

I had no idea what that meant and at that point, I didn't care. I was so close to exploding, all of my concentration was on preventing that from happening. I felt a finger sliding through my wetness, then two, and that's when my hips surged up and my legs started to close around Trey's head. His fingers drove in and I did not care he was courting suffocation when my thighs clamped tight. I needed his fingers where they were, I needed his tongue to keep doing what it was doing, and I didn't know how to communicate that.

"Open," he demanded, but he didn't lift his head so he spoke that demand against my sensitive clit, and the vibration that one word caused sent shock waves through me.

I fisted the blanket and let my legs fall open.

"Ride my fingers, Addy."

I didn't know what that meant either, but my body did because it bucked at his command and his fingers slid in deeper then he curled them, rubbing against a magic spot I had no idea existed. And it was magical—it made my neck arch and my eyes close, and I fought with all my might to hold on.

"Let go, baby."

"Can't."

"Adalynn. Let. Go."

"Can't."

Trey was not one to be denied. So many things happened at once I couldn't fully comprehend what he was doing. But I felt it. All of it. His mouth latched onto my clit. His fingers curled more. And his other hand reached up and yanked down my bra. His fingers found my nipple and pinched it so hard my back came off the bed. Then a flash of color danced behind my eyelids, my lungs stopped working, and every single muscle in my body seized.

It was *glorious*.

It was scary.

It was wild.

It was out of my control. I couldn't stop what was happening to me. I didn't want it to stop. I was babbling nonsense.

My mind completely blanked, and when I came to, Trey was covering me. His hips were cradled in mine. Balanced on his elbows, his palm cupped my face and his thumb stroked my jaw. All of that felt great, but it was Trey staring right at me that made me shiver.

"Ready, baby?"

Some of the haze of my orgasm started to fade and when Trey came into focus, my heart that was already galloping started to thunder. Pure, unmasked hunger. Trey Durum was looking down at me like he wanted to eat me—well, technically he *had* eaten me, but he looked like he wanted to do it again.

Holy, holy crap.

"Addy?"

"No, I'm not ready," I whispered, and his body went taut. "I'm still fuzzy."

"Fuzzy?"

He was holding himself still, fighting his desire, waiting on me. That knowledge did something crazy to my heart. It made it swell in a way it shouldn't. I couldn't fall in love with Trey. I'd been teetering on the edge since the day I met him. I had no experience but I didn't need any to know that sex and love were worlds apart.

But even knowing that, I still told him, "I want to remember this."

His body relaxed, his forehead dropped to mine, and he muttered, "Fuck."

Then he resumed rubbing the head of his dick around my opening.

"Gonna slide in now."

I nodded, and boy did he slide in. More like he slammed home, and when he did, he groaned and I lost his eyes because he closed them.

"Goddamn."

Oh, no.

My body locked, his eyes snapped open, and his hand moved from my jaw to my hair. He gave it a sharp tug and forced me to look at him.

"I'm gonna tell you straight, so you don't twist what's happening here."

That didn't sound good so I closed my eyes.

"You can try to shut me out, but I won't let you,

Adalynn. You're gonna give me more. You're gonna come around my cock the same way you did in my mouth." He pulled out and drove back in. "And you're gonna give it to me fast because your pussy's so fucking tight and hot I don't have much time. Wrap your legs around me."

I did as he asked. His hand glided over my hip and grabbed my ass and grinded down.

Sweet Jesus, that felt good. So good, I locked my ankles and reached for more.

"Fuck, yeah. Dig your heels in my ass and do that again."

I did as I was told and Trey pulled back only to drive in harder. Then I stopped worrying altogether if I was doing it right because I felt it build again. Only this time it was different. I felt my inner muscles contracting, clutching at his dick, and every time it happened, Trey groaned.

"Jesus Christ, Adalynn, give it to me."

"Trey."

He pounded into me harder. The force of his thrusts rocked my body, so I wrapped my arms around him and held on with all four limbs. Trey must've liked this because his hard thrusts turned into out-of-control.

"Fuck," he snarled and planted himself deep.

I had just enough cognitive thought left to feel his dick swell and jerk. Then when Trey swiveled his hips, that last thread snapped and I was thrown into a sea of pleasure.

I was right. Totally right. It was different. So different, I chased it and bucked my hips, not wanting it to end. Never wanting to lose the feeling of being wrapped around Trey. Surrounded. Tethered. Bound.

"Adalynn," he moaned long and low.

I didn't hear Trey say my name. I felt it. And try as I might I couldn't stop that feeling from settling in my soul. It was a stupid thing to do. It was dangerous. But I still couldn't fight against it.

6

Christian.

Adalynn.

My mind blanked as I emptied myself into her. But I had the presence of mind to savor the feel of Adalynn's legs locked tight around my hips, the ripple of her pussy as it clutched my cock, the way her body moved with mine.

I slowly came back to myself and started gliding in and out, not wanting to lose her wet heat. Not wanting to lose any part of her.

I was an asshole and I knew it.

I shouldn't have barged into her house. Hell, I shouldn't have come, period. I knew I wasn't good enough for Addy but I was taking my shot anyway. I'd fought my feelings for her long enough. She was the only thing right and true in my life. The only person who didn't feel sorry for me or put up with my shit. I hadn't repaid her care with kindness, but that was going to change. I'd do whatever I had to do to make things right. I'd show her I wasn't the dick she thought I was.

"Trey."

The sound of Addy moaning my name while my cock was still hard and gliding inside of her sent a trail of heat up my spine. Before I could fully appreciate the lightness that heat brought with it, Addy uncurled her fingers from where she'd found purchase on my shoulders, flattened her palms on my upper back, and I froze.

Fuck.

Down her hands went, and knowing what she'd encounter, I held my breath. Not wanting her to feel the puckered burned skin but knowing I wasn't going to stop her left me cold. Ice-fucking-cold.

Fuck.

"Trey?" That time my name wasn't a soft, sexy moan, it came out in a shaky, tentative question.

"Yeah, baby?"

"Why are you shaking?"

Am I?

Christ.

Instead of answering, I lowered my mouth to hers and pressed my lips against the corner of hers, then moved to the hinge of her jaw, and finally to her neck. I inhaled and willed my body still.

"You okay?"

"Shit, yeah."

"Then why—"

"What do you feel?" I interrupted her, unable to stomach her hesitant tone.

"Feel?"

"Yeah, Addy, what do you feel?"

"I don't understand."

Her ankles unhooked and she started to move her legs, but before she could disengage, my hand went to her thigh.

"I need you wrapped around me."

"What?" she whispered.

"To have this conversation, I need you to hold on." When she didn't move to lock her legs tight, I pulled my face out of her neck and looked down at her. "Goddamn, you're beautiful."

I hadn't meant to utter the words out loud, but when her face went soft and her eyes turned hazy like they had right before she told me she wanted to remember the moment I entered her, I was glad I had.

"Under your hands, tell me what you feel?"

"Your skin."

Jesus fuck.

"What else?'

"Um...you're hot."

Fucking shit.

"What else?"

"I don't understand what you're asking. I sense this is important to you. But I just feel *you*. Your skin, your heat, I guess you're kinda sweating, but, Trey, I don't know what you're asking, honey."

"Fuck," I muttered, and my eyes closed against her sincerity.

She didn't understand.

Fucking Christ.

Addy's legs wrapped tight, her hands on my back roamed, and I was cocooned in her innocence. And at that moment, my life changed. I felt the shift and I didn't fight it, I let it settle over me.

Right and good. That was Adalynn.

I would not fuck this up.

"My scars." I stopped to clear my throat of the emotion threatening to choke me.

"Oh."

Oh. Just, oh.

Christ.

There was a beat of silence before she said, "Look at me, Trey."

I opened my eyes, surprised to see her glaring at me.

"Your scars?" she prompted. I started to pull away but her thighs pressed tighter. "I've done everything you've asked." Her tone was low and soft. "I trusted you with something I've never trusted anyone with. Now I'm asking you to do the same. What about your scars?"

Her gently spoken words felt like a sharp jab to the gut. She had trusted me and the results of that trust had been spectacular. She'd irrevocably proven the other two idiots she'd been with didn't know shit about women. There was not a damn thing wrong with Addy. It had taken nothing more than a kiss to get her to ignite. And when I got my mouth between her legs and my tongue in her pussy, she'd gone wild. Everything about her was sexy as hell.

I owed her the same trust she'd given me and I'd give it. I just didn't think she'd appreciate it while my cock was buried inside her. And the talking we'd done, had done nothing to alleviate my erection. More proof, the woman was crazy good.

"I need you wrapped around me a different way," I told her, and rolled us to the side. She whimpered when my cock slid out of her. I smiled and she frowned.

I gathered her close and ran my fingers through her hair. I couldn't get enough of feeling the silky strands. I'd never felt anything so soft.

"In the beginning, I admit some of my hang-ups were my ego," I started. "I wasn't used to looking in the mirror seeing a face full of scars. Over the months, they've faded but their existence is a reminder I fucked up. Liberty made a call and I didn't act fast enough. My inaction almost cost Luke his eyesight, did cost him his career in the Navy. And because of me, Logan and Matt left the teams. I put us all in danger that day. If I would've moved when Liberty radioed, Luke and I would've been away from the blast. Instead, they had to triage us on the street and carry us to the extraction point. From there it was a clusterfuck."

"And your back?"

"Burns and shrapnel."

Addy nodded against my chest and pressed herself closer.

"There's no such thing as perfect, Trey. We're all flawed. Some of those imperfections we wear, some are hidden inside of us, and some are buried so deep they're dormant until something triggers them awake. And sometimes, the things we bury are the very things that should be brought to light."

Instead of lashing out, I clenched my jaw and closed my eyes.

"Guilt and blame will eat you alive unless you talk about it," she continued.

"Addy—"

"Shh, Trey." Her hand slid from my chest to my ribs, then farther until her palm rested on the small of my back. I screwed my eyes closed and stiffened. "I'm not saying I'm the right person to talk to about it. I'm not even saying you're ready. But when you are, I know some pretty great guys who are waiting for you."

Fuck.

"I want you to know I was being sincere when I apologized for being an ass. I said some stupid shit about you living a perfect life. I knew it was stupid when I was saying it. I knew I was lashing out at you because my head was twisted. And as fucked-up as this is, maybe I was trying to push you into hating me. Every day it was getting harder and harder to keep my distance. I wanted to see you as much as I wanted to avoid you. I have a lot of shit to work out but I promise you, I will never take that out on you again."

There was a beat of silence before she asked, "What changed?"

So much. Everything. Too much.

Instead of answering, I told her, "You know, I've never laid in bed with a woman naked and talked." Unsurprisingly, Addy's hand stilled and her body went taut. "Never, Adalynn. And since I've never done that, you can take from that I've never laid naked with a woman and been open about my feelings. So what changed? Everything and it started the day I met you."

"You thought I was Hadley."

There was accusation in her tone and she was right.

"I did, for about a nanosecond. I'm getting the sense that bothers you, but, Addy, you two are identical twins, and until someone knows you, the mix-up is easy. But as I said, it took me barely a second to see you were not your sister, and when I did, the change in me started. I went from a cocksure prick to a man who felt unworthy."

"Unworthy?"

"Before the explosion, I wouldn't have hesitated. I would've turned on the charm and worked you."

"And I would've turned you down," she vowed.

"I know you would've." I smiled. "And knowing made me feel unworthy."

"That doesn't make sense."

"It does to me. Simply knowing that you're the type of woman who sees past all the superficial bull-shit made me fall for you. It went beyond attraction, it was a feeling that settled over me, warm and comforting. Something I'd never felt. I told myself I was insane, no one fell for a woman they didn't know anything about. Then I reminded myself I wasn't good enough for you. Not anymore. And that pissed me off. It made me resent my new life. It made me feel less of a man. And from there, the change in me went south until I hit a new low. A place I didn't want to be. I became a person I didn't like. I was ungrateful, and as you pointed out, a quitter. And, Addy, I have never in my life quit.

"But you were right, I quit being a man I was proud of. Everything I was doing was counterpro-ductive—I wanted you to see me but the man I was showing you was a fucking dick. I spent a lot of time this last week thinking about how it was possible I fell so hard and fast for you. But it comes down to this. What we're doing right now—I've never held a woman in my arms and been open and honest about anything because I never trusted or felt comfortable enough to do it. And beyond that, I've never wanted to share any part of my personal life with a woman. I never wanted a woman to hold me close. I've never asked another living soul to wrap themselves around me and beg them not to let go."

"Trey—"

"Got more to say, baby. As you pointed out, you trusted me with something precious and I want you to know I cherish what you gave me. You also talked about burying perceived imperfections. I hope after what we shared, you know what you had buried in you wasn't yours to hide. I've given enough head-space to the two twats who you've been with, so this is the last I'm giving them, but hear this, Adalynn. God's honest truth, you are phenomenal in bed."

"Trey," she whispered, and tucked her chin.

"Look at me." I took my hand out of her hair and lifted her chin until her gaze met mine. "Trust me, I got off on every moan, every move, every touch. All of that was sexy. No other way to say it other than to state it plain, you're crazy beautiful, you're unbeliev-ably tight, so tight I was worried I wasn't gonna get you off before I went. But, baby, how wet you got just from my mouth and fingers—off-the-charts hot. You kiss great, you smell good, you taste good, you feel good. What I'm saying is, you can let go of whatever you've been twisting around in your head."

Addy's face had turned a pretty shade of pink and I thought she should know how fucking cute that was.

"And one last thing, the fact that you're blushing is crazy fucking sexy."

The pink in her cheeks turned red, her lips tipped up, and her beautiful green eyes danced with humor.

Good God, she was gorgeous.

"We done talking?" I asked.

"I don't know, are we?"

"We're done talking." My hand moved back into her hair. I gathered it in my fist and I watched her eyes flare. I gave it a tug and the eye flare turned hungry. Perfect. "Gonna kiss you. Then you're gonna get on top and ride me."

"Again?"

"Fuck, yeah."

She didn't respond—at least not verbally.

The kiss was great.

Her sweet, wet pussy sinking down on my cock— better. Her going wild riding me—fucking magnificent.

7

My eyes popped open and I didn't need a moment to get my bearings. I knew exactly whose hard chest was under my cheek, whose leg my thigh was draped over, whose hand was on my hip, and lastly, I knew why I'd dozed off.

Surprisingly, I didn't feel embarrassment. I felt great. Sex with Trey had been eye-opening. No, it had been wondrous, astonishing, marvelous.

"How are you feeling?" Trey's rough voice wrapped around me like a warm blanket and I smiled.

"Great," I chirped, uncaring my voice sounded squeaky and excited.

I didn't even care when his body started to shake and his next statement came out full of humor.

"You sore?"

"Sore?"

"Yeah, Addy, sore. I took you pretty rough that last time."

Pretty rough?

Holy Hannah, if he called that 'pretty rough' I was scared to experience what he called out-of-control.

Scared, but not unwilling.

After round two—which was incredible once Trey coaxed me out of my head and I got over being on full display, I found that I thoroughly enjoyed being on top. Part of that was seeing that Trey thoroughly enjoying me being on top. He wasn't shy communicating this to me. I never in my life pictured myself as someone who would enjoy dirty talk, but sweet baby Jesus, the dirtier his words, the more turned on I got. But it wasn't just his words—his eyes, his hands, the sounds he made, the way his body bowed—spawned my excitement. So, needless to say, round two was a pleasurable success...which led us to round three.

If round one was all about me, round two was about him getting me to loosen up and have fun, then round three was all about him. When Trey told me to get on my hands and knees I didn't hesitate, I trusted him to take care of me, and holy crap did he. It was rough, it was a shade dirtier, there was no coaxing. Trey took from me what he wanted and he did it while pulling my hair and whispering filthy things in my ear. I didn't think he could top the first three orgasms he'd given me. I was wrong. The fourth one was by far the best. Hence, why I passed out after round three.

"A little," I admitted.

"Want me to run you a bath?"

What the what? Did big, macho Trey just ask me if I wanted him to run me a bath? I didn't want to think his offer was sweet, I was in unchartered territory and trying to keep my wayward emotions from creeping in. Which was seriously hard after some of the stuff Trey had said to me. Especially the part about him falling for me at first sight. I wasn't sure what exactly he meant by that. Did he mean he fell in lust with me? Did he fall in love? Did he love the idea of spending time with a woman like me? There'd been no time for me analyze then obsessively over-analyze what a man like Trey meant when he said he'd never lain in bed with a woman naked and talked. What I thought he meant was when he was in bed with a woman he didn't waste time with heart-to-hearts and dove straight to orgasms. But again, I didn't have the experience to know for sure so I wasn't allowing myself to think about it. I had to keep my wits about me and not start thinking Trey was sweet.

He was good in bed.

No, he was magnificent, and I had to remember that was what this was about.

"I don't have a bathtub," I told him.

"You don't have a tub?"

"Nope."

"Baby, how is that possible?"

"This is a condo."

"And?"

"The woman I rent from is ninety-two. She couldn't get into the tub, not without being lifted in. She didn't want to go into a nursing home and she didn't want to impose on her daughter-in-law since she really didn't want her son lifting her in and out and the aide that came in to help her couldn't do it, so her son tore out the tub. Actually, he redid the whole bathroom so she could get into the shower with her walker and the chair she used to bathe would fit. He added extra spray heads as well."

"Where is she now?"

"Mrs. Parker?"

"If that's the ninety-two-year-old woman you rent from, then yeah."

I smiled against his chest, not because of his smartass retort but because Trey's hand had meandered from my hip and he was now rubbing my butt.

"Sadly, after the bathroom remodel, she had a fall and she broke her hip. It freaked her son out and he put her in assisted living. But it's one of those posh facilities that looks more like a resort than old folks' home. She loves it there and says if she'd known her boy was gonna spring for such a nice place she would've given in years before."

I left out the part about her grandson, Bass, who was my kickboxing instructor, also having a freak-out, and it was him who'd talked his grandmother into moving into an assisted living facility. This was supposed to be short-term, until her hip healed, which was why I was offered the condo. In the beginning, it was basically me housesitting. I wanted my own space but didn't have the money saved to set up a place, so it worked out great. Then Mrs. Parker loved her new surroundings, having friends, not having to cook for herself, and decided to stay. So now I rented the condo. But last week Bass told me they wanted to sell it and asked if I wanted to buy it. I was on the fence.

The condo was in a great location, nice quiet neighborhood, nice neighbors, the price was doable, but I wanted a yard. My mom had a green thumb—growing up, our front yard was the best in the neighborhood—but it was the backyard that was the showstopper. Some of my best childhood memories were of my mom and me working on the flowerbeds. I wanted that again. I wanted a fresh canvas so I could invite my mom over and we could create something beautiful together.

Trey's body went stiff under mine, and all thoughts on flowers flew out of my head as he rolled to the side, swung his legs over the bed, and yanked the covers over my naked body.

What in the world?

"Trey?"

"Shh."

He was standing next to my bed gloriously naked and reaching for his jeans when I heard it. I blame my delayed reaction on Trey's mind-boggling, muscular body. My eyes were transfixed, my brain was muddled, so I missed what Trey obviously hadn't. Only, he'd miscalculated the time it would take for Hadley to reach my bedroom door—which was open by the way, because, hello, we were alone in my house and there wasn't a need to close it.

That is, there wasn't a freaking need to close it if you didn't have a nosy twin with a key to your front door and wasn't afraid to use it.

"Oh my God!" Hadley shouted, and my gaze went from Trey's semi-erect dick to my sister.

She was stumbling back, her arms wheeling, trying to catch her balance.

"Fuck," Trey clipped while at the same time tried to untangle his jeans.

In my quest to block Hadley's view, I tossed the covers back, not caring I was naked, too. It wasn't like my sister hadn't seen me naked. But it was then and in the subsequent moments when I truly understood what the word 'mortified' meant.

That was because the moment my feet touched the floor, Brady appeared—at my bedroom door—while I was naked.

Naked.

I was naked as a jaybird with nothing close to cover myself with, and my sister's fiancé was standing in front of me.

"Jesus Christ."

So what did Trey do?

He dropped his useless jeans, straightened, and shoved me behind him. This I knew was a gallant effort to save my modesty. However, it left him fully exposed to my sister, who was now chanting "you're naked" coupled with "he's naked" and she added an "ohmigod" to that before Brady growled, "Close your eyes."

To which my sister responded with, "Ohmigod, they were doing the nasty."

This was said with humor. Brady didn't find the situation humorous and I knew this not because I could see him, but because there was no mistaking his tone when he repeated, "Woman, close your eyes."

Obviously, Trey didn't find anything funny. After all, it was his pecker standing at half-mast—or maybe since the commotion had started it was now flaccid—either way Hadley had gotten an eyeful.

"Shut the door," Trey barked and I jumped.

His hand went to my hip to stay my position.

As if I would move.

I heard the door slam and Trey's back muscles relaxed a skoosh and he shook his head.

"Did that just happen?"

"Yeah, baby, it did."

"My sister and her fiancé just walked in and saw us?" I asked, seeking clarification. "I wasn't hallucinating? Say, from an orgasm-induced haze where I imagined Brady standing in the doorway seeing my boobs and...other parts."

"Orgasm-induced haze?" He chuckled.

"Well, I don't know. I've never had an orgasm before. I was hoping that they came with side effects like: hallucinations, hot flashes, maybe paranoia, and delusions."

"Baby."

Trey started to turn and I pressed deeper into his back, not wanting to face him. Partly because I knew my face was flaming red. I was completely nude, and while we were in bed I didn't seem to have an issue with this, but standing in front of him I was now shy.

The other part was because I was enjoying the feel of his massive body shaking against mine.

"Adalynn," he called.

"Hm?"

"Baby, let go?"

"No way."

"The door's closed."

Too late. It was way too late to care about the door. Hadley had seen what she'd seen. Brady had seen what he'd seen. And they knew what they knew.

"Oh my God, they know."

"Baby." He laughed.

Not chuckled. Not snickered. A straight-out, gut-busting rumble. Loud, gruff, and for a long time.

When it finally died down, he said, "You're killing me."

"I wish someone would kill *me*," I muttered. "I don't ever want to see Brady again. And I don't care if that makes me sound like an immature idiot. He saw my boobs, Trey."

"And Hadley got a nice full frontal of my cock."

"Gawd!"

"We need to get dressed," he reminded me.

We did, we totally needed to get dressed. Then I could crawl out my bedroom window and run away. Maybe Trey would go with me and we could hole up at a hotel or catch a flight to the Bahamas. Yes, the beach sounded wonderful. Sand and surf and fruity drinks on a beach full of strangers who had not seen me naked.

I was so lost in my misery I missed Trey turning to face me. But I didn't miss him slide his hands up the sides of my neck and thread his fingers into my hair.

"You have nothing to be embarrassed about," he told me.

"Brady—"

"Addy, your sister barged into your house uninvited and unannounced. Brady should've seriously known better. They saw what they saw. It's done and over."

"Hadley's always invited." I defended my sister. "Never in her wildest dreams would she imagine she'd walk into...you know...what was going on."

"And what was going on?" He smirked.

"Don't be a jerk."

"I'm not, baby, I just like seeing your cheeks turn pink."

"That's you being a jerk."

"No. That's me being a man who loves knowing that when I get you in bed you burn hot, but out of it, you blush. You're bashful and shy and sweet. That's what everyone sees. But you're also wild and sexy and you like when I pull your hair and talk dirty to you. That's mine. That's the part of you *I* get. So I'm not being a jerk. Smug, maybe. Grateful, definitely. Happy as fuck to be standing next to you—unquestionably yes."

Man, Trey really needed to stop saying stuff like that, or I'd get the wrong impression. It was hard enough for me to keep my emotions locked down when I'd been daydreaming about the man for months. I will admit, it was his looks that caught my attention, but probably not the same way they caught most women's. It wasn't the scars that marred his beauty—they made him more interesting, masculine, dangerous. It was his perpetual frown when no one was looking that had captured my heart. I wanted to know why he was pretending and what he was hiding. I also wanted to help him work it out.

Then I got to know him. He wasn't pretending, he was straight-out lying to his friends. He smiled and joked with them. But with me, the real Trey came out. The anger, the guilt, the feelings of inadequacy. I wondered if he realized his vulnerability was what had endeared me to him. It was his raw honesty that made me overlook the times he'd behaved like a jerk. And I overlooked them, not because I was a spineless twit but because I knew I was the only person he showed his pain to. And deep down in a place I didn't want to admit I had, I liked that.

"Trey," I started, but said no more and averted my gaze.

"Need to ask you a favor."

"What's that?" I asked his bare chest.

"Ride this out with me."

"Huh?"

His hands tightened and he tilted my head back until I was forced to look at him or close my eyes.

Since I wasn't actually as immature as I was behaving, I lifted my eyes and I froze.

His green eyes were intense. Deeper, darker than they normally were. Even darker than they were when we'd been in bed. More intense than when we were arguing about his PT.

"Take a chance and ride this out," he repeated.

"I still don't understand."

"You and me, Adalynn."

"Like, be your girlfriend?"

Trey's brows pulled together and his jaw ticked. Seeing that, my gaze skidded over his shoulder, and embarrassment set in. Not as much as Brady seeing me naked but enough that I wished I could rewind time and not make myself sound like an idiot.

"Haven't had a girlfriend since the sixth grade."

Sixth grade. Cripes, Trey started young. If he had a girlfriend before he even hit middle school, God knows what he was doing in high school. Of course, that would explain his superior skills in bed.

Since I was at a loss for words, I didn't say anything. I just lamely bobbed my head and studied the large canvas print that hung over my bed. Which was now crooked to the side, probably due to my bed rocking against the wall.

Sweet mother of God. Sweet, old Mrs. Landon

next door must've thought there'd been an earth-quake. She was older than Mrs. Parker and very rarely left her bedroom. A room that shared a wall with mine.

"Addy, swear to God if you're booking a flight to the Bahamas thinking you can crawl out your bedroom window so you don't have to talk to me, I'll hunt you down!" Hadley shouted and I closed my eyes.

Damn.

There were a great many things I loved about having a twin—Hadley knowing what was in my head at all times was not one of them. Being as she knew what was in mine, I knew what was in hers, and if I didn't hurry up, she'd start talking to me about Trey through the closed door, not caring Trey was in the room with me.

"I need to get dressed," I told him.

"Adalynn," Trey called.

I forced my gaze back to him.

His was soft and gentle.

Oh my.

Soft and gentle on Trey was the very definition of male perfection. I'd seen Trey loads, I'd spent time with him at family gatherings, in the gym, and now in my bed. But right then, it was like I was *seeing* him for the first time. I thought he'd shown me the real him. I thought I'd seen him raw and vulnerable. I had not.

God, he was handsome. He looked like he should've been a movie star.

"Baby," he whispered.

Any lingering harshness softened and I shivered. Trey felt it and smiled. It lit his eyes and I knew it was the first genuine smile I'd seen.

"Fuck," he muttered, then went on as if talking to himself. "The whisper of a promise."

"What?"

"We have a lot to talk about," he returned instead of elaborating. "Before we get dressed and go out there, I need to know you understand me."

Crap.

I didn't understand but we didn't have time to dally. Hadley was impatient. I was surprised she hadn't barged back into my room and demanded an explanation. Hadley remaining in my living room reminded me that Brady was out there, too. She wasn't being patient, her fiancé was likely containing her.

Crap and crap.

"Trust me, Trey, we have to hurry."

"You're naked." My shoulders tensed at his

weird statement. "You're standing in my arms completely naked and you're comfortable doing it. Remember that."

"Why?"

"I'm a lot of things, Addy. Stupid isn't one of them. I know the second you're dressed and out of this room, you'll find a hundred excuses to push me away. You'll tell yourself what we shared was all about sex. You'll tell yourself that you should keep your distance. So, *I'm* telling you straight out, what we shared was not about sex but intimacy. *I'm* telling you, I want more. More in every sense of the word. *I'm* telling you I want the opportunity to explore what we have and I want to do that in a real way. Not hiding from each other and not hiding it from our friends and your family."

"Trey, that's—"

"Baby, you are not a secret. I will not keep us in the shadows. Hadley and Brady knew what was going on in your bed before they showed up. I will not lie to them—not about you. I will not brush it off or pretend me being in your bed doesn't mean what it means."

"And what does it mean?" I asked even though I was scared to know.

"Being as I'm not stupid, I know that Adalynn

Walker is not the type of woman you fuck and leave. And that isn't because essentially you're my boss's daughter, and everything to do with the woman *you* are. I wouldn't have come here, and I sure as shit wouldn't have taken you to your bed unless I was sure I was ready to give you what you deserve."

"Addy," my sister snapped.

"Hadley," Brady snapped back. "Shut it."

"Don't tell me to shut it. They've been in there *forever*. How long does it take to get on clothes?"

"It's gonna take longer you keep interrupting them."

I needed to move. Not to the Bahamas, Hadley would find me there. Finland. Yeah, she'd never think to look in Finland. I was wondering if Finns were welcoming to Americans, when Trey's body started to shake. Then I stopped wondering about Finland and started wondering if I could handle *more* with Trey.

The answer was—no.

I absolutely couldn't handle a man like Trey. His experience alone put me at a disadvantage. But it wasn't him having a girlfriend in sixth grade and how he'd gained the vast skill he'd learned between then and now that worried me. I already had feelings for him, feelings that ran deep. Meaning, it wouldn't take but a gentle nudge to turn 'like' into 'love.'

The whisper of a promise.

Darn it all to hell.

"We'll talk later," I told him and watched him smile.

Crap. I'd been wrong again. That smile lit his eyes.

8

"Trey."

"Don't," I warned and tore my gaze from Addy and Hadley to Brady.

We were standing outside on a slab of concrete that couldn't have been more than a ten-foot by ten-foot square. The women were in Addy's living room and I'd been watching Hadley animatedly flail her arms and pace. Contrary to her twin, Addy was standing still with her arms crossed over her chest.

I wasn't big on Addy's posture. I also knew I couldn't get between the sisters, and not because it wasn't my place or they'd work it out. I had to deal with Brady, which didn't make me happy. But out of all the men closest to Addy, I was thanking all things holy it had been Brady who had walked in on us.

"You hafta know we're gonna talk about this," Brady retorted.

"I'll tell you two things and I'm gonna do it once. After that, you have a problem with me being with Adalynn, then it will be just that, your problem."

"*Being* with Adalynn?"

"You think I'd fuck Addy?" I asked, unable to keep the irritation from my tone.

"Brother, I am not dumb. You were in there—"

"I was," I confirmed. "You saw what you saw, and, Brady, I cannot say I'm pleased you walked in and saw my woman naked. The same as I don't reckon you're too happy Hadley saw what she saw. But I want you to think about what I'm asking you. Do you really believe I'd *fuck* Adalynn?"

"Your woman?" he pushed out.

Jesus, he was pissing me off.

"Now you're just ticking me off."

"Christ, Trey. The last I saw, you two were circling each other, snarling. I wasn't sure which one of you was itching for a showdown more—you or her. What the hell am I supposed to think?"

He wasn't wrong. But Brady didn't understand why I'd been circling, trying to keep my distance, and he certainly hadn't known the showdown I'd been itching for was the horizontal and naked kind.

"I had some shit I had to work out," I told him.

"And you've done that?"

"Wouldn't be in her home and absolutely wouldn't have been in her bed if I hadn't."

Brady's stare turned contemplative. He was a man who, until recently, lived with some pretty dark secrets. That was, until Hadley worked her Walker magic. Now Brady was a man who knew the goodness he had at his side. He was also smart enough to know if he wanted to keep it, he had to let his past go. And somewhere along the line, Brady had changed from the withdrawn, tight-lipped man I'd first met to a man who said what was on his mind and openly showed his love for his fiancée.

Even knowing all of that, I didn't brace.

"I get you think that. But I know what happened in Lebanon—"

"Actually, you don't, Brady. I understand you're looking out for Adalynn. Hell, I *like* that she has people watching her back. But you don't know jack-shit about what happened."

I was seeking patience; trying to remember that Brady had known Addy for years. He'd been part of her life and family long before he pulled his thumb out and got involved with Hadley. Something unpleasant slithered up my spine, something that felt a lot like jealousy. Not the tingle a man got when he noticed other men checking out his woman—the kind that morphed into pride, knowing the woman by your side was so special other men were jealous of *you*.

No, my jealousy stemmed from the knowledge that Brady had had years to get to know Addy. He'd spent time with her. He'd seen her smile and heard her laugh more than I had. He'd shared meals with her. He'd been invited into her family. And Brady had settled into life. Brady had been able to let go of his demons. Brady was where I wanted to be.

"I read the reports—"

"Really? You did? You read the after action reports; about the rescue, the mission, the explosion. Did it tell you about how I failed to react in time to Liberty's warning? Did it tell you that she made a call that I ignored, and because of that, I almost got my team killed? Did it tell you how I fucked Luke's career? Tell me, Brady, what exactly did the report tell you?"

Brady's face turned to stone when he mumbled, "Right. You've worked your shit out."

"Yeah, Brady, I have. As much of it that's gonna get worked out."

"By that, I assume you mean you intend to keep

holding on to something that's not yours—" Brady's hand came up and I bit back my interruption and my desire to break the finger he was jabbing my way. "Not, done, brother."

My jaw clenched as I waited for him to finish whatever it was he had to say. "You're not doing her or yourself any favors keeping that shit locked up. It is not your fault Luke left the Navy. It's not your fault some asshole carried out a suicide mission. It's not Liberty's fault she didn't warn you sooner and it's not your fault you didn't jump the second she figured out what was going down. And just to add, Luke had comms, he could've bolted his damn self. He didn't need to wait for you to make the first move. Both of you were fucked before Liberty made that call. And you're both fucking lucky you weren't blown to hell."

I tried to let Brady's angry words settle in. I tried to push them deep and let them soothe the guilt. But my body rejected them, deflected the reprieve of responsibility. I wasn't blameless and every fiber of my soul knew it.

There would be no liberation, no absolution, no amnesty for what I'd done.

"Brady..." I wasn't sure what I intended to say beyond his name. I wasn't sure I could keep the lid on my emotions. Hell, the vibration in my voice told me I was failing at this endeavor.

Always failing.

"The longer you hold guilt, the harder it is to let go."

"No shit?" I snarled. "But what am I supposed to do? Pretend it didn't happen? Disrespect my brother and brush his injury off like it's nothing? Christ, Brady, Luke damn near went blind and I'm supposed to what, say sorry and move on?"

"Yeah, Trey. That's exactly what you're supposed to do. Move the fuck on because you didn't do a fucking thing to Luke. And if you think you pulling away from your brothers, shutting them out, acting like a bear with a thorn up his ass isn't disrespecting them, then you're straight out stupid. And if you think Jasper's not gonna call you out on this shit, you're even stupider. He'll sniff you out and put you down, he thinks your shit will fuck his daughter. The man is rabid when it comes to his girls. So you better brace, Trey. Once he catches wind you and Addy are starting something, he's gonna come at you."

I had nothing to say to that. Brady spoke the truth. Jasper Walker was a pit bull when it came to his girls. He was a man whose bite you'd feel—he could be ruthless when someone threatened his family.

And I'm a threat.

Fuck.

My gaze went back to Addy.

So sweet and innocent.

Christ, Jasper would have my balls in a vise if he knew what my intentions were. Shit, who was I kidding? Once he found out what I'd already done, I was as good as dead.

I was not good enough for his pretty, shy daughter.

Fuck.

I never should've come to Georgia. I never should've accepted a job at Triple Canopy.

"I see the wheels turning," Brady said, all of the anger in his tone gone. "I didn't tell you that to make you run. I'm warning you because you're gonna have to be way more convincing if you want Jasper's blessing."

Jasper's blessing.

Addy's head turned and our eyes met. Instead of feeling the beauty of her gaze, dread hit my gut like a lead weight. Heavy and suffocating. I should've kept my distance. I never should've touched her perfection. I knew one taste and I'd be addicted. I'd want more.

Though I'd been wrong and selfish, Adalynn Walker wasn't just addictive, and I didn't just want more—I wanted *everything*. I wanted forever. I wanted to be worthy of her.

Before I could respond to Brady, Hadley broke away from Addy and moved across the small dining area.

When she opened the sliding glass door, she didn't come outside but she did smile big.

"We've decided we're having dinner."

"You mean, *you've* decided." Brady chuckled and Hadley narrowed her eyes.

"No, *we've* decided," she reiterated her lie, completely unfazed Brady had called her out. "*We* were thinking Indian."

"Now I know you're full of shit because Addy doesn't like Indian and you've been trying to get me to take you there for weeks."

That ugly green monster started to fill my gut again. I hadn't known Addy didn't like Indian food. Not that the knowledge wasn't welcomed, I, too, didn't care for Indian. But I hated Brady knew and I didn't.

"I'm not eating there," Addy called out.

"Fine," Hadley huffed. "You two pick because Addy's being difficult."

Hadley's definition of her sister being difficult meant that Addy hadn't given in right away. The assumption was proven correct when Addy came to stand beside her sister, hands on her hips, brow pinched, her annoyance sparking.

"Just because you don't want to hear me when I remind you I hate Indian food so I don't want to try the new place even if it has rave reviews, doesn't mean I'm being difficult. Further, I told you I had plans but you bowled right over that and horned in on dinner."

"I just want—"

"I know what you want, Hadley, but you're not hearing me when I tell you I'm not ready to give it. And that doesn't make me difficult, either. It makes you a nosy pain in the butt."

Hadley smiled and Addy shook her head at her twin's obvious ability to deflect her insult.

"I think I saw—"

"Hadley," I ground out with more bite than I'd intended. Both women jolted but it was Hadley's startled eyes that came to me. "Don't embarrass your sister."

Hadley's gaze sliced to Brady's then to Addy

before it came back to me. Her eyes settled but her mouth didn't. It tipped up into a big, bright smile and she muttered, "Right."

"Come on, Hadley," Brady started. "I'll take you to the Indian place."

Hadley took in her man, then her sister, and said, "We can order in." Then Hadley's face went soft and her eyes turned pleading and I made a mental note to brace if Addy ever decided to look at me that way. "I feel like I haven't seen you in forever."

Yep, I'd need to brace if Addy had a mind to look at me that way, with her pretty eyes and beautiful face slack and her tone beseeching. I had no doubt I'd cave in under a minute and give her whatever she wanted. Therefore, it was no surprise when Addy sighed and her shoulders slumped forward. Hadley's latest play worked, Adalynn was giving in, but she looked nervous about this.

"Baby?" I called, and her gaze lifted to mine. "What do you want? If it doesn't deliver, me and Brady will go pick it up."

Relief.

I wasn't sure if it was from the knowledge I had no plans of leaving her, or someone else made the choice, or it was obvious I was okay with them stay-ing. Whatever it was—and it might not have been any of that—I learned something new about Adalynn Walker. Unlike her sister, she didn't use her eyes to get what she wanted—she used them to offer gratitude. Now I had a new dilemma, a new addiction—I wanted to see that look turned my way and I wanted it often. And so I knew I'd seek it out, give her anything and everything she wanted, *anything* to earn those soft, green eyes alight with a beauty I knew with certainty I wanted to see for the rest of my life.

That wasn't the first time I'd had that realization. Hell, it wasn't even the first time in the last five hours. But this time, after Brady's reminder, it was the first time pain sliced through me.

"I'd like a burger from The Station," Addy told me.

"They deliver?"

"No."

"Call in the order."

Hadley happily slipped back into the house, smile firmly in place, knowing she'd gotten her way. Addy's movements were slower, still unsure. Then she stopped and turned.

"Um. What do you want?"

"Patty melt, onion rings, and a cream soda."

She didn't smile like her sister, but some of the

unease slid from her posture as she made her way into the house.

"Maybe I was wrong," Brady muttered.

He hadn't been. Brady had been spot-on in his assessment. I was an asshole who didn't deserve the likes of a Walker. Especially the sweet shy one.

Jasper Walker would bury me, and *that* I deserved.

9

"Addy and Trey..." Hadley's singsong voice filled my kitchen. I rolled my eyes to the ceiling and wondered how much trouble I'd get in if I hog-tied and gagged my sister.

My mom would likely frown on it. My dad would totally get it and my brother would wonder what the hell had taken me so long. My sisters would laugh, so would my cousins. My sister was a known 'shit talker'—she loved to get a rise and worked hard at it. But she absolutely didn't like being teased in return. Total poor sport when she was on the receiving end. So, likely I wouldn't get in any trouble because everyone in the family would understand, even my mom.

But Brady wouldn't; he loved my twin more than reason, and I liked Brady and didn't want Thanksgiving and Christmas to be uncomfortable. So I decided against hog-tying and gagging Hadley. For now.

"Seriously, are we in fifth grade?"

"You didn't have a boyfriend in fifth grade," she reminded me. "You didn't even have one in ninth grade."

I hadn't. My dad had strict rules about dating and I'd followed them to the letter. However, none of my siblings had. Though it was worth noting that my older brother, Jason, didn't have the same rules as us girls had. Mom grumbled about this on our behalf, my aunts had taken her back, but my dad was unmovable when it came to his girls.

"And..." Hadley continued. "I've never, not once in all my life have caught you *naked* with a guy."

Heat hit my cheeks and I shook my head.

"We're not talking about this."

"Um. Yes, we are. We're talking about it in minute detail. Spill, Addy. We have less than a half-hour before they get back and I want every last juicy—"

"No way!"

"Addy," she whined. "When Steve Keller shoved his tongue in my mouth and proceeded to instigate the worst kiss in the history of worst kisses, I told you. And when Tony fumbled his way to second base and made that weird sound when he touched my bra, then shuddered before he jumped away from me and covered his crotch, I told you. And when the mac-daddy of them all—"

"Please, God, stop. I don't need a walk down TMI Memory Lane."

"Point is, I tell you. But you never tell me anything."

Hadley had a point, she did tell me everything. I knew every detail about her limited sex life. Everything except Brady.

"Fine. I'll tell you after you tell me about Brady."

I held my breath and prayed she didn't call my bluff. I absolutely, unequivocally did not want to know a single thing about my future brother-in-law and I hoped Hadley wouldn't share.

"What do you want to know?" She smirked.

Drat. She knew me too well. This was a game we'd played too many times—me challenging Hadley and her rising to the challenge then doubling down.

"Nothing," I mumbled, too afraid to take the game any further.

It was a crapshoot—either Hadley would spill her guts, making it difficult for me to ever look at Brady again, or she'd back down. Hadley rarely backed down, so really it wasn't a crapshoot. I had no choice but to admit defeat.

"Well, seeing as you don't have to tell me what he's—"

"Please stop," I interrupted her. "I'm embarrassed enough that Brady saw...what he saw. I know what you saw. I don't want to talk about it. As in, not talk about it at all, never, ever talk about it."

"Fine." She gave in. "We'll skip the horizontal tango, but I want details about the rest."

"There's nothing to tell," I lied.

"Addy," my sister whispered. "Last I *saw*, you were stomping out of his office fit to be tied. Last I *heard* was, you told him to find another therapist. Then I heard and saw more when I was at Triple Canopy and Trey was sulking around pissed as hell. Even though I didn't need him to, Brady confirmed what I saw and told me that Trey was unbearable at work and everyone was giving him a wide berth including Matt, who he's closest to. Now, I'm happy for you if you're happy. But that doesn't mean I'm not worried about you. I'm not saying this to be a bitch but it is not lost on anyone that Trey's got some experience, and not just a little—a goodly amount. And, sister, you do not. I don't want to see you get hurt."

Crap.

I wanted to talk about this less than I wanted to give my sister details about Trey's skills. Not that I actually had to tell Hadley anything—as she'd said, she knew Trey had seen a good amount of action, so it could be assumed he'd be good at it.

But maybe it would be good to get her advice. My sister, Quinn, would've been my best option, she was no-nonsense and straight-up honest. She'd tell me the truth even if it scored deep. Delaney was a dreamer, she'd been in love with her husband Carter since forever. She hadn't lived a fairy tale, far from it. But in the end, she'd gotten her happily ever after. And being as she'd been in love with one man her whole life, she'd only been with that one man, making it so she had less experience than I did.

There was also the issue of discretion. I hadn't planned on telling anyone what happened, but seeing as Hadley had barged her way into my house, the cat was out of the bag. My twin could give good advice when she had a mind to give it. But normally she just tried to shield me from any blow life could land.

"He thinks I'm beautiful."

"Addy—"

"Not in an 'I want to get in your pants' way," I talked over her. "It was after. When we were talking about something important and he stopped mid-thought and told me. But it was more, Hads, it was like he couldn't stop himself from saying it. He's full of something ugly. He calls himself an asshole. But he's shockingly honest. So honest it hurts my heart. And it's not just the words he says that hurts, the pain he doesn't hide. He says it and shows it and it hurts so bad knowing he carries all of that inside of him. He wants more. He straight out said that, too. He said he's been fighting it since we first met. He asked me to stick with him and explore what's between us. I don't know what that means."

When I stopped speaking, Hadley's smile split her face and I realized then that Delaney wasn't the only dreamer in our family. My twin had found her happily ever after, too. She was now shrouded in the love of a good man she'd worked to get, and seeing her smile I knew she wanted that for me, too. Which meant she wouldn't be much help.

"Stick with him," she told me, not surprisingly.

"Did you miss the part where I said I don't know what that means?"

"It means he's got something ugly inside of him. Something that hurts you to see. And, Addy, it wouldn't hurt you if you didn't care about him. What he's asking is for you to stick with him while he works that out. But what that really means is, he's asking you to stick with him so *you* can work that out of him."

That was what I was afraid it meant. Something I very much wanted to do, even if that meant losing myself while I was doing it.

"That scares me."

"It should."

I felt my jaw drop at my sister's honesty. I figured she'd sugarcoat the battle I'd have on my hands and tell me I could handle it. What I hadn't expected was for her to agree with me. And that didn't just scare me—it scared the pants off me.

"Hadley—"

"Wait." Her hand came up and I did what she asked. I waited. Then I waited longer, until the silence was uncomfortable and I'd thought about all the reasons I was scared.

"I see you planning your retreat, Addy. But that'd be a mistake. Brady had so much ugly buried inside of him. Thinking back on it, it's a miracle he got through the day. It was hard to hear, it was harder to witness. But if I'd given up, I wouldn't have him. And, sister, I cannot imagine my life without him. There's one thing I know for certain, Trey would not lie to you. Not about thinking you're beautiful—which, duh, of course he'd think that because you're gorgeous."

Hadley's compliment wasn't a compliment as such considering she was my identical twin, therefore, her telling me I was gorgeous was really self-serving because she was calling herself gorgeous. But I didn't call her out on it when her smile faded and she pinned me with a serious stare. "He wouldn't ask you for more if he didn't mean it. Actually, I don't believe he would've nailed you unless he intended to make an honest woman out of you."

Nailed me? Honest woman out of me? I wasn't sure which quip sounded worse. Again, I found myself rolling my eyes to the ceiling, this time wondering how it was possible that Hadley and I could be so different.

"He's a man," I pointed out.

"A man who respects you, his friends, his job, our family. A man who wouldn't fuck you, then roll out of your bed and walk away."

I cringed at Hadley's vulgar description of what Trey and I had done. There was no arguing it had been rough and deliciously dirty, but there was something more to it. Tender didn't quite explain it, but that was the best I could come up with. It was in the way he'd looked at me, the way he touched me—even though it had been anything but gentle, it had been done with reverence.

"I don't think Trey knows what he wants. I think he's struggling with a lot of stuff and he's confused."

"I agree, he's struggling. But he's not confused. He reached out to you because he sees in you what all of us know."

"What's that?"

"Adalynn Walker isn't shy and she isn't a sweet wallflower. She's strong and fierce and loyal to the end. He sees it, recognizes it, and knows if there is someone who can heal what he's got inside of him, it's you."

"I think you're describing yourself," I whispered.

"I'm impulsive and loud and unrelenting. Your strength is quieter. You bring peace where I bring mayhem. You'll coax and soothe whereas I'll force and demand. We are the same in so many ways, different in others, but one thing that cannot be denied is, we are Emily Walker's daughters. She taught us how to love hard, how to be strong, to be smart. But just like Mom, the two of us need something different than Quinn and Delaney."

I didn't want to ask because I was afraid I already knew the answer, but I found my lips forming the question before I could stop it.

"And what's different about us?"

"Like Mom, we found ourselves men who need us. Not like Carter needs Laney or Brice needs Quinn. Mom taught the two of us something different, she taught us to feel deep, to see past the surface and into the heart of someone. And, Addy, Mom also passed down something else important—the tools we need to heal the men that we would eventually find."

Damn if Hadley wasn't right. Mom gave me and Hadley something a little more than she gave our sisters. Delaney had Mom's inner strength. Quinn was all Dad, she had his determination. Hadley also had parts of Dad in her, but I was all Emily Walker. Mom had found herself a man who had demons and she didn't delay in eradicating what would take him from her. Mom saw a broken man and there was a driving force in her that needed to fix him. I'd known all my life I had that in me, too. I needed to be needed. It was essential to who I was. I wasn't *needy*, but I felt so deep, cared so much, *loved so hard*, I sought out a certain type of man.

A man like my father—strong, bold, protective, who had a soft spot, a vulnerability that my mom had to protect.

No man will live up to Jasper Walker. In your eyes, no man will ever love you like he does.

Crap.

Jake was right.

I did compare all men to my father. But Jake was wrong about one thing, one day I would find a man who loved me. Not the same as my dad loved me—the same way my dad loved my mom. And I wouldn't apologize for wanting that. My parents' love was timeless. It was full of ups and downs, twists and turns, heartache and happiness. They were unshakable.

One day I would find that.

One day I would find a man I could love like my mom loved my dad. And I wouldn't stop until I did.

"He thinks he's an asshole," I repeated. "I hate that he thinks that. But I'm so scared to commit to what I'm feeling because I'm not sure I'm as strong as you think I am."

"You are."

"He thinks I'm...he said..." I stopped myself from

telling her any more of what he said. It felt like a betrayal, a breach of the fragile trust Trey had given me. "I feel like he's put me on a pedestal and now I'm looking down and the fall would be painful."

"He'll catch you."

I looked at Hadley and narrowed my eyes.

"You're not helping."

"I'm totally helping. Climb up that pedestal he built for you, Addy, and stand tall and proud. You deserve to be there. Or jump off it and Trey will catch you. I know he will. Trust him the way he's trusted you. It's gonna be hard though. I'll bet you a hundred bucks, by tomorrow he'll have come up with reasons to push you away."

Just when I'd started to relax at my sister's adamant proclamation I could trust Trey, she went and freaked me out. No, scratch that, freaked me *way* the heck out. Freaked me out so badly, my palms started to sweat and I felt the muscles in my shoulders bunch.

"What?" I stammered.

"What, what? You're not new, Addy. You were right there with the rest of us watching Carter's decades-long battle with Delaney. That boy made an art out of pushing her away. Quinn and Brice started as a fuck buddy arrangement—which is hilarious that

Brice fell for that line of BS from our sister. As if she would've ever *really* agreed to that. When Brice caught on to her game, he bailed like a scared rabbit. And it took Brady four years to give in to what he was feeling, and even after that, I had to stand my ground and force him to open his damn eyes. He didn't run, but boy did he shut me out. Point is, you've seen it time and time again, the struggle to wrangle these men into facing their fears. What I'm telling you is you have it in you to stay the course and win the prize, but you have to stand strong. Shore up your defenses and don't *let* him give in to his fear."

I wasn't sure it worked that way—not with Trey. It wouldn't be about me *letting* him do anything. I couldn't force him to face something he didn't want to face. PT proved that one. Perhaps Hadley hadn't been paying enough attention to the type of man Trey was. My sisters all had an advantage I didn't have; Carter, Brice, and Brady had been in love with them before they'd started their game.

A whisper of a promise.

You're the type of woman who sees past all the superficial bullshit.

Made me fall for you.

I was staring at my twin, contemplating my options. I could pack a bag and flee. I had a multitude of places that didn't include Hadley where I could hunker down and hide. I could rummage through my kitchen and look for a roll of duct tape— which I was ninety-nine-point-nine percent positive I didn't actually own, but hope springs…and all of that—to tape Hadley's mouth closed to prevent her from freaking me out more than she already had. Or I could simply tell her I was done with the conversation, though I knew she wouldn't listen even if I demanded her to stop.

But to my absolute shock, it was Hadley who changed the subject.

"I see you're freaked out," she wisely noted. "Enough about that. Let's talk about Delaney and Mercy."

Freaked out? *Understatement.*

Enough about that? *Was she crazy?*

"I hope Laney has a boy this time," Hadley continued as if she hadn't given me whiplash.

Delaney was pregnant again, this news was met with excitement. My sister had waited a long time to claim her man. And it seemed they were wasting no time building a family. But it was my sister-in-law Mercy's pregnancy that had rocked our family— rocked in the best kind of way. Jason and Mercy had been married a donkey's years and everyone had been impatiently waiting for them to get around to making babies. Laney being Laney didn't take offense to Jason and Mercy's news overshadowing her and Carter's second pregnancy. Actually, it was Laney who was celebrating Mercy and Jason's unborn baby the loudest. She was making this special time in our family all about our brother and his wife.

I, however, didn't want Laney to have a boy this time. I thought that Carter needed girls—pretty little girls he could spoil.

Instead of sharing my opinion, I asked, "Is Mercy feeling better?"

"Not even a little bit. Morning sickness is kicking her ass."

Darn. I didn't know much about pregnancy other than what a never-been-pregnant-woman knew, which was to say, not very much beyond the basics seeing as I'd never grown a human before. But my mom had said that her morning sickness ended at twelve weeks. It would seem Mercy hadn't gotten that lucky.

I made a mental note to text her tomorrow and ask if there was something I could do for her. Jason had said the only thing Mercy was holding down was cereal of all things, but that was last week. As I'd learned with Laney's first pregnancy, cravings could change daily.

"Has anyone started planning her baby shower?" I asked as the front door opened and Trey came through.

I suppose Brady followed. Though I didn't notice.

I suppose my sister answered my question. Though I didn't hear a single word she said.

No, all of my attention was on Trey. Whatever mood he'd been in when he left had worsened.

Sure, he'd tried to hide it like Trey tried to hide a lot of things. But something had changed. He looked crushed, and when his gaze met mine, the oxygen in my lungs crystalized and I stopped breathing. He was crushed…no, he was something different. If I could conjure up an image in my mind of what a man whose dog he'd had since birth, gone everywhere with, hunted with, went on runs with, watched football with, and had trained to fetch beers from the fridge—in other words, his very best friend in the whole world—had just dropped dead right before his very eyes—that would be Trey.

A moment later, Trey blanked his expression and gave me a careful grin.

Grin, not smile.

The desire to do bodily harm, after I shook some sense into him, bubbled to the surface. But before I could tell Trey to wipe the stupid, fake, ugly grin off his face, my sister nudged my shoulder.

"What?" My head whipped to the side. Hadley was close and she gave me wide eyes and a sharp jerk of her chin.

"How was traffic?" she asked the guys and pushed me forward, completely ignoring my 'what.'

"The Station's only two blocks up, babe," Brady answered.

I could hear the smile in his tone but my attention was back on Trey. He had to be the hottest guy I'd ever seen. Way better looking than Jake. But right then with that fake grin on his face, his posture stiff, his eyes distant, his social mask firmly in place, he was downright unattractive.

Emily Walker had taught me a great many things. To my way of thinking, the most important lesson was to pay attention. To look beyond what people showed you—to the hurt that lies beneath. Not to listen to the words people spoke but to hear the meaning behind those words.

I held Trey's icy stare and contemplated Hadley's certainty I had what it took to stay strong and break through his force field—to dig out what pained him.

Confidence took root.

I see you, Trey Durum.

I. See. You.

10

Addy saw it.

She saw everything I didn't want her to see, and instead of feeling annoyed, I felt a shiver of excitement. But when Brady entered the kitchen and dropped a kiss on Hadley's forehead before he dropped the bags on the counter, that excitement turned to guilt, then to anger.

I'd never be accepted into the Walker family like Brady had. And that pissed me right the fuck off. Like his daughter, Jasper saw too much. He knew I'd fucked up on my last mission, he knew the result of that put his niece, Liberty, in grave danger, and he knew my reputation. It pissed me off because had I been in the right frame of mind and thinking, I would've remembered all the reasons I needed to stay away from Addy.

My latest fuck-up was arguably bigger than my last. Addy would be caught in the crossfire. Shy, innocent Adalynn who'd sweetly given herself to me despite all of her hang-ups.

Now what am I supposed to do?

"Trey?" Addy called.

"Yeah?"

"I asked if you wanted a plate."

"A plate?"

Addy blinked, then her eyes narrowed and again she saw too fucking much.

"Would you like a plate for your patty melt or are you good to eat it over the wrapper?"

Jesus, how much of the conversation had I missed?

"Wrapper's fine."

Addy handed me my sandwich, which I lamely took but didn't move. Then she went about sorting the rest of the food. When she was done and Hadley and Brady had walked to her table, leaving the two of us alone in her kitchen, I felt the heat of her stare and looked up.

So damn beautiful.

So damn sweet.

I wanted to promise her the world. Promise I'd bury all the bad shit that infested my brain if she'd promise I could wake up every morning next to her. Promise I'd make her happy if she promised not to give up on me.

For the first time in my life, I wanted what Carter had. I wanted a pretty wife, I wanted our children to fill the home I gave her. I wanted to go to sleep next to Adalynn knowing she saw too much, knowing she knew me, the real me. And she knew, not because I told her but because she saw past all my shit straight to the heart of me. She didn't care about perfection, she wasn't impressed by my military service, she didn't care I had scars and marks on my soul.

"What's wrong?" she muttered quietly.

"We'll talk after they leave."

"And during this talk, will you let me down easy and tell me it's you and not me?"

Fucking hell.

Pain stabbed my heart. That was exactly what I'd planned to tell her.

"Baby—"

"Just so you know." She paused and leaned closer. "You can save the speech. I know it's you and not me. I know it's you who asked me to trust you, but once you had that trust it scared the crap out of you. I might not be experienced but I am not naïve. So you have until Brady and my sister leave to come up with a new excuse why you're gonna bolt," Addy finished and straightened but decided she wasn't done and continued. "Think real hard, Trey. You've got one shot."

One shot?

Addy was more right than she knew and I'd had my one and only shot at her. I'd taken it and now I was going to do everything she said I was going to do. But she'd never know I was doing it because I loved her. Because I didn't want to cause problems for her.

I'd do it because her dad and most likely all of her uncles would form an impenetrable wall to keep me out. And they'd be right to do it.

Being as I was already an asshole, I watched Addy's hips sway as she walked out of the kitchen. I did this with a new appreciation from all the other times I'd watched her strut her fine ass around Triple Canopy, the gym, and family get-togethers. The woman had an exceptional ass—it was hard not to stare at it—but it felt better cupped in my hands. And it had never looked better than when she was on her hands and knees in front of me, my cock dipping in her pussy and coming out wet with her excitement.

Christ.

I wasn't an asshole. I was a motherfucker with an erection.

And if you think Jasper's not gonna call you out on this shit, you're even stupider.

Jasper Walker.

Nothing could kill my hard-on faster than thinking about the man who'd cut off my dick if he found out I wanted to keep his daughter.

Yeah, that was what I needed. I needed to have the man's name tattooed on my palm so every time I looked at it I'd remember to keep my filthy hands off Addy.

"By the way, I didn't know Jake moved back to Georgia," Hadley said and I froze mid-step.

"Come again?"

Three sets of startled eyes swung my way but I was focused on the pair that belonged to Addy. Hers were wide and pleading.

"Shit. Sorry," Hadley mumbled.

"Who's Jake?" Brady's inquiry wasn't so much a question as a demand to know. The guy was far from dumb and I wasn't trying to hide my irritation as much as Addy was trying to hide her plea not to bring up what had happened.

I was of a different feeling. The more people who knew her ex was in town and had made threats, the better. Hell, I'd planned to tell the team first thing tomorrow morning.

"Jake is Adalynn's ex-boyfriend. Who happens to be a fucking dick. I caught him shouting at Addy. I intervened. Jake didn't feel like backing down and made threats."

"Trey!" Addy seethed.

"Oh my God," Hadley gasped.

"What the fuck?" Brady said over them.

"Was gonna bring it to the table tomorrow. I want eyes on this asshole while he's in town. And if he's moved back, I'll be having words with him to make clear he's never to be in Addy's space again."

"*We'll* make clear," Brady returned.

"You're up for that, I won't say no. I don't want it clear, I want it crystal clear he gets up in Addy's face again, he won't take another easy breath, ever." I glanced back at Hadley and asked, "Where'd you see him?"

Hadley fidgeted in her seat and diverted her eyes, not looking at anyone in the room but on the burger in front of her.

"Hadley?" Brady pushed.

"Out front," she muttered.

"Out front? You mean out front of Addy's?" I forced out.

"Trey," Addy whispered and my insides hollowed.

Fuck.

I wanted to be the man who deserved to hear Addy breathe his name like that. I wanted to be the man who earned her fear.

But I hadn't earned jackshit. I'd fucked up again by not following her home. And when I showed up after getting more than halfway to work, only to give in to my selfish need and turn around, I hadn't checked the street before I banged on her front door.

"Baby, he is not gonna get in your face again," I vowed.

"I'm not worried about me." Addy shook her head and frowned. "He threatened you, not me."

"You don't need to worry about me."

Addy took a deep breath and let it out on a long exhale before her fear-filled eyes locked with mine.

"I think you should be worried. Before he yelled at me, he was poorly explaining why he'd broken up with me."

"Poorly explaining? What does that mean?" Brady rejoined.

Addy looked like she wanted to talk about Jake only less than she wanted her fingernails plucked out.

"Wait," Hadley huffed. "Was he trying to get back together with you?"

I felt my muscles bunch at Hadley's question.

Over my dead body.

"I don't think so. He was at the VA and asked me to lunch. I tried to decline by telling him I had a class. He said he'd wait."

"Why the hell didn't you tell him to shove it? He broke your heart."

"I was curious." Addy's gaze sliced to Hadley's. "He said he wanted to apologize and explain."

"Well? What did he have to say for himself?" Hadley's snotty response made Addy cringe.

"He said he wasn't in the regular Army. That he wasn't infantry, not even back when we were together. When I reminded him who Dad was and that I of all people would understand, he got pissed and said he remembered who Dad was and said some stuff about how Jasper Walker was a hard act to follow. From there it went downhill. Jake didn't come out and say, but the inference was there that he was Special Forces. He said he even lied to his family about being in the infantry." Addy looked back to me and the pleading returned when she said, "You need to take his threats seriously."

I planned on taking them very seriously, just not in the way Addy was implying. I wasn't scared of some piece of shit who talked shit about Jasper because he wasn't man enough to handle his woman while he had her. There was no doubt Jasper taught his daughters how a man should love them, how they shouldn't settle for anything less than the best. But in no way did Carter, Brice, or Brady cow behind some fucked-up excuse like, Jasper was a hard act to follow.

Lame ass punk.

Lame ass punk who knew where Addy lived.

"I'm staying here tonight," I announced.

"Good idea," Brady agreed.

"What? Why?"

"Because you live here alone."

"She can—"

"Hadley," Brady cut his fiancée off. "Trey's staying here tonight. Tomorrow, he'll bring it to the table. We'll discuss it and come up with a plan."

Something warm hit my chest but I shoved it

down, unwilling to entertain the idea Brady trusted me with his soon-to-be sister-in-law.

"Right. That sounds good."

"No, it doesn't. It sounds like my privacy is getting ready to be invaded. No, not my privacy, *my life*. After everything that went down with you, and with Quinn, and with Delaney, and with Tuesday, Mercy, Honor, and Meadow, I will be locked in a safe house."

Hadley grinned a sad smile. "You're probably right. But I'll come visit."

"No, you won't because you won't know where Dad's stashed me. And who knows what Jake's doing in town. Maybe he did get stationed here again. And you know...*you know*, if that's the case Dad will pack my shit and move me back into his house. He won't care I'm a grown woman. He will not care that's not what I want. He will not listen to reason. He will freak the hell out, get the uncles on board, and I'll live with my parents until I'm an old maid."

"She's right," Hadley muttered and nodded. "That's what's gonna happen when Dad finds out."

"And?" Brady asked the question I was thinking.

Jasper's plan sounded perfectly reasonable to me. I wasn't around for Quinn or Delaney's trauma. Though I was intimately familiar with Carter's pain at what happened to her. And I was well acquainted with what had happened to Hadley because I was around for that. Brady had nearly lost his mind and Jasper wasn't far behind him.

I didn't know about the rest, but what I did know was Addy's family had suffered more than their fair share and they would not take Jake lightly.

Addy would be protected.

"And?" Addy scoffed. "I don't want to live in lockdown."

"You can move in with me or I'll move in here," I offered before I thought better of it. "We'll rotate security for her while she's working. The VA is off-limits until we know why Jake was there. Tomorrow I'll get Dylan started. What he can't dig up, Blake can. I know she and Levi are officially retired but I think she'd help on this. As a matter of fact, the new gym's complete. Addy can transfer all her PT patients there. That way she won't have to leave the Triple Canopy compound."

"I agree," Brady said. "The compound's a better option. Security's already set up."

"Is this really happening?" Addy looked outraged.

"Yup," Hadley answered her sister.

"I don't want any of this," Addy protested.

"Baby, you got two choices. Tonight I stay here and tomorrow I hand you over to your father until I handle Jake. Or tonight I stay here, tomorrow I move in with you or you move in with me and your PT sessions get moved to the compound."

"Neither," she snapped.

"That wasn't one of your options."

Adalynn pushed away from the table and stood. Then she showed me a side of her I'd never suspected. One I wish I'd never seen. Sweet Addy enthralled me. The Addy who pushed me over the edge in madness was addicting. But the accretive, aggressive Addy was a game-changer.

And the fuck of it was, I despised aggressive women who wouldn't back down and take no for an answer. But coming from Adalynn Walker, it was hot as fuck.

"I see you haven't met me," she spat. "You think I'm some weak-minded nitwit who will bow down to the men around me. That what, Trey, since you've given me choices, it makes your demand more palpable? That I'll feel warm and fuzzy that *you've* given *me* options about how *you're* gonna take over *my* life? That's not a no, that's a *fuck* no. No to all of it. No to you taking it to the table—whatever the hell that means. No to you spending the night and moving in.

No to me moving my patients. And a big, fat, huge no to my dad thinking he's gonna move me in. I am under no delusion he's not gonna try, he will, and I'm telling you right now, you go into work tomorrow and make a big deal out of this, you'll be the cause of World War Three. No, come to think of it, it'll be more like Armageddon. Dad's gonna push, I'm gonna dig in, and when he tries to pull what you just did, I'll set him straight, too."

"Baby, I do not think you're weak-minded or a nitwit. I don't think you bow down to anyone. But I know you're smart," I stated calmly.

"Damn right, I am."

I'd underestimated Adalynn. I'd never thought any of the things she'd accused me of. But I had wrongly thought she was easygoing. Maybe I'd even mistaken her shyness for something else and thought she needed to be shielded.

"Being that you're smart, I know you didn't miss the threats. But more, I know you didn't miss that something's not right with Jake."

"Trey—"

"Let me finish," I spoke over her. "You're smart, damn smart. So I know you didn't miss the way he was looking at you. That worries me more than him squaring up. I'm a man, I can handle myself if it came down to that. But he lost his shit in a café full of people. I calmly and clearly communicated he was done speaking to you. He was of another mind, and made that clear."

"Right. But, Trey—"

"Not done, baby." Addy clamped her mouth shut but plainly conveyed with her squinted eyes she was not pleased I'd once again interrupted her. "So, being as you're smart, you didn't miss his outburst. But beyond that, I know you love your family—all of them. You know they'll worry and you don't want that for them. No one's—or I should say, *I'm*—not taking over your life or invading your privacy. What I'm doing is helping you give them peace of mind while we look into this douchebag. And while I'm helping you do that, I'll have you covered so if he does think to approach, he'll think twice. If he thinks on it and is still stupid enough to try to get close, I'll have your back. Which means it will be me dealing with him and not you."

"He's right, Addy," Hadley interjected.

"Hadley," Addy sighed. "You know—"

"What I know is a man yelled at my sister. A man who invited her to lunch to explain why he left her. His excuse was he wasn't in the regular Army, but something far more dangerous. Which means, *he's* dangerous. Then he shows up at her house unin-vited after Trey made it clear he wasn't to get near you. Obviously, I wasn't there, but I have a feeling Trey didn't mince words when he told Jake he wasn't to get near you again."

Hadley was breaking through. Addy bit her bottom lip and her gaze skidded from her sister to Brady then to the wall. "What I was going to say is, you know I don't want everyone to worry. But maybe Jake just wanted to apologize."

Was she insane?

"Don't do that," Hadley scoffed. "I get that out of all of us, you're the one who wants to see the best in people. But don't be stupid."

"I'm not being stupid," Addy defended herself.

Before I could get a lid on a Walker Twin argu-ment—which I knew from experience could get heated and loud. Not to mention both women were stubborn in their own ways. Addy silently. Hadley loudly and more determined to win. Hadley went in for the kill.

"I almost died."

I heard Addy draw in a breath. But more, I felt so much fury rolling off of Brady it filled the room and coated my skin.

"Hads," Addy croaked.

"Don't be stupid like me. Don't put Mom and Dad through *that* again. Let Trey keep you safe, even if you think it's not necessary. Let him do what he feels he has to do. How long can it take for them to track down Jake? A week, tops. Isn't that a small price to pay to give everyone around you, including me, peace of mind?"

I was wrong. *That* was the kill shot. Emotional manipulation—*sister style.*

Addy's gaze came back to me, assessing, evaluating; in other words—not happy.

"Want to stay here," she started then stopped. Her lips twisted as she weighed her next words. "But it freaks me out he knows where I live. I didn't tell him, so either he looked it up somehow, or he followed me. Neither of those is good."

I nodded but wisely kept quiet.

"I don't want to give him more," Addy grumbled.

"What was that?"

"I don't want to give him more," she repeated louder. "I've given him all that I want to give him. I wasted a lot of time after he broke up with me licking my wounds, blaming myself, wondering what I did to make him leave me. It ticks me off thinking about giving him more. Uprooting my life, using Triple Canopy resources, taking up valuable—"

"Adalynn, there is nothing more valuable than you," I broke in.

I watched as Addy's shoulders stiffened, her head tilted to the side, her eyes widened and this time she studied me far more thoroughly. And I let her. Didn't move a single muscle, didn't mask my sincerity, nor did I close down. I needed her to know I was serious. I wasn't blowing sunshine trying to get her to do what I wanted.

"Straight up, Addy, you're more important than resources and manpower. Me looking after you isn't a waste, it would be an honor. I get you wanna stay here, and we will if that's what you want. But you're right, he knows where you live and that's creepy as fuck. Beyond that, it's stalking. You didn't give him your address. You didn't invite further communication. So I'd feel better staying at my place, but the choice is yours."

"Your place."

Thank fuck.

"But you have to promise me something?"

Anything. "What's that?"

"You won't tell my dad."

Except that.

"Not gonna play that game, Addy. Either you tell him what went down or I do." Addy started to protest but I kept talking right on over her. No fucking way was I hiding this shit from her family. "I think you feel me when I tell you, I get you're a grown woman. I also get you're independent. But this has nothing to do with that and everything to do with playing it smart. The more people who understand what's going on, the safer you are, and the faster this shit gets sorted. And that's what you want, right? To get this shit done, so Jake doesn't take up more of your time, and you can get back to livin'?"

Addy's face turned a bright shade of red. This time it wasn't sexy. But it sure as fuck was cute.

It also meant I'd won this round.

So I'd take it.

But later, I'd turn her pretty cheeks pink in a better way.

11

I didn't know what I'd expected. Truthfully, I hadn't really thought about where Trey lived. Well, I had wondered in a none-of-my-business-but-I-wanted-to-know-everything-about-the-man sort of way. But like all things having to do with him, I'd shoved it to the back of my mind.

However, someone could've given me a list of ten properties and I wouldn't have picked this one as the house Trey lived in.

This being a brick home in a gated community.

Gated community.

A five-bedroom, five-bath home with a covered front porch. A covered porch with two rocking chairs.

Rocking. Chairs.

Trey had a McMansion with rocking chairs.

I was so stunned I didn't know what to say. I mean, what was there to say? A former Navy SEAL, current commando-slash-PI, lived in a family-style home, albeit a huge family home, with rocking chairs.

How in the heck was this even possible?

"Addy, you okay?" Trey inquired.

My gaze skidded from the fabulous archways, to the pillars, to the gourmet kitchen I could see through the open dining room, to Trey. He looked perfectly comfortable in the vast space. Right at home in the monstrous living room. My eyes left Trey and traveled up the stonework that surrounded the fireplace, going up, and up, and up, reaching the cathedral ceiling.

"It must cost a fortune to heat this place."

"Luckily, it doesn't get too cold in Georgia or you'd be right." Trey chuckled.

"You live in a gated community." I told him something he very well knew.

"Yep."

"In a brick mansion," I went on, pointing out the obvious. "It has five bedrooms but there's only one of you."

"Wouldn't call it a mansion."

Was he nuts? It was huge.

There I was, contemplating buying Mrs. Parker's condo or wondering if I was financially ready for a bigger investment. But my bigger investment would've been a two-bedroom cottage, not in a gated community. Apparently, I was seriously behind in the home-owning game.

I stopped staring at the fireplace only to gawk at the huge windows that ran along the front of the room. Floor-to-ceiling windows that allowed natural light to spill into the room making a huge room look warm and inviting.

And his furniture was to die for. Big oversized suede couches. The perfect shade of thundercloud gray that complemented the soft smoky gray walls. But there were splashes of blue and yellow thrown in to give the room a jolt of color.

Not only did Trey live in a beautiful family home, he was also a master interior decorator. And he'd been to my house. My boring, plain-Jane condo that had no personality. Nothing on the walls, nothing special or inviting about my furniture, no splashes of color, nothing. Just plain.

"Addy?"

"Hm?"

"Look at me, Adalynn."

I did not look at Trey. Instead, my eyes kept

roaming the room, and the more I took in, the more embarrassed I became. Then I was forced to obey his command because I was no longer staring at his super cool, ornate, glass inlaid coffee table, I was staring at Trey's jeans covering his thighs.

"Baby, what's wrong?"

What *was* wrong with me?

I'd never been self-conscious about where I lived. I didn't live in a hovel, but it certainly wasn't a mansion. I'd never cared about money or social status. I had friends who had money, friends who had less money, but they were just that—friends.

"Your house is really nice," I stupidly noted.

"It's not me," he said, and my gaze darted to his.

"What's not you?"

"This place. I don't intend to keep it." Before I could tell him I didn't understand, he went on. "It's an investment. I got this house for a steal. It came fully furnished. I don't know it for a fact because I didn't buy all the shit in this place separately, but I'd guess the furnishings alone shoulda added another hundred-grand to the listing."

Investment.

That didn't make me less embarrassed, that reminded me that I'd been lollygagging through life. I rented a condo from an old woman. In the time I'd lived there, I hadn't even settled in and put my stamp on the place. I didn't have any investments, though my Uncle Levi who was a genius with money had offered to help me. I'd paid for my education while I was getting it. But like my parents had done with my siblings after graduation, they'd given me a check reimbursing me and paid off the loans I'd had. It was their gift to us and it was two-fold. The first part was to teach us responsibility, allow us to muddle our way through, juggle work and school. The bigger lesson though was not to quit. If we quit, we were responsible for the loans. The second part of the gift was obvious—they'd gotten us out of debt. They'd done that to teach us to plan for the future so you could take care of those you loved.

We'd never taken extravagant vacations, Mom and Dad drove decent vehicles, they had a nice home, beautiful backyard, they had five children to take care of and we were not rich. So I knew that saving college tuition for all of us cut deep. But they'd sacrificed and saved. Giving us the opportunity to start our lives free of financial burden.

But I hadn't started planning for my future.

Trey had.

The evidence of that was a brick mansion in a gated community.

"This house has five bedrooms, four and a half baths, a pool, and an HOA board that should be BUD/s instructors they're so quick to jump on your shit. If I so much as leave my trashcan at the curb past eight a.m., there's a letter in my mailbox. I'm not an HOA kinda guy. As I said, I got this place so cheap I actually bought the seller a five-hundred-dollar bottle of scotch I felt so bad. But the seller had retired. He and his wife wanted to move to Missouri where their daughter, son-in-law, and five grandchildren lived. They wanted to downsize and didn't want the hassle of moving all their shit. They also didn't want to wait for the market to go up. They bought this place at a good price, so even giving it to me for what they did they still made a whack. And even if they didn't, Leon and his wife were far from hurting."

When I remained silent, Trey prompted, "Does that explain the house?"

Being as it did, but it didn't take the sting out of how I'd squandered the blessings my parents had given me, I only nodded.

"Good. Now, would you like a tour of the house?"

I wasn't sure I wanted a tour. I wasn't even sure how I'd ended up here.

Jake.

That was why I was standing in Trey's fabulous living room.

I glanced over his shoulder and my eyes caught on the fireplace. It really was too bad he wasn't an HOA kind of guy, because that fireplace rocked. It might not get super-cold in Georgia but it still got chilly. And I'd bet sitting on that huge, gray suede couch with a fire roaring, cuddled under a blanket with Trey, would be awesome. So awesome, I'd never want to get up. So awesome, I could probably drag my backside out of bed on whatever day the trash-cans had to be pulled in and do that at the butt-crack of dawn so there wouldn't be a letter left in the mailbox.

"Yeah, I'd like that," I answered.

"You gonna go silent on me again when I show you the sauna?"

"You have a sauna?"

"Yep. There's also a Jacuzzi, a wine cellar—though it's more like a big closet with racks, something called a butler's pantry, and a library."

My gaze skidded back to his and my stomach clenched. I'd known Trey awhile, I'd seen a whole lot of different expressions pass over his handsome face, but I'd never seen him wary.

"I'm sorry," I grumbled. "You have a beautiful home."

"House," he corrected. "This is just a house. A home is where you raise a family."

Something flashed across his face and I wondered if he wanted a family.

"It's beautiful nonetheless."

Trey dipped his chin, tagged my hand, and pulled me through the huge, formal dining room. Then he took me for a tour of his mansion and I'd found I was right—it *was* a mansion. Nearly six-thousand square feet. Way too much for one person. I found out his definition of a "big closet" and mine were two different things. The wine cellar was the size of my childhood bedroom. The walls were painted a deep maroon, the racks were mahogany, and in the middle of the room, three round, high-top tables sat four each. Presumably for tastings or entertaining. I wasn't a wine person, nor was I into formal entertaining, however even I could appreciate the beauty of the cellar.

The sauna was, well, a sauna. The Jacuzzi was to-die-for with a Japanese-style pergola surrounding it. One side had an intricate privacy screen, the other sides had curtains that were right then tied open. You could sit in the warm bubbling water and either have complete privacy or a view of the beautiful backyard.

Trey completed the tour in the master bedroom. If you could call a room so large it had a king-sized bed, two nightstands, an armoire, a twelve-drawer dresser, a couch, two chairs, and an accent table a bedroom. Maybe it was called the master suite. Maybe it was simply called insanely huge, over-the-top, and unnecessary. Then again, I grew up in a *home*. Not big, not small, but there were six of us packed in and there was no such thing as personal space. Mom and Dad didn't allow it, they wanted us close—physically and mentally. Even after Dad left the Army and started Triple Canopy and my parents could afford to scale up, they didn't. They kept our family home.

"You've gone silent again," Trey teased.

"It's a lot to take in. Especially this." I lifted my hand and swept the room. "This room alone is half the size of my condo."

Again Trey's expression settled on wary.

Crap.

"I don't know why you're looking at me like that," I said. "I don't mean to be offensive. I'm just surprised. And not because I thought you would live in a crappy bachelor pad full of empty pizza boxes and beer cans. It's just...this isn't you. I don't know how to explain it, but I promise I'm not doggin' where you live. It's beautiful."

His lips twitched and he stepped closer to me, forcing my head to tip back so I could continue to look at him. But when that lip twitch turned into a full-fledged smile, I was glad I'd tipped my head back. And when his mouth lowered to mine, I was doubly glad. I wouldn't call what he did a kiss so much as a lip touch. The sweetness of it so earnest, I quivered.

"What's happening?" I whispered.

"You know what's happening, Adalynn."

"I don't think I do."

"I made myself pretty damn clear what I wanted to happen."

He had made himself clear—crystal clear. But then he'd left with Brady and when he came back he didn't look like a man who wanted to 'take a chance and ride this out.' He looked like a man who'd changed his mind and wanted to find a way to extradite himself from the situation as quickly as possible.

"You said we'd talk later," I reminded him.

"Are you ready for that talk now?"

No. No, I was not ready. I was standing in Trey's master suite in his huge house with a thousand troubling thoughts running through my mind, stupefied why I'd brought up the talk he'd said we'd have in the first place. Maybe I'd thought he'd blow me off. Maybe that was what I secretly wanted. And suddenly I figured out what my problem was. I was not embarrassed about my small condo with no personality. I wasn't shocked Trey lived in a show-stopper in a gated community. I didn't even really care he seemed to have his life together and invest-ments and I absolutely did not.

I was scared.

Utterly terrified.

And not of Jake. I thought everyone, most espe-cially Trey, was making way too big of a deal about nothing.

No, I was petrified that Trey had changed his mind.

12

I should've let Addy off the hook. She thought she'd offended me, when she'd done the opposite. I wasn't insulted at her surprise I lived in a big house. I was ecstatic she noted it wasn't my style. I was pleased as fuck it didn't impress her. It didn't change her opinion of me. It absolutely didn't change her. If anything, it made her withdraw, and even that made me happy.

Addy was who she was. She was nothing like any other woman I'd ever met. It wasn't lost on me I was good-looking. I had a mirror, and even if I didn't like the way women had thrown themselves at me—going back as far as I could remember—I didn't have to work very hard—actually I didn't have to work *at all* —to get a warm body in my bed. In high school, that worked for me. In my early twenties, that seriously worked for me.

Then it got old. Then it got annoying. Then it became annoying as fuck I couldn't sit in a bar with my friends without being approached. That was when my dislike for aggressive women started. There was no challenge, no chase, and for a man like me who needed both, I took little to no pleasure knowing all I needed to do was jerk my head to the exit sign and women would follow.

That was not Adalynn. First, she wouldn't catch that play. She'd be utterly clueless even if I'd pointed directly at her, then the door—she wouldn't understand the meaning. And if by some miracle she'd caught on, she would not wordlessly follow me out the door. She would not get in her car and let me follow her home. And she unequivocally would not fuck a man never having spoken to him. All of that was refreshing in a way that made what we'd shared earlier even sweeter.

I was not a man she thought was hot and wanted to fuck. I was Trey. Now that she'd seen my house, which was so in-your-face and screamed money, she couldn't miss I had some, and not a little, but a lot. Yet, she didn't give the first fuck. She was still shy, unsure, sweet, innocent Addy. If anything, she didn't like knowing I could afford a house like this. And that turned me the fuck on. I was still *just* Trey.

I'd been a lot of things to a lot of women, but never had a single one of them just seen me.

But Addy did.

So, Addy looking around my house with curiosity, trying her best to disguise her mild distaste, wasn't refreshing, it wasn't a turn-on, it was *everything*. Which was going to make the conversation we needed to have, suck.

"Bathroom's through there." I pointed to the door. "I'm gonna go down and get your bag. You can change. After that, your choice, we can talk up here, on the couch, or out by the pool."

"You should've told me you had a pool. I would've brought a suit."

Visions of Addy in the yellow bikini I saw her wear last summer assaulted my mind. The image so vivid, I remembered down to the minutest of details how the bottoms had sat low on her hips, how the triangle top had teased me all afternoon. I felt my cock stiffen the same way it had that day when I fought the need to take her somewhere private and slide the material to the side while leaving it tied around her neck.

"Trey?"

"The yellow one," I demanded.

"Huh?"

"Tomorrow, we're going to your house so you can get your yellow bikini."

"Yellow—"

"The one you wore at your Uncle Lenox's."

"You remember what color my bathing suit was?" Her pretty eyes widened.

"Baby, that suit is burned into my memory. I hope to God I don't lose my mind when I'm an old man because I want you in that yellow bikini to be the last thing I see while I slip from this life."

With that, I turned and left a gawking Addy standing in my room. We had things to talk about, and if I didn't hurry and wrangle my cock into submission, there would be no discussions. I'd have her bent over my bed, balls deep, not thinking about bathing suits, what her father would do to me when he found out I was in love with his daughter, or Jake Belview—the motherfucker wouldn't be a thought. And that would be a mistake. I had to stay sharp and keep Addy safe.

I checked the doors, set the alarm in case Addy wanted to have our talk in my bed and I wouldn't have to leave her again to come back down and arm it. I grabbed her heavy-ass bag and started the trek back through a monstrous house that was not a home. I used this time—and there was a lot of it—to get my head straight. She needed to understand where I was at, where I knew her family would be at, and how we were going to proceed.

How I was going to accomplish all of that with Addy in my bed, I wasn't sure.

Heaven and hell.

I wasn't sure how I could be in both at the same time but I was. After Addy changed, she couldn't hide her yawn so I made the decision for her and opted for our talk to happen in my bed. With her in a pair of cotton sleep shorts and a tight tank-top thing that I was sure had a specific name, but since I had a dick I didn't have the first clue and truthfully didn't care to know what it was called. I had two eyes and 20/20 vision so even if she wasn't cuddled to my side, I wouldn't have missed she'd taken off her bra, and the thin elastic digging into the flesh of her shoulders was working overtime keeping her full breasts contained. The color was pinkish, though Addy would likely call the shade some specific name that, again, me having a dick prevented me from knowing. Though, the way the hue complemented her skin tone was not missed.

So, I was in heaven and hell at the same time and I'd put myself there. And the fuck of it was, I'd take this kind of hell every day of the week and twice on Sunday if it meant I had Addy at my side. Just like this. Her tucked to my side, her head resting on my shoulder, our legs tangled together, and her arm heavy across my stomach. She was stiff as a board, unsure, uncoordinated, and I would absolutely, without a doubt, take this over some overtly sexed-up woman making a grab for my cock. Addy was hesitant about what to do, where to put her hands, her legs, and I'd had to arrange her to the position we were currently in or she would've been on the other side of the bed making sure no inch of her body touched mine.

"Know you're tired, babe, but we hafta talk about a few things that are gonna happen tomorrow."

"Oh-kay," she said on an exhale. And if it was possible, her body grew stiffer.

"Relax."

"Not sure I can. You're scaring me."

"You've got no reason to be scared. You're not the one in danger of losing body parts."

"What?" She started to sit up but I tightened my arm around her and held tight.

"I'm kidding."

I wasn't, but I didn't want to get into all the ways a human body could be dismembered—Jasper knowing all of those ways and how he wouldn't hesitate.

"Before I start, was there something in particular you wanted to talk about?" I offered, sensing her discord.

There were a few beats of silence before I gave her a squeeze and told her, "You can be straight with me, Addy. Anything you have to say I want to hear. Especially if it's scaring you."

I let the quiet stretch and finally she relaxed—not much, but I'd take it.

"Why'd you look upset when you got back from The Station?"

I blew out a breath and didn't hesitate. The only way to get Addy to fully trust me was to earn it. She would give me some trust to start with, but the rest— the real trust, I'd have to work to get. And I planned on having all of Adalynn. Top to toe. Heart and soul. Unbreakable trust. I needed that from her.

"Brady pointed out your dad was gonna have an issue with us."

"My dad?" Gone was any minuscule amount of tension she'd released.

Fuck.

"I've got mad respect for your dad. It has nothing to do with him owning the company I work for, his time in the Army, or him being your father, and everything to do with the kind of man he is. I respect he loves his family, he's protective of his girls, that he'd lay down his life for his wife. He treats the people around him the way a man should, with care and understanding. With all that said, I get why he's gonna have a problem. I just don't care."

"Maybe you should explain that," she said and jerked out of my arms. This time I let her go but only because I wanted to be able to look at her when I did as she asked.

But I didn't allow her to get far and I communicated this by trapping her hand on my chest and tightened my grip on her hip. She was sitting up, mostly on her side, looking down at me. Her hair was pulled up into a ponytail and honest to God, I had to use every inch of concentration I had to not let my attention wander to the graceful slope of her neck. Her pretty exposed throat, collarbone, and chest had me at a whole new level of alert. A place where my body was very aware of hers, but deeper still to a place where I was simply cognizant of her. Of all that she was, all that I had close, all that I wanted to have, keep, and hold for a lifetime.

Ultimately, my need for her trust and understanding won out over my desire to greedily drink her in before I did very filthy things to her. So I was able to hold her gaze as I explained.

"Jasper knows me. He knows as much as he can know about my military service, he knows I fucked up and almost killed his niece, he knows I just plain fucked up, but he also knows my reputation. And that I figure is going to be the black mark he hones in on. He wants better for you because you deserve better. I know that, too. I know you deserve the best, and I fall short of that in every way, but I don't care about that either. I know I should've continued to protect you from me and kept my distance. I didn't do that, but I can't say I regret giving in to what I've wanted since I first saw you because that would be a fucking lie."

I squeezed her hand resting on my chest. "I also wish I could blame what happened on something stupid like my control snapped, but it didn't. I went to your house with the intent to make you mine. I did it willfully and fully aware it wasn't right, but I didn't care because I'm selfish as fuck and I know—knew it the very second I laid eyes on you—that you were the woman who was going to challenge me, frustrate me, push me, and I was gonna love every minute of it."

She shifted, but I wasn't done. "I knew, Adalynn, just by one single look that you were what I'd been missing. So, I don't care your dad's gonna have a shit hemorrhage. I'm not gonna waste his time or mine trying to talk him around, because the man he is, that will not work. He'll need proof you are who you are to me and that's gonna take time. That I intend to give him. That's the respect I'm going to extend to him. I'll show him with time and deed what my intentions are.

"But, baby, Brady was right, and we both better brace, because the wrath of Jasper Walker is gonna scorch the earth. And he'll be coming at me with an assault team. Your uncles will take his back and I'll feel the full weight of your family."

"Trey—"

"Let me finish," I cut her off. "I welcome it."

"Welcome it?"

"Yep. Not only do I welcome it. You need it. And I'm fully prepared to give you everything you need including time, deed, and proving to your family I'm exactly what you've been missing."

"I don't think I need that," she whispered.

"You do, Addy. Not only does your dad know my reputation, you do as well. And it fucks me to say it, but that reputation was earned. I don't deny it, I won't make excuses for what I've done in the past, mainly because I don't regret it. I was young, single, and never lied to a single woman I've been with. I will tell you that, since I've been in Georgia, I've only been with one woman—you. Haven't touched anyone else, haven't thought about it, didn't want it."

"You haven't?"

Her wide eyes and disbelief pissed me off more than Brady thinking I'd fuck Addy.

"Did you miss the part where I told you I fell in love with you before I spoke a single word to you?" I snapped.

"Are you mad?"

"Gettin' there, baby."

"Why?"

"Seriously?"

Addy flinched at my biting tone, then served up her own attitude when she responded, "Yes, seriously. I can't imagine why you'd be mad at me being surprised you haven't slept with someone in, I don't know...months and months and months."

"Adalynn—"

"Don't growl at me, you caveman."

That was it.

I was done.

I surged up, Addy let out a squeak, and I flipped her on her back, pinning her to the bed.

"Serious as shit, woman—you think I'd fuck another woman knowing I'd found *The One*?" I gave her my weight and she wheezed something illegible. But I didn't give her a chance to repeat herself before I went on. "You think I'd fuck some random chick when I knew I was gonna make my play for you, knew I'd found someone special? Finally after years of living with nothing, I found something—someone who made me want to be better. You think I'd seriously stick my dick—"

"No," she rasped and I propped more of my weight on my elbow. "Not when you put it like that."

"And me telling you I took one look at you and fell for you wasn't enough?"

"I've been told that before," she whispered. "Twice. The first one left me after he took my virginity and gave me some lame reason. The second bided his time, got me into bed, told me I was frigid and not very good at it, and...it um...ended badly. However, both told me they were in love with me. But obviously, they weren't."

I felt my chest cave in at the humiliation and

embarrassment she couldn't hide. I also got the sense there was more to the story than the second relationship ending badly, but I didn't question her because she looked positively mortified.

Motherfuckers.

"Now why do you look mad?"

"I'm not," I told her and stared down into the most amazing pair of green eyes. Christ, she was beautiful—every inch of her—but it was her eyes that did it for me.

"You look like you are," she pushed.

"Okay. I'll amend. I'm not mad at *you*, I'm pissed as fuck at both those assholes. But more, I'm pissed I only have a shot at shoving Jake's teeth down his throat, and not the other idiot, too."

"You can't—"

"Shh. I can and I will. First, because he's going to understand that you're off-limits and that understanding is gonna come direct from me. Seeing as he's a douchebag idiot, he's gonna puff his chest and square up. Something I'm looking forward to him doing. Thankful even, that he's gonna provide me with the golden opportunity to teach him a lesson about how to treat women."

"He didn't—"

"I don't know how he treated you when you were

together and I don't ever wanna know. But in the end, he made you feel insignificant, he made you feel bad about yourself, he threw a precious gift you gave him in your face and he did that in the dirtiest way a man can do to a woman. He tarnished something special and beautiful. So, yes, Addy, he did. And years later, it's still fucking with your head. And don't deny it, because you're lying under me, and instead of knowing that you are sexy as fuck, beautiful, crazy-good in bed, you're looking up at me like it's the first time you've heard it."

"Because it is."

Jesus Christ.

How was *that* possible? It pissed me off Addy didn't understand her allure—not her sexual appeal, her innocence, her beauty—none of it.

"You look madder," she whispered.

I was wrong.

Now I was done.

Done as in, I was done talking.

It was time to show her.

"Shirt off, baby."

I lifted to my knees, her hands went to the hem of her shirt, and she tore it over her head. Then I took in my fill. My eyes roamed, eating up every inch of skin she'd revealed. Soft, silky skin I couldn't wait to touch and taste. But first, she needed to know a few things, so maybe I wasn't done talking.

"You know what I see?" Addy didn't answer but I didn't need her to. "Pure beauty. Soul-deep beauty. The kind you cannot create with the shit women put on their faces and in their hair to glam it up. The kind you can't fake. Pure of heart and mind. Straight up good and clean."

I heard her swift inhale and continued. "You know what else I see? The woman who was made to be mine." My hands went to her waist and my thumbs skimmed the soft skin of her stomach. "Made to enjoy my touch." I leaned forward and dipped my tongue into her belly button before I licked all the way to the curve of her breast, over the swell, and circled her nipple. "Made to enjoy my mouth." I traveled to her other breast, pulled that nipple between my teeth, and softly grazed it until she arched her back, silently asking for more.

When she finally made that sexy-as-fuck mew I loved so much, I pulled away. "Made to moan for me. Do you get it yet? You weren't meant for *them*, you were made for *me*."

I was then seriously fucking done talking.

13

Luxurious.

I was floating on a cloud—a soft, fluffy, *luxurious* cloud. My head was tipped back in offering, Trey's mouth was on my throat, and he was moving slowly, lazily, gently. And both his hands were engaged in the action. One was resting on the side of my neck, his fingers wrapped around the back and pressed deep, his thumb softly skimming under my chin—a gentle command to stay as I was.

His other hand had slid up from my hip and was now cupping my breast, that thumb was also softly skimming, only it was skimming my nipple.

All of it sublime. His heat, his weight, his touch, his mouth—perfect. All of it was also lazy, gentle, slow—in other words, pure torture. Trey was taking his time like he'd cleared his schedule for the next week for the sole purpose of driving me mad. He was in the mood to explore and to do it at his leisure.

Trey shifted down and my legs automatically opened to make room for him. This movement caused friction between my legs, and without meaning to I lifted my hips, needing more.

I heard his chuckle as he brushed his lips over my nipple and continued this torturous event until my back bowed and I let out a frustrated groan.

"Hm," he hummed and swept his mouth over my nipple, featherlight.

"Trey."

He didn't reply.

He didn't give into my non-verbal demand to get the show on the road.

He didn't engage his tongue or his teeth.

He just continued at *his* pace, doing what *he* wanted, not giving *me* what *I* wanted.

It occurred to me there was a way I could get what I wanted—all I had to do was take control. I brought my knees up, planted my feet on the bed, and bucked my hips while twisting. This maneuver failed when Trey gave me more of his weight, effectively pinning me down. It also had the unfortunate side effect of bunching my shorts, which gathered in the perfect position to rub exactly the right spot. The unfortunate part was it felt so good, I did it again, which had the adverse reaction I needed and slowed Trey down.

Apparently, I wasn't above begging. I found this out when I did just that—begged.

"Please, Trey."

"Slide your hand in your panties."

Say what?

"Hand in your panties, Adalynn," he repeated.

I didn't think I vocalized my query, however, my anxiety-addled mind was in a haze so maybe I had. When I didn't move, Trey made the decision for me. His hand found mine, guided them to my chest, placed my palm on my breast, and used his over mine to slowly steer them down over my ribs, my belly, then into my shorts and panties.

He didn't stop there. Together, our fingers glided over my clit, not pausing even when I moaned and shafts of electricity shot through me. He didn't slow until he reached his destination, and even then he used our fingers to tease my opening until I felt another gush of wetness surge. Through all of this, Trey remained silent. I, however, was beyond silence and was now panting my groans.

"More, please."

Trey dipped our fingers through my excitement and pushed in. If I hadn't been so turned on I would've been embarrassed at how wet I was. However, I was beyond that, too. Further, I was so far gone I didn't wait for him to start moving and took over fingering myself. I adjusted so my palm rubbed my clit as my finger moved in and out and tangled with his.

"Do not stop." Trey's gruff demand sent tingles down my spine.

Then he roughly yanked his hand out of my panties, sat up, and jerked my shorts and panties down. He did not need my help doing this. In a flash, they were magically gone and his hands were on my thighs, opening me to his gaze.

Holy freaking-A.

All I was doing, all he could see, would've freaked me the heck out if I hadn't caught the look on Trey's face. It was the first time since he told me what he saw when he looked at me that I'd come out of my daze long enough to focus on his face.

There was hunger for sure. Desire, absolutely. He liked what I was doing and he liked what he'd driven me to do. But more, there was pure, unleashed affection. It made his already handsome face infinitely better. Knowing that all of it was for me—the best.

"Do not stop."

Oh, yeah, right.

I'd been so lost staring up at him, I'd forgotten what I was supposed to be doing. Not because it didn't feel good, but looking at Trey with his face soft, his eyes gentled, knowing what I knew—how he felt about me, what he saw, and what he wanted—was way better.

That was, until he shoved his lounge pants down and his rigid dick sprung free. My mouth watered and my hand between my legs moved faster.

"Christ, you're so fucking hot, I don't know what to do with you."

My gaze locked on his and I watched with no small amount of attention as Trey started stroking himself. He did this slowly, like he was taking the week-long vacation he'd set aside to drive me mindless and was now inflecting the same torture upon himself.

"When you look at me with those beautiful eyes of yours, I want to hand you the world. But, baby, when they darken and turn wild, knowing all that beauty is just for me, you make me lose my mind." His other hand left my leg and he cupped his balls, giving them a not-so-gentle tug, eliciting a groan from him that made my inner muscles spasm. "You're gonna finger yourself for me until you come."

Freaking, freaking-A, that's hot.

So incredibly hot, my back bowed so deep my hips left the mattress and my eyes drifted closed.

"No, baby, watch me." My eyes snapped back open and I hazily took in Trey's sexy smile. *Sweet mother of all things holy.* "Watch me stroke my cock." Slowly, my gaze dropped to his hand and I watched. No, I didn't watch—I was riveted. So engrossed, I wasn't paying attention to the show I was putting on for Trey, totally enthralled at his instead. Long, firm glides, stopping every few strokes to thumb the tip before he started again.

Then I saw the bead of moisture leak and that was so freaking out-of-this-world hot, I snapped. I don't know what came over me, except that I was so turned on watching him while he commanded me to touch myself while he watched. Instinct and need washed over me and I rubbed harder and faster until my climax built. I slid my finger out, added another, and went deeper. I was nearly there, so close I was pulsing, preparing to shatter any moment, when Trey broke the silence.

"Goddamn beautiful. Give it, baby."

And I gave it. I couldn't stop it if I wanted to. My hips bucked and my fingers stilled as my orgasm rolled over me. Seconds later, Trey pulled my hand away and in one rough thrust, he was inside of me. My ass was off the bed, he was still on his knees, his hands gripped my hips and he drove in and out while holding me where he wanted.

Holy shit.

"One more."

"Can't."

"One. More."

Each word was punctuated by a thrust. I didn't think it was possible but at that moment, hearing his coarse, desire-filled tone, I'd give him anything, including the impossible. Somehow, someway, I'd give Trey everything he wanted.

But in the end, I didn't have to give anything. He took it.

"Silk," he grunted. "So goddamn slick and tight."

Trey lifted me higher. I felt my pussy start to flutter and it was building again. This time better. So much better than what I could give myself. He must've felt it, too, because a low groan rumbled from him and he pounded harder.

"Trey."

"Fucking Christ, Addy."

I righted my head and blinked to clear the fog, needing to see him as he took me over the edge. And that was all it took for the throbbing to turn into pulses that tore through me until my body seized and fire seared my skin.

"Fuck," he groaned through gritted teeth.

His eyes closed, his head tipped back, and I watched the most beautiful thing I'd ever witnessed in my life. Trey Durum's big, muscular body shuddered and trembled, totally unmasked and open. Long moments later, I was still staring up at him, reveling in the splendor of Trey giving me a gift, one he hadn't given the first three times we'd been together, one that even in my limited experience I knew was huge. When his eyes opened, they immediately found mine. And it was then I watched the second most beautiful thing I'd ever witnessed—Trey Durum laid bare. Not a shred of pain was to be seen. No guilt. No shame. No anger. Just *him*.

My breath caught, my belly melted, and I frantically memorized every nuance. All the light that he hid behind the shadows. The beauty he'd unveiled. Every shade and hue that couldn't be seen when his darkness blotted out all the color. *Everything*. I tattooed it on my soul so I'd never forget.

That moment was what I'd fight to keep. That

shine in his eyes that said he was happy, deliriously so. I would fight to earn that look.

"Thank you," I whispered.

To my surprise, he did not shut down the way I thought he would.

His response was heartbreakingly honest.

"Only for you, Adalynn."

He knew what he was showing me. And he knew I understood how precious his gift was.

Oh, yes, I was going to fight until he showed that shine to the world.

14

The next morning, I yanked my tee over my head, turned to leave, and froze.

The bed was made. Not like I normally "made" it, but well and truly made. Comforter pulled up and straight, pillows fluffed and arranged neatly. Then my gaze drifted to the suitcase. Then I thought about what I'd found in my shower that morning—Addy's shampoo, conditioner, and something called "body scrub" the bright pink label proclaiming it contained sugar. Being as I was a man and I'd never had woman-shit in my shower before, I had no clue the significance of the proclamation, nor did I understand why a woman would want to slather sugar over her skin. Though, having felt Adalynn's silky smooth skin, I fully appreciated the effects and would stock her up so she never ran out. Her electric toothbrush was on the vanity, plugged in and ready for future use. There were two hair ties, five bobby pins, lotion with a pump top, a small green screw top bottle that claimed to be "eye cream" whatever the fuck that was, and lastly, her brush. All of that in my bathroom.

The bed was made—by Addy. And her suitcase that still needed to be unpacked was on the floor near the outrageously huge armoire that I'd yet to figure out its proper use.

Bottom line was, I liked Addy's things being in my bathroom. I liked seeing her belongings in my bedroom. But I'd fucking love it if she'd unpack and stay indefinitely.

On those thoughts, I exited a bedroom that had never felt like anything but a huge room, in a huge house, in a luxury community that I sure as fuck didn't belong in. But that morning, the first morning I'd woken up to a soft, warm Addy cuddled to my side, that huge room felt like something more. Like it was *ours*. Almost like a home. And from the moment my eyes opened, I wanted to give this huge house to her. I wanted her to fill it with our kids. No, I wanted her to fill it with her laughter—her happiness.

I made my way to the kitchen and more warmth

spread. Addy was at the stove with her back to me. That sight filled me with the same unnamable emotion I'd experienced seeing her stuff in my shower. It had nothing to do with her cooking, it didn't even have anything to do with her wearing a tight pair of workout pants that molded to her ass. It was just her in my kitchen.

Before I could call out my greeting, she set down the spatula and reached for her phone. With her back still to me, she finished what she was doing and set it on the counter beside the stove. Ringing filled the vast space; she was calling someone. I hadn't moved, not because I was being nosy but because I was *moved* by some unnamable emotion her mere presence elicited.

It was unfortunate I didn't tell her I was there.

A man's deep voice replaced the ringing and that warmth turned into fire.

"Addy," the guy cooed.

Fucking *cooed*. At *my* woman.

"Bass. Hey. Sorry to call so early but I need to cancel."

Bass? Was that the guy's name?

"What's going on, sweetheart?"

Sweetheart?

What. The. Fuck?

"I had some stuff come up. I'm really sorry. We'll do lunch after next week's class."

"Anything I can help with?"

Still motherfucking cooing.

"That's sweet of you to offer but I have it under control."

Sweet?

Hell, no. I'd show Addy sweet and it wasn't some dude's offer to help her.

I moved around the island, made my way to her, and bent to kiss her neck.

"Morning, baby."

My greeting wasn't quiet—the guy on the phone was meant to hear it and Addy caught on immediately. Her head swiveled to the side, her eyes narrowed, and she gave me an adorable annoyed scowl.

"Adalynn?"

"Sorry, Bass. I'm here. Again, I'm really sorry I have to cancel today. Hopefully, by next week I'll have everything sorted and I'll be in class."

"Who was that?"

The adorable went out of Addy's scowl and her lips pinched. So when she answered this Bass guy, her tone was clearly miffed.

"Trey," she answered.

"Trey?" Gone was Bass's cooing and his tone had slid straight to unhappy.

Addy's shoulders jerked and her gaze sliced to the phone. She hadn't missed it either.

"Yeah. You might've heard me talk about him, he works at—"

"I know who he is," Bass cut her off then followed up with a question. One he could disguise—total fishing expedition. "Are you working at TC today?"

"Eggs are burning, baby, you want me to turn them off?"

Even though that was the God's honest truth, Addy snatched her phone off the counter and pushed me back so she could escape.

"That'd be helpful," she snapped before she walked out of the kitchen.

I turned off the burner, salvaged the eggs she'd made, and felt zero guilt for making it crystal clear we were getting ready to enjoy breakfast—together.

I had the eggs plated and a mug of coffee halfway to my lips when Addy returned. It didn't take a genius to see she was seriously pissed. Still, I smiled.

There hadn't been a time when I'd looked at Addy and didn't think she was sweet, shy, and beguilingly beautiful. But pissed, she was smoking hot.

"What was that?" she asked and marched her fine ass straight to me. Shoulders square, back straight, eyes flashing a new kind of fire—*that* was extremely sexy—and lastly, her face was set to granite.

Oh, yeah, my little devil was out and she was pissed as fuck.

Totally cute.

Addy wasn't stupid, nor was I. She'd caught on to my play the second I'd said good morning. There was no reason to deny it, so I didn't.

"That was me making it clear whose kitchen you're in."

"And why would you do that?"

"Because that dude has the hots for my woman. Not only that, but he's got it bad. Figured it was best to kill any hopes he has that he's gonna get in there. The sooner the better. So I killed the dream he's been conjuring up in his asshole brain that he's gonna get you into his bed."

"Bass is not an asshole and he does not have the hots for me."

"No? So you're telling me he doesn't like women?"

"What?"

"Women, Addy. Are you telling me that Bass doesn't like women?"

"I assume so, considering I've seen him with a variety of girlfriends in the years I've known him."

She was no less pissed, but some of the venom had left her tone.

"Is there a reason you don't want him knowing you're in my kitchen making breakfast?"

"Of course not. I just don't like you pissing on my leg."

That made me smile. Which was the wrong thing to do if her downturned lips were anything to go by.

I couldn't resist. "Baby, as kinky as that sounds, I'm not into golden showers. You wanna give that a go, we can—"

"You're gross. I don't—"

She let out a squeak of surprise when I tagged her around the waist and jerked her forward. Her hands hit my chest to brace her fall.

"Adalynn, straight up, that guy's into you. Heard it the second he said your fuckin' name. What I don't know is, are you into him?"

Her hands spasmed and her body locked tight.

Seeing her reaction sent tiny, sharp spikes into my heart.

What the fuck?

"No, I'm not into him," she spat. "He's my kickboxing instructor. He's also a friend and his grandmother owns the condo I live in. Sometimes we have lunch after class."

I believed that they were friends, but there was something more there.

"Addy," I pushed.

"What?"

"Sometimes you have lunch after class?" I prompted.

The change in Addy was immediate. It was also violent and way over the top. Her hands left my chest, then they were back and she shoved me hard enough I had no choice but to let her go so I could keep my balance. Her hip hit the corner of the island, her face registered pain, and the audible groan that followed had me reaching out to stop her retreat but my arms arrested when she flinched away from me.

What in the actual mother fuck was that?

"Addy, baby, what's going on?" I gently asked.

Her answer was to retreat further, not physically, but emotionally. She closed down and locked herself away from me.

She looked like a doe caught in the sights of a crossbow—certain death imminent with nowhere to run.

Again, what in the actual mother fuck?

"Adalynn, what's wrong?"

"You don't get to tell me who my friends are," she rasped.

Her voice was not her own—none of the shy, sweet Addy could be heard. None of the pissed, cute, devilish Addy present. No, this was new, it was hurt-filled and ugly. And my gut roiled at the reason why she'd respond the way she did. It wasn't a kneejerk reaction, it wasn't her being pissed Bass knew she was cooking breakfast in my kitchen.

It was the reaction of a woman who had experience with a man telling her who she could be friends with—the severity of that experience was what had me on edge.

"Baby, I need you to explain why you're telling me that."

Still rooted, body strung tight, fear in her eyes, she didn't delay laying it out.

"I get to be friends with Bass if I want. You don't get to tell me I can't. If I want to go to lunch with someone, I'll do that, too. And I'll go to kickboxing, and I'll teach my classes, and you can't tell me not to do that either. Never again will you tell me I can't have friends."

Never again will you tell me I can't have friends.

The bile started churning.

"Addy, that wasn't where I was going with my question. The way you said it, the way he sounded on the phone, gave me the impression one of you was feeling the other out. Bass is interested in you for sure. So I'm thinking he was angling for an in using lunch to get it."

"So what if he is? You still don't have a say, Keith. I get to be friends with who I want."

Bile turned to acid. A deadly poison polluted my blood as it pumped through my veins.

She'd called me another man's name. And when she'd done it, she had motherfucking fear in her eyes. Fear. My Adalynn.

Now, what in the motherfucking shit was that?

"Addy, baby, need you to tell me who Keith is."

Her torso swung back as if I'd power-punched her to the stomach. Her head also snapped back so fast I was afraid she'd given herself whiplash. However, she no longer seemed to be in her fear-addled trance when she asked, "What?"

"Who is Keith?" I repeated.

"How do you know that name?"

Is she serious?

"Addy—" The words died in my throat when her eyes lifted and locked with mine.

Sadness. Fear. Regret. Shame.

Jesus fuck.

"How?" she pressed.

I could've very well lied and told her I'd heard the name from a family member, then dig and figure out who this guy was on my own. And it was on the tip of my tongue to do so. I wanted nothing more than to erase the shame. It was that emotion that gutted me. We all have regrets. Everyone felt sadness. And fear was unfortunately a part of life. But my sweet, shy, innocent Addy wearing shame —fuck no.

But in the end, I couldn't lie. I didn't want to dig, I wanted Addy to trust me enough to tell me. I wanted the story straight from her.

I also wanted to end this conversation for her, shelve it, and pick it back up when she wasn't blind-sided and overcome with emotion.

"You called me Keith," I told her and watched her face register shock.

"Trey," she whispered. "I'm sorry."

"I don't want you to apologize. I also don't want to talk about it right now."

Addy nodded once and her shoulders hunched forward.

Goddamn.

"Is it okay if I come to you?" I asked as gently as I could muster with all the nasty shit coursing through me.

"Maybe I should just get my stuff," she mumbled.

"That's not gonna happen."

Addy came out of her hunch. Steel infused her spine as she stood tall.

There was my Addy.

"Few things," I quickly said before she could say anything. "We'll talk about Keith at a time and in a place where you feel safe to do so. You feeling trapped in my kitchen is neither. Something else—I am not him. Whatever he said and did to you was jacked. And I don't need you to tell me a goddamn thing about him to know that. You are absolutely, unequivocally correct. I don't have the right to tell you who you can be friends with, where you go, what classes you take or teach. More than that, I'm not a motherfucking dick, so I wouldn't try.

"That swings us back around to Bass. I explained already, but I think it bears repeating—the guy wants in your pants. He's obviously not getting in there.

And don't twist that into me being a motherfucking dick, that's just straight-up the truth. If you wanted Bass in your pants, you wouldn't be in my kitchen after the night we had. He wants it, so that means you're the one that pumped the brakes on that.

"And lastly, you're not going up to get your stuff so you can bolt. And you're not gonna do that because you don't run when times get tough. I know that, not because you're a Walker and Walkers are not cowards, but because you're Adalynn. And my Addy is *strong*."

There was some emotion that sprinted across her face, but it was so quick I couldn't decipher if it was good or bad or if I'd pissed her off again.

"Baby, you know what we're starting," I told her softly, much calmer now that she no longer looked like bones were rattling in a closet she'd dead bolted closed.

"Maybe it's not the right time to start something," she murmured.

"I'd believe you meant that if last night hadn't happened."

"People have sex all the time without being in a relationship," she told me, only her cheeks turned pink and her eyes dropped to the floor.

It hurt, it really did, keeping my gut-busting

laugh to a minimum. I tried not to roar with it but her adorably angry scowl told me I'd failed, and failed miserably.

"Addy," I said through a chuckle. "I'll give it to you, lots of people have sex who are not in a relationship. But you're not lots of people, you're not even most people. You're my Addy. And my Addy doesn't have sex with a man because she's got an itch to scratch. So, yes, we are most definitely in a relationship. But I wasn't talking about the sex and you know it."

She had nothing to say to that because I was right, she knew it, so she didn't bother crafting a rebuttal that would be bullshit and a straight out lie.

In her silence, I continued, "Now, the eggs that you cooked are probably cold but I'm gonna eat them anyway because I'm starving. Would you like me to make you something fresh or are you good with cold eggs?"

"Cold eggs," she mumbled.

"Gonna come to you now," I warned and did just that.

Once I had her in my arms, I kissed her forehead, then I told her the last thing she needed to know.

"I will never hurt you. Swear it on my life, Adalynn. I can't promise I won't be an ass, do shit that pisses you off, but I vow to you, I will never hurt you. Not physically, not emotionally. And I'm gonna prove that to you."

Addy said not a word.

But the full-body shiver told me everything I needed to know.

She didn't believe me.

And my gut told me Keith was to blame.

Motherfucker.

15

"You're quiet," Trey noted as the big, metal guard gate slowly swung open.

However I wasn't watching the gate. I was quiet because my mind was back in Trey's kitchen. He'd been cool about me calling him Keith. He'd even been cool not pressing me for an explanation. And it was especially cool because it went against his nature.

My whole life, I'd been surrounded by men like him—men who pushed, demanded, and refused to take no for an answer. They were men like my dad, uncles, cousins, and brother, who had honor and held the women in their lives in high regard so their brand of bossy, assertive, and overbearing—while annoying—came from a place of deep love.

Then there were men like Jake who pretended to have honor, showed you only what they wanted you to see, and didn't care enough to be bossy, assertive, or overbearing in a way that protected you.

The third kind of man was like Keith.

He hadn't pretended to have honor because he'd had none. I just didn't know it at the time. He hadn't shown me what he wanted me to see, he'd flat-out lied about who he was. And he didn't hold women in high regard, therefore, every word, every touch, every demand, every accusation was done with cruelty. His intent—to cause maximum damage. But I hadn't known any of that until it was too late, until he'd inflicted his pain both in word and deed.

And I never told a soul.

Keith Richardson was my biggest regret and my darkest secret.

My deepest shame.

"Do you have siblings?" I asked after he'd pulled through the gate.

"Yeah. A brother, CJ," Trey answered.

"Older or younger?"

"Younger."

"I'm the youngest by three minutes."

Why I imparted that factoid I had no clue other than I was nervous, and with every revolution of

Trey's tires, we were getting closer to Triple Canopy —a place I didn't want to go. I didn't want to face my cousins, and my big brother would likely be there, and maybe even my dad if Brady or Trey had called him.

"Did you already talk to my dad?"

"Yeah, texted him this morning and asked if he had time to come in."

Son of a motherless goat.

He'd have time.

My dad always had time for the people he cared about, so I didn't bother to inquire if he'd received a reply, I knew he had.

"Did you tell him what it was about?"

"No. Just said I needed a word."

Maybe there was hope.

"Listen, I really don't think we need to involve my dad. I mean, I'm staying with you. You live in a gated community and I noted the security guard last night. I'm sure I'm perfectly safe there, and really, Jake acted like a jerk but I know him. He was blowing smoke to save face."

"He was unhinged," Trey returned with steel in his tone.

Darn.

"I think unhinged is overstating his state of mind."

"You don't gauge a man's sanity by the words he says or threats he makes. People lie. They try to hide shit they don't want you to see. And he was trying to mask the fact he was off his leash, he just wasn't very good at it."

Boy did I know people lied.

"And just to point out a few things," he continued. "Lenny, the security guard is a great guy, but he's sixty-eight and retired from the force about twenty years ago and he did that because his eyesight is shit. Which means the unsuspecting residents are lucky he is unarmed. The man admits he can't hit the broadside of a barn and never was a good shot. And that big gate you see is for appearances. It's not meant to keep people out as much as it is to deter unsolicited visitors. Not to mention, that gate is it. The rest of the property is open—no electric fences, razor wire, or armed militia. So while you are safe in my house, you're only as safe as my locks, my alarm, and me and my guns. The next issue for you is, I'm asking my team for help. Period. I will not waver on that. And being as most of my team are your relatives, I hate to say it, babe, but the chance of one of them not telling your dad is zero. Not to mention, as

I think I explained yesterday, I respect your father and owe him honesty."

Always comes back to my dad, doesn't it?

God, I wanted to slap myself for even thinking that horrible thought.

"Right," I mumbled and looked out the window.

We were almost there, and once Trey explained the situation, my life as I knew it would be over. One or all of them would move in to take over and lock me down.

"There a reason you don't want your dad knowing what's going on?"

There were a million. But instead of exposing my ungrateful, bratty side, I kept all my reasons to myself.

"I already told you why."

"No one's gonna make you do anything—"

"Yes, they will and you know it," I cut him off. "Heck, even you got your way. And I don't mean that in a thankless, ugly way, I'm just pointing out facts. I don't want my family to worry. I don't want *you* to worry. Even though I don't think Jake would actually hurt me, I still agreed to move in with you until you check him out and he leaves to go back to wherever he's stationed, or deployed to, or whatever it is that he does. But you know them. The *second* they catch wind there's danger, all of them will swoop in."

Silence fell, and when it stretched, I regretted my outburst.

Trey wouldn't understand. Heck, it was happening to me and *I* couldn't verbalize my feelings in a way that made a lick of sense. I knew down to my soul I was loved. I knew my family—all of them were protective, kind, loyal, giving people. I was blessed beyond measure to have all of them. But it was stifling, and I felt no small amount of guilt for feeling that way.

Who in their right mind complained they were loved too much?

No one.

Not a single, normal, sane person would whine about being protected and cherished.

"No one is going to make you do anything you don't want to do, Addy. Not even me."

"Really? And who's gonna stop them from trampling over my life and taking over?"

"I am."

I went rock solid at the vigor in his tone. He was serious. He would stop them—not *try* to, he would simply make it so.

I remained frozen in my seat in an effort to

contain the hope that was threatening to break free. Hope that I promised myself I'd never have again.

A heavy silence fell and neither of us tried to fill it.

I didn't know what Trey was thinking about and I didn't dare ask. My head was too muddled with all the garbage I'd sworn to myself I'd never think about again.

Keith had no place in my life. Yet, neither did hope, but there I was sitting next to Trey trusting him.

Man, I really messed up. I knew down deep in my bones Trey wouldn't give up. Not on me, and he'd be relentless in his pursuit of the truth.

Crap.

"HE SAID *WHAT*?" my brother seethed.

Oh, heck, Jason was pissed. Madder than I can remember seeing him in recent history. This was because ten minutes after we'd walked into Triple Canopy, Trey had called a meeting. Not just any meeting, he'd requested everyone's presence. That meant Jason, Nick, Carter, Brady, Logan, Matt, Drake, Luke, Dylan, Trey, and myself were jammed into the conference room, which was not small, yet with all the testosterone seeping from the men, the room turned stifling.

Trey hadn't even let the men settle before he launched into the scene Jake created at the café. Through this, I didn't speak or fill in the blanks because there were none to fill in. Trey was thorough, as in *thorough*. The only thing he'd left out was me finding Jake with another woman before he shipped out. Which, I was fairly certain, was only because I was in the room and he would later dish out that tidbit. Of course, that would only fuel my brother's anger. Not to mention my cousins'.

Trey didn't repeat Jake's threat. Instead, he turned to Dylan. "Need you to start digging. I want to know everything there is to know about Jake Belview."

I didn't bother protesting this as it would be a waste of my breath. The men were now in full battle mode and they would move as they saw fit.

"You're coming to stay with me and Mercy," Jason commanded.

There it was, I'd lost. My dad and uncles hadn't even gotten into the mix and my brother, being a mini-Jasper, was making demands.

"Actually, Adalynn's staying with me. She moved

in last night and will stay there until we sort out the situation."

Those words came from Trey—strong, resolute, stubborn.

"Trey—"

"Not up for discussion," Trey spoke over my brother. "You know I got mad respect for you and your family. But this isn't about you, it's about Adalynn and what she wants."

The vibe in the room shifted from uncomfortable to downright hostile. With all the hostility coming from my brother. It was thick and ugly and I knew from experience when Jason felt like he was backed into a corner he lashed out and he did it *ugly*. It had been years since I'd seen his temper flare, but that wasn't to say I didn't remember.

"Right, and *Adalynn* came to the conclusion she wanted to move in with *you*, instead of, say, her brother or parents. Or, hey, even one of her cousins," Jason sneered.

His insinuation was hard to miss. And if the insinuation didn't smack you in the face, his condescension did.

"Jason," I called out to get my brother's attention. But once I had it, I flinched at the fury I saw. "I want to stay with Trey. It was my choice. He offered to stay with me, and Brady and Hadley already gave me the option of staying with them."

I lost Jason's gaze when it sliced back to Trey. But when he spoke, his question was aimed at me and it was beyond ugly.

"And did you make this decision before or after he talked you into his bed?"

"The fuck?"

I ignored Trey's deadly tone and decided it was time to end this. I was well over an age where my big brother got to play the role of the almighty protector.

"Between the first time and second time," I told him.

"Come again?" Jason's body tensed and once again I had his full attention.

"When I made the decision, Jason. It was between the first time and the second time I found myself happily in his bed. Though, just to clarify, the first time was in *my* bed. And just clearing up something else, *I* decided to move in with him instead of the other way around because I was freaked out Hadley saw Jake outside my house. But frankly, *I* made the decision to even entertain the idea that I needed to stay with Trey because Hadley pointed out that with everything our family has been through, it's best to err on the side of caution. I also don't want to worry Mom and Dad. *Me*, Jason. I made those decisions."

"Adalynn. You have to know, he's—"

"If I were you I'd stop, brother, before you let that foul temper of yours get you into something you cannot undo," I warned.

"Straight up, Addy, you're my baby sister. It's my job to look after you. Especially when you're too naïve to see what's going on."

"And straight up, Jay, you just crossed the line I warned you not to cross. You'll always be my big brother and I will always love you. But what you just said is total bullshit. I am far from naïve, and the fact you'd say that to me is the very reason I'm staying with Trey and not you."

"Addy." My brother softened his tone but it was too late.

I put my hand up to halt Jason from continuing.

"You know I'll forgive you for that," I whispered, too hurt and angry to care the room had gone still. "But when you calm down and think back you'll know that not only did you embarrass your sister in front of a group of men, but you'll also kick yourself in the ass for being incredibly insulting. My sex life is none of your goddamned business, brother. And fuck you for thinking I'm so stupid I'd jump into bed with a man who I didn't have feelings for and knew returned those feelings. I want no part of this. I think Trey's being over-protective, Brady's on board to blow it up, and now you'll take it further. And when Dad catches wind, all hell will break loose. Have fun digging into Jake's life—in the meantime, I'm living mine and I'm doing it any damn way I see fit. And so help me God, if any one of you tries to stop me, I'll never forgive you."

I'd made it to the door when Trey called out. I stopped and craned my neck so I could look over my shoulder.

He gave me a small smile and I swear to all things holy, he looked proud. I wanted to soak up that look and lock it in so I'd always have it, but I was too ticked off at my brother to fully appreciate it.

"Baby, please don't leave the building."

Gah. I wanted to steal his keys, get in his truck, and go back to his big house where I could hide in his big room in his big bed and not think about the monumental butthole Jason was.

Instead, I nodded.

"Thank you."

Those two words hit me in the chest, and I knew he wasn't thanking me for not leaving the building.

Hope built.

16

The door quietly clicked behind Addy. As pissed as she'd been at her brother, I admired her self-control. I, on the other hand, was unsure if I possessed the same restraint.

But then, I wasn't pissed. I wasn't even angry. I was motherfucking furious.

"Trey—"

"Do not speak to me, Jason."

The room, so quiet you could hear every inhale, turned strained. Tension so high, one move would inflame an already hostile situation. A room that was filled with deadly men who were no strangers to violence, death, and destruction.

"Razor," Carter called.

The old nickname cut me to the quick, I wasn't Razor—not anymore.

I wasn't anything.

I found Carter through the crush of men, still sitting at the head of the table while the others had stood, prepared to lock down the combatants if the need arose. Nick was moving around the table to take his cousin's side, Matt was moving in behind me. But I didn't take my eyes off Carter. During my contemplation, I hadn't thought about what Carter would think of me being with his cousin. He knew me; we'd served together for years, he'd had a front-row seat to my indiscretions.

"How big of an issue do you think Belview's gonna be?" Carter asked.

"Gut says a big one," I returned, happy Addy was no longer in the room, yet not pleased about why that was.

"Right, and are you saying that because you want to keep my sister in your bed?"

Carter's jaw clenched, Matt moved closer, Nick slid in behind Jason, and I vaguely wondered what Addy would think if her beloved brother left the office with missing teeth. Likely she'd be pissed, though after the shit he'd slung her way, she might not. But Emily Walker would be out of her mind pissed. Although she might be more pissed when she found out why her son needed dental work.

"I'm gonna say this one time, Jason. I respect you and your family. I understand you're looking out for Adalynn. I even get why you don't like me with your sister. I have a lot to prove to all of you. But I swear to Christ, you take one more dig at my woman, you'll be eating through a straw."

Jason reared back and his eyes narrowed. "And that's how you're planning on proving you're good enough for my sister?"

"No, that's me telling you, brother or not, I will not stand for anyone disrespecting, embarrassing, or talking shit about Adalynn. And you of all fucking people should know that the shit you said to Addy both embarrassed and hurt her. She's Addy, so she'll forgive you. Me, not so much. It's gonna take a long time before I forget. A long fucking time, Jason. And for the record, Addy's not in my bed, she's in my life. And I know without having to explain it to you, you know the difference. So that brings us back to my point—you don't like me for your sister and you wanna take jabs at me, I'm man enough to take them. But you ever embarrass, hurt, or disrespect Adalynn again, you and I will have bigger problems than we have now."

"You're fucking my sister," Jason angrily returned. The electricity that had been bouncing around the room ignited. Matt's hand curled around my bicep and Nick flanked Jason, stopping him from moving closer. "And you've got the balls to tell me how it is."

"Last time, Jason. I am not *fucking* your sister. And if you knew her as well as you think you do, you'd already know that."

"She's in your bed."

"She is, absolutely," I confirmed. "And what we do there is none of your fucking business. But I'll repeat, I am not *fucking* Adalynn."

"*Fuck!*" A voice boomed from behind me.

Good goddamn.

I didn't need to turn to know Jasper Walker had entered the room.

"There a reason the two of you are shouting so goddamn loud I heard you from the parking lot?"

I didn't doubt Jasper heard more than I wanted him to hear, but I doubted he heard because we were shouting. It was likely because Jasper had well-honed fatherly instincts that pinged when one of his children was in distress. Seeing as two of his offspring were involved, that ping would be huge.

I remained rooted, my gaze locked with Jason's,

unwilling to back down even with Jasper in the room, until Addy's brother understood I was serious. I gave zero fucks what Jason thought about me. It was going to suck, losing the budding friendship, suck more if he decided to fire me, but I wouldn't stand for him being a prick to Addy—that included him being an ass when she wasn't around to hear it.

"Jay, man, stand down," Nick muttered.

Unwilling to budge, Jason didn't stand down. Further, he continued, uncaring his father was now in attendance. Or maybe he felt that now that Jasper was in the room, he'd have backup therefore he was emboldened.

"Adalynn cannot survive a man like you."

"A man like me? Tell me, Jason, what kind of a man do you think I am?"

"The kind that doesn't know how *not* to fuck. Tell me, Trey, how hard was it for you to play my sister, hook her deep, and have her bending to your demands? Shy, sweet, innocent Addy in your bed. How convenient—Belview pops up, hurls some insults her way, doesn't like you intervened so he makes his displeasure known, and voilà, you have the perfect excuse to move her in. Hook her deeper. But tell me, when you use up all that innocence, get bored, and cut her loose, where does that leave my sister?"

"Way over the line, cousin," Carter's voice rumbled.

It took a full minute to beat back the driving urge to strangle Addy's brother. That minute was filled with complete silence. Not a single man spoke, including Jasper. When I got a lock on my temper and my body's natural response to eliminate the enemy—in this case, the enemy being Addy's family —I exhaled, but otherwise didn't move.

"I see you don't know your sister at all. No one bends Adalynn to do anything she doesn't want to do. I can see how you might think that, since *you've* run roughshod over her all her life, and being the type of person she is, she likely caved to you without much argument. Don't bother denying it because she begged me not to bring this to the table because she knew you and everyone else would take over, boss her, and trample over her. Those were her words."

I drew in a deep breath. "So, tonight when you're thinking about what a motherfucker you were to your sister, think on that, too. There's not a damn thing convenient about Belview hurling insults at your sister, think about that tonight, too. You okay with some asshole shouting at your sister in the middle of a café, talking shit to her after he fucked her over? Fucked her over in ways she never told you about. But she told me. You can stand there and look at me like I'm scum, and my guess is you think that because of my reputation—"

"You fuck anything that moves," Jason cut in.

"I do? I'd like to think I'm a little more discriminating than that. The fact is, I know how many women I've had—I was there. Wanna know who wasn't? You. If my sexual history is what your problem is, let me help you with that. I have fucked a lot of women—a lot. I was single, my field was open, and I enjoyed the fuck out of a variety of women on a variety of different continents. So with all that experience, I can assure you I know the difference between a woman I'd fuck and Adalynn."

Matt tightened his grip on my arm but I wasn't done. "Straight up, Jason, she's your sister, I get it, you want what's best for her. But I also do not need your approval. I don't want there to be tension and bad blood between us. I don't want that because it would fuck with my woman's head and I want to cushion that for her. But serious as shit, you can hold on and be pissed and it will not make a bit of fucking difference to me.

"But you know what will? If you drag your feet

on dealing with Belview. If you make it harder for me to get a lock on him and communicate to him if he so much as glances in my woman's direction, I'll slit his throat. The guy is fucked up, he's dangerous. He hurts Addy again—mentally or physically—and he got his chance because you're too busy being a dick throwing up roadblocks to keep me from her instead of helping, I swear to God, Jason, I'll bury you right next to him. Now, I'm gonna go find Addy, make sure she's okay, get to work, and, Dylan, I'd be obliged you ran those traces. If you don't, I will."

I jerked my arm free and gave Matt a lift of my chin. I waited until he dipped his in return before I turned to leave. I appreciated his support, even if he was effectively there to stop me from losing my shit and doing something stupid like actually getting into a fight with Addy's brother. The momentary pleasure of pounding on a man I considered a loose friend but a good man would be just that—momentary—until the regret set in. Addy didn't need that kind of trouble.

I was near the door when Jasper stepped in front of me. Hard, cold, calculating familiar green eyes took me in. The green a reminder that this was Adalynn's father. The color so similar, yet Jasper's held none of the warmth and beauty his daughter's did. His jaw was set, his expression furious, his posture un-fucking-happy.

Not good. Particularly not good when I'd planned on having a civil conversation with the man about the relationship I'd entered into with his daughter.

Jasper was a man of integrity, deep loyalty, and honor that was so ingrained into him he wore it like armor. I owed him the truth and he'd get it, but it would have to wait until I sorted through my simmering anger.

Jason's being a good brother, looking out for his baby sister, I reminded myself to no avail. No good brother would humiliate his sister in front of a room full of men, most of whom she didn't know very well. Had Jason said what he'd said to Quinn, she would've handed her brother his ass. Hadley probably would've kicked him in the balls. And Delaney would've cut him off at the knees. In her own way, Adalynn had told her brother she was unhappy at his remarks, but she wasn't as vocal or vicious as her sisters would've been. And that pissed me right the fuck off that Jason knew, out of all his siblings, Addy would be the least likely to lash out and more apt to hold in her hurt.

"I'll come find you after I sort this."

"Respect, Jasper, but I need some time."

"I'll come find you after I sort this," he repeated heatedly.

Shit, goddamn.

"And I need some time to check on Adalynn."

"Then you better see to that and *I'll find you after I sort this.*"

Unyielding.

There was no budging a Walker. Unless the situation was one where emotional manipulation could be carried out. And somehow, I found it hard to believe anyone, man or woman, could manipulate Jasper.

Except maybe Addy.

She was a daddy's girl. But I wouldn't hide behind my woman, it was my job to stand tall so she could use me as the buffer should she need to.

"See you then," I confirmed, and Jasper stepped aside.

―――――

I FOUND ADDY, ascertained she was pissed and didn't want to discuss what happened, and like her father, she was firm. I pushed just enough for her to explain that her feelings were hurt and being that they were she needed to hold onto the anger so she didn't cry. Something she didn't want to do at the office where someone could see her, and certainly not right before a patient met her in the Triple Canopy gym for PT.

I walked her to the new building, got her situated, and went back to my office to wait for Jasper. He didn't make me wait long, but while he did I thought about my future and what it would look like if Jason, Nick, or Carter pushed to have me fired. Or if one of the original four principals one being Jasper, the others Addy's uncles, wanted me out. Financially, I'd be more than fine. I'd invested wisely. And with Matt's help, I'd followed his lead buying and flipping houses. Though, I'd kept a few after I'd fixed them up and they had renters in them. If I had to, I could sell my house, downsize into something more appropriate, and use the profit to buy a few more houses.

I'd be fine financially. But mentally, losing Triple Canopy would cripple me. I needed the routine, the brotherhood, the teamwork, the training, and it was worth repeating—the *brotherhood*. I held guilt for what happened in Bruit, Luke's injury, my monumental fuck-up. For my own peace of mind, I had to find a way to make that right. But more, I needed my brothers. We were a team in more ways than blood, sweat, and battle. They were my family, my real family, not like my father and brother. I would be fucking lost without them. So, I needed to keep my calm and I probably needed to apologize to Jasper for a few things I'd said to Jason, though it would be a cold day in hell before I gave Jason a free pass—he needed to make shit right with Addy, then I would think about forgiving him for the bullshit he spewed at her.

There was a knock, then the door to my office swung open. Jasper silently entered, lifting his chin in greeting. I kept my seat and waited for him to pull a chair around the front of my desk and settle into it.

"Few things about Belview," Jasper started and I perked up, wanting all the intel I could get. "I knew he was SF when he was dating Addy. I also knew what assignment he was being sent on. And I knew before he broke it off with her, he was going to do it."

So much for remaining calm.

"Did you encourage him to break up with her?" I asked.

"If by 'encouraged' you're really asking, did I demand it, then no, I didn't. But when he came to me, I certainly didn't persuade him to stay with her, which I could've easily done."

Fucking shit.

"Does she know he came to you?"

"No. And I don't want her to know."

"Then we need to stop this conversation here," I told him.

"Because I can't trust you to keep a confidence?"

Was he for real?

"No, Jasper, because you can trust I will not lie to Addy."

He nodded and his stare turned knowing. Jesus, fuck me, I had to hand it to him. The man had been out of the game for a long time, yet he still had it. I fought the urge to squirm under his heavy scrutiny and wondered if that was the father in him or the warrior. My guess—both. He'd found a way to mold those two together and the effect was enough to make me want to look away.

"I'm gonna be straight with you, Trey. I like you. I think you were a good operator, you served honorably, I'll forever be grateful for your role in saving Liberty, and I think you're an asset to Triple Canopy." Jasper paused and I braced for the 'but' I knew was coming. "My son was out of line, but he was not wrong."

There it was.

I wasn't good enough for Adalynn.

Fuck, that stung. And before I could stop my hand from moving as if it had a mind of its own, it left my desk and landed square in the middle of my chest.

"His delivery was piss-poor, but his concerns valid."

"Right," I ground out through gritted teeth. "Just so you know, she's staying with me until this is over."

"I'm thinking she should come home and stay with her mom and me."

He would think that, but he was wrong.

"Obviously, you can talk to Addy about that, but she made herself clear so I'll reiterate what I told Jason and what I promised her. No one, including you or her brother, are going to make her do a damn thing she doesn't want to do. She didn't want me to bring you in on this. Please don't make me regret my decision."

"What the fuck does that mean?"

Well, here goes nothing.

It wasn't like I had to worry about Jasper's approval. I didn't have, nor was I ever, going to get it.

So, really, I had not a damn fucking thing to lose.

Except Addy.

Christ.

"It means she knows you love her. She knows the

man you are, the father you are, so she knew the second you caught the scent something was wrong you'd make moves to protect her. That is exactly what she doesn't want. She expressly stated she was not going into lockdown. It took Hadley guilting her for Addy to take Jake's threat seriously. Which, I know Jason thinks I'm blowing smoke, because he has it in his head I'm jacking his sister around, but I'm telling you, Jasper, the motherfucker is deranged. I cannot put into words what I saw in him, except to say he's vacant. He will not get another shot at ripping Addy apart. She's agreed to stay with me so that's where she's staying. I've also asked her to change all of her PT appointments to the Triple Canopy gym, which she's done. She also agreed she won't be going near the VA until Jake is dealt with.

"One last thing—this morning on the way over here, Addy was struggling. To ease that I promised her I wouldn't let anyone make her do something she didn't want to do. The same way I will not lie to her, I sure as fuck will not break that promise."

"That a threat or a warning?" Jasper grunted.

Mother fuck, the Walkers and their goddamn stubbornness.

"Wouldn't dream of doing either of those two things to you."

"But you have no problem threatening to bury my son?"

"Nope," I told him honestly. "Tell me something, Jasper, you heard a man talking ugly shit to Emily, you wouldn't make your displeasure known?" Considering the question was not one I needed an answer to, I didn't wait for one. "Actually, you wouldn't have bothered with a warning, you simply would've buried him. Brother or not, I got a serious issue with my woman's face turning red with embarrassment, her body strung tight, and her eyes full of hurt. All of that caused by a man who has her love and trust, one that should always handle her with care. Jason doesn't like me, doesn't want me with Addy, then he should've found the time to have a quiet word with me like you did. He shouldn't have done what he did."

Jasper sat back in the chair, and knowing turned into unease. Normally upon seeing Jasper's jaw set, eyes glittering, his muscles coiled tight, I'd beat a hasty retreat, not wanting to be in the firing line. But considering I was the one who put him on-edge, I didn't move.

"And now that I've had my quiet word?"

"By that, you mean now that you've made it

known you agree with Jason and you think I'm not good enough for Addy?"

Jasper dipped his chin and there was more confirmation. I wasn't good enough, and that didn't sting, it fucking *hurt*.

Never good enough.

Not for my dad. Not for Addy's family. Not even good enough for my little brother.

"Now nothing," I returned.

"Nothing?" Jasper asked.

"What were you expecting? Respect, Jasper, but Adalynn is a grown woman. For her sake, I hoped this would go smoothly and you'd give me an honest shot at proving to you I love your daughter. But she's not of an age where I need to ask your permission to date her. As much as I respect you, Emily, Jason, and the rest of your family, I'd be a punk ass bitch if a few words and a scowl veered me off-course and made me break my promises to Addy. We both know I'm not that. And we both fucking know that you being the type of father you are, it hasn't escaped you that your other daughters didn't choose punk bitches to spend their lives with, so it baffles me as to why you'd think Adalynn would."

Something passed over Jasper's expression, but

like the master he was, a nanosecond later it was clear.

"Adalynn is not like her sisters. She's special—"

"She sure as fuck is. But what she absolutely is not, is naïve. Your girl knows her mind and has no issue communicating exactly what she wants and doesn't want. She might be the youngest but she's not a baby. And she might be shy but she sure as fuck isn't stupid. I'll give you this and hopefully, it will give you a sliver of peace. I know how special Addy is. I know the beauty she brings to my life and I'll do everything in my power to protect it. What I will not do is give her up because her brother has a problem with me. And no bullshit, Jasper, I wish you had it in you to see past a reputation I earned when I was unattached, had no commitments, and made no promises. But you don't, you don't. That's on you, and it will not stop me from giving your daughter everything she needs and deserves."

"I think we should end this conversation here."

"Sure," I agreed. "Anytime you wanna talk, you know where to find me. Now that that's outta the way, I have a favor. I need information on Jake Belview. Dylan's looking into him but we both know he's not gonna find dick, because there'll be nothing but bullshit in Belview's service records. You have contacts none of us do—I'd appreciate it if you can make some calls."

"You don't have to ask that shit," Jasper grunted.

"Sorry, but I feel like I do have to ask. Jason's made it clear he's not taking this seriously. I cannot stress this enough; I've faced down my fair share of soulless men. Never once did I flinch. Jake Belview gave me a shiver. Here's the thing that worries me—you know him, he dated your daughter and lived to tell about it, which means he's changed. You confirming he was SF means he didn't change, something inside him broke. He was looking at Addy like he wanted to tear her head off and he had no problem doing that right there at the table, then sitting back down and finishing his meal. I want to know why that motherfucker is in Georgia and what he was doing at the VA. I also think it's important to find out if his superiors know there's something seriously fucking wrong with this guy before he's sent back out."

This time Jasper didn't try to hide his anger. He leaned forward, narrowed his eyes, and spat fire before he stood.

"You better fucking have this, Durum."

I didn't get a chance to answer before he was gone.

Fucking shit.

———

I HELD OPEN the door to my truck and waited for Addy to get in. When she didn't move, I stopped scanning the parking lot and looked at her.

"You're quiet," she said. It wasn't lost on me that eight hours ago, I'd been the one to note her silence. "Everything go okay with my dad?" she inquired

I felt my brows pull together and asked, "You didn't talk to him?"

"No. I saw him walk past the gym but he didn't stop in."

Interesting. I figured after Jasper left my office, Addy would be his next stop.

"We'll talk when we get home."

Addy dropped her chin and looked at the tarmac when she muttered, "It went bad."

"Baby, look at me." When her gaze lifted, my heart constricted painfully. "I told you he wouldn't be happy. I also told you I didn't give a fuck. Thinking on that, without meaning to, I lied. I do care, because obviously, you care. I know your dad, it's gonna take a while before he's ready to give me a chance. There's nothing I can do about that. But I promise you, I'll put the work in. In the meantime, nothing changes for me."

"Okay."

"You gonna be able to wait that out with me?"

"Yes."

Thank fuck. Some of the pain in my chest started to recede.

"We haven't had a chance to talk since it went down, but you okay after that scene with your brother?"

"We'll talk when we get home," she repeated my earlier response.

"Okay, baby, hop in."

"Trey?"

"Yeah?"

"Thank you," she whispered, and rolled up on her toes.

Her soft lips brushed mine and I was lost. So fucking lost I was oblivious to my surroundings.

Which was unfortunate.

JASPER WALKER WATCHED, feeling no remorse for intruding on his daughter's privacy.

He knew what was coming but forced himself to watch.

Trey brushed Addy's hair off her shoulder, craned his neck forward, and kissed the side of her neck before his hands framed her face. He said something that made her smile—that was his Addy, always smiling to hide her pain.

Jasper's gut tightened as it always did when he thought about his girl keeping a secret—one that meant she was suffering alone, keeping things that troubled her bottled up. It had been years and he expended no small amount of effort to draw that secret out, to no avail. Whatever was eating away at her, she wasn't talking. Not to anyone.

He continued to watch as Trey dropped another kiss, this one on her forehead, then straightened. As he did, Trey shifted his weight to his good leg, hiding *his* pain.

Fuck.

He did not want this for his girl—not his Adalynn.

He wanted her to have easy. Soft. Gentle.

She needed someone who could heal whatever caused her to bury the pain that had been etched onto her soul.

It was a toss-up which one of the two was hiding more than the other.

Jesus, *fuck*.

Jasper Walker did not want this for his girl, and he wasn't sure he had it in him to accept Trey Durum into her life.

He closed his eyes and clenched his fists in an effort not to intervene. Therefore, Jasper missed it when Trey spotted him. He also missed the hurt and determination Trey *didn't* hide.

17

"I can help," I told Trey as I sipped my beer, even though I didn't actually want to get up.

What I wanted to do was continue to sit my booty on the stool he'd pulled out for me, placing me on one side of the big island in his kitchen, him on the other with his back to me as he cooked. I wanted to continue to do this because I found it fascinating Trey knew how to cook. Not mac-and-cheese-from-a-box kind of cooking, but chop up vegetables, dice chicken, and make his own stir-fry sauce kind of cooking.

"Rather have you sit where you are and stare at my ass while I make you dinner."

I choked down a gulp of cold liquid and sputtered, "What makes you think I'm staring at your butt?"

"Cute," he muttered back.

"What's cute? Your butt?"

"No. You."

Trey craned his neck to look at me, and when he did, I caught that shine in his eyes. It'd returned now that we were back at his place. It wasn't as bright as it was last night. But nonetheless, it was still there, and for whatever reason, he was grinning at me. I liked Trey grinning at me—couple that with the shine and I was in heaven. I could sit my behind at his island watching him cook me dinner for the rest of my life and be happy.

I didn't know what it was about him that made me feel that way. I just felt it and I felt it from the very beginning. It was weird, it made my stomach cramp, and it scared the heck out of me. The two times I'd opened myself up to a relationship, I'd been burned. The first time hurt. The second time left thick scar tissue around my heart.

Yet Trey got through. That was the weird part. Not even Bass, who I did have a mild crush on when I first met him, was able to peel back even the thinnest of layers. I wasn't dumb or naïve like my brother accused me of being. I knew Bass asked me to lunch in an attempt to 'get in there' as Trey called it. He was a nice enough guy, but I knew from the first lunch I'd never let my guard down and let him in.

"Babe?"

"Huh?"

"What are you thinking about?"

"Bass."

"Come again?"

Mother trucker. My hand slapped over my mouth and I closed my eyes, praying I did not just say that.

"Adalynn." Trey's voice rumbled and my prayers went unanswered.

Crappity, crap, crap.

"I was thinking about how you were right. Earlier, you said Bass wanted to get in there. You're right, he does."

"Okay."

Trey leaned his hip on the counter and settled in. That meant he was waiting for me to explain further.

"I was thinking about that because I was thinking about how much you scared me."

Trey's eyes got squinty and his lips formed a flat line as he silently waited for more.

Darn it all to hell.

"I was remembering that I'd tried this relationship stuff twice before and it didn't go too good for me. Both times I got hurt, and after the second time, I wasn't all that fired-up to try again. Bass is a nice guy, good looking, sweet..." Trey grunted something I didn't catch but I didn't need to, to understand he was seriously unhappy, so I rushed to continue. "Anyway, point is, he's nice and he tried to get me to open up to him, or at least be open for a date, but I never gave it to him."

"Let's get back to the part where I scare you," he suggested.

I wasn't a fool so I read his demand, even if he tried to disguise it.

"Since the day I met you, my stomach's been in knots. You frustrate me to no end. You make me lose my temper. You excite me. And that scares me. But the other times when I know you let me see a side of yourself you keep from everyone else, that you trust me with that part of yourself, when the real Trey breaks through—those times scare the bejeezus out of me. Those are the times when I want to wrap you up and run away with you. When I wish you knew how strong I was so you'd let me battle by your side to beat back all the garbage in your head. But times like last night, when you open yourself bare and let me see all that light you're hiding and I feel how warm it is, freaks me the frick out because I want that so bad, to feel it for the rest of my life, I forget to be scared. That's—"

I didn't finish my explanation. I was plucked off the stool and my booty was planted on the counter. I still hadn't gotten my bearings when Trey's hands went to my thighs and he roughly opened them before stepping between them.

Face-to-face, our eyes locked and he gave me everything.

"Takin' my back."

That was all he said before his mouth slammed down on mine and his tongue invaded. Then his hands started moving, but not to grope—to pull me even closer when my front was already plastered to his. One arm was diagonal across my back, holding me so tightly I could barely breathe. His other hand was fisting my hair, holding me where he wanted. I gave myself more and melted into him, taking from him as surely as he was taking from me. My fears liquefied and then evaporated. Another thing I didn't understand, but with Trey's tongue in my mouth I didn't take the time to contemplate how I could be scared and happy at the same time.

Through this, a phone rang then until it stopped.

Just as Trey was grinding his erection between my legs it started again. He tore his mouth from mine and I dazedly stared up at him wondering how upset he'd be if I tossed the ringing phone in the garbage disposal.

"Cute." He kissed my nose and tagged his cell off the counter, not taking himself away from me when he answered.

"Lenny?" There was a pause, and even if I hadn't been studying his handsome features, had his body close, I would've felt it. The room filled with ugly. "Right. Sorry about that. Let 'em in."

Trey tossed his phone on the counter, it bounced off and landed on the floor. So maybe he wouldn't have cared if I'd chopped it up in the garbage disposal.

I lifted my gaze from the face-down cell back up to him and I wished I would've taken my chance with the disposal.

"Fuck," he clipped. "Fucking *hell*."

Trey not being one to shy away from using the f-word, the use of it twice didn't concern me. But the look on his face did.

"My parents are here," he announced, like Ivan the Terrible and his army were getting ready to storm the premises and we needed to find weapons and shields to beat them back.

"I take it this is not good news."

"Fuck. No."

All righty then. Another f-bomb. This one unmistakably irate.

"Okay. So, they're here and they'll be pulling up any minute. What do you need from me?"

"Fuck."

"Not sure we have time for that, honey, but is there something else I can do?"

"Goddamn cute," he huffed. "And takes my back."

I didn't know what to say to that so I remained quiet, though I feared we were running out of time. If Trey didn't explain what was about to happen, I'd have to wing it and I'd never been very good at improv. I needed a clear picture or I tended to put my foot into my mouth and choke.

"My dad's an asshole. He'll likely say shit that is inappropriate and it will piss me off. It will also hurt my mom, she'll try her best to hide it, but I'll see it and it will piss me off more."

Um. That didn't sound good.

"Why are they here?"

"Fuck if I know."

"Where do they live?"

After I asked, I wondered why I hadn't asked sooner.

"Maine."

"Maine?" I repeated.

"Yup."

There was a knock at the door and Trey stiffened. When another loud bang reverberated, I jerked. Trey saw it and his lips flattened.

Oh, boy, even the knock sounded mean.

"I will not let him fuck with you."

That didn't sound good.

"But you'll let him mess with you?" I inquired.

Trey didn't answer, which *was* his answer.

Crap. Maybe Ivan the Terrible *was* here.

"Seriously, baby, if he opens his mouth and says something, I'll set his ass out. You do not need to worry."

A third pound came and Trey took a deep breath before he came to me, kissed my cheek, and asked, "Do me a favor and turn down the burner, yeah?"

"Yeah."

He left the kitchen and I went to the stove to do as he asked. I also flipped the chicken and pushed around the vegetables in the other pan. I took my time, making sure every broccoli floret was turned over.

"Babe?" Trey called, and I jolted before I gave myself a mental pep talk, plastered a fake smile on my face, and turned.

Holy crap.

Not what I was expecting.

At all.

Not being mean, but Trey was exceptionally good-looking, so I'd envisioned a devastatingly handsome older man and beautiful, graceful older woman.

Trey's father was shorter than him by at least three inches, he had a beer belly that strained against the buttons of his shirt, and his hair was gray. Not in a devastatingly handsome way that makes a man look interesting and arresting. No, in an unkempt, uncared for way that looked almost oily.

His mother was pretty with delicate features. She was indeed aging gracefully, but not gracefully enough to be considered a beauty.

I noted all of that and felt like a royal twit for thinking it. It was mean, but I only thought it because I couldn't imagine how the two of them had created a man as beautiful as Trey.

Next to them was a younger man. And he was

openly staring at me in a way that made me want to take a shower to wash the ick off. He was not good-looking, or handsome, or beautiful. He was average and that was at a push. I didn't know how old he was, just younger than Trey, but he still had acne and it could be described as *not* attractive.

"Hi, I'm Adalynn." I introduced myself, not knowing why, just wanting to get it over with so the three of them would stop staring at me.

"Fucking-A, brother. Even with your face all fucked up, you still nail down a hot piece."

"CJ," Trey rumbled at the same time his mother gasped.

"What? Dude, just saying it like it is. Thought for sure after you got mangled, your options would dry up. Clearly, they haven't."

"Clearly," Trey's dad agreed.

Yuck.

"This is your only warning. Both of you. One more comment like that and you're gone."

"Hello, Adalynn, I'm Paige. Trey's mom."

I glanced at Trey's mom and took her in. Weary. That was the first thing that came to mind. Weary and bone-tired.

"Paige. Nice to meet you."

"This is Carl, his dad. And CJ, his brother," Paige continued.

"Carl. CJ."

I didn't add the 'nice to meet you' part because so far it hadn't been pleasant and my mama taught me it wasn't right to lie.

I turned to Trey who'd made it to my side and asked, "Should we order something in?"

"Why?"

Why? How was it possible he was asking that? Three guests had arrived and the meal he'd been making surely wouldn't feed five. And as mean as it was to think, but I wasn't too torn up about it because Carl was more of a butthole than Trey had explained. He alone could eat all the stir-fry that was on the stove.

"Have y'all eaten?" I asked.

"Been driving ten hours. I'm starved," Carl answered.

"Well, Trey made dinner. It won't be enough to feed us all, but how 'bout we use it as an appetizer and we'll order—"

"Trey cooked dinner?" CJ snickered.

"Hm?" I glanced up at Trey to find his jaw clenched.

"What can I help you with, Adalynn?" Paige asked.

I didn't know the answer to that. I wasn't the one cooking, but I felt it was in everyone's best interest not to bring that up again.

"Trey, honey, you wanna tell me what needs to be finished, or do you want me to call in an order?"

"What are you doing here?" Trey asked instead of answering me.

"Driving down to Florida. Thought we'd stop and spend the night," Carl replied.

Anger started rolling off Trey so I stepped closer and slid my arm around his middle. His hand went up, rested on my shoulder, and he pulled me to his side. Only then did he speak.

"Florida?"

"It's your Aunt Betty's birthday. We're going down for the weekend. Big bash for her seventieth."

"Right. So you thought what, you'd use my house like a hotel? No call? No invite? You just show up unannounced and uninvited?"

"Not like you'd go anyway," CJ said, as he opened Trey's refrigerator and shoved his head in. The next part came out muffled, "You got anything besides Rolling Rock? Bud? Coors? Something fuckin' drinkable?"

Apparently, CJ had no issue dropping the f-bomb either.

Good to know.

Except nothing was good at the moment. Trey had gone statue-still and I hadn't heard or felt him exhale in several seconds.

Evidently, CJ had no issue complaining about his brother's beer and drinking it anyway. With bottle in hand, CJ turned around and finished with, "You never did like going to family shit, and after you got your face fucked up and they kicked you out of the SEALs, you pretty much stopped going to anything. And it's not like you don't got the room in your big-ass house. Guess it pays. I mean, I'd take a bomb to the face if it meant I'd get a wad of cash. Guess bitches really do love the dolla—"

"Are you for real?" I asked. "His face isn't *fucked up*, you moron."

"Addy—"

"No, Trey. *A bomb to the face?*" I screeched. "Who *says* that?"

"I do," CJ piped up. "Since that's what it was, a fucking bomb to the face. You can't be blind. You see all those scars. It's fucked up."

"Please, Trey, tell me I'm stuck in some sort of

weird dream after I was force-fed mushrooms. You know, the kind that made you go all wonky."

"'Fraid not, baby."

"No? So no one handcuffed me, rolled a fatty, and forced me to inhale? And now I'm so high I'm imagining I'm standing in your kitchen with your brother?"

"No, baby." I watched his lips twitch and I didn't understand how that was possible.

"So this is the real world, the normal one, and your brother's talking to you about taking a *bomb to the face*?"

"Yep." He smiled.

"Has he lost his mind? Dropped on his head as a baby? Played some full-contact sport where he sustained multiple concussions that rendered him stupid?"

"Yes, not sure, no, and no."

"She might be fine but she sure is mouthy," CJ blurted out.

"Are we gonna eat?" Carl asked.

I stared at Trey a beat, then I busted out laughing. I couldn't help it. There wasn't anything funny about Trey's brother being a big, fat jerk. And to top it off, his father was worried about food instead of how incredibly insulting his younger son had been.

"This can't be real life," I sputtered.

"Unfortunately, it's mine."

That sobered me.

I didn't understand how Trey came from these people. And I wasn't talking about looks. Trey was not rude, he was not inconsiderate, he wasn't an asshole. Sure, he was gruff and a little rough around the edges. There was a hard exterior but he was kind, gentle, and good at his core.

"Tell me what you need me to do," I whispered.

Trey's eyes drifted closed, and when they opened, that light shone so bright it blinded me.

"Just this."

I didn't know what 'just this' meant, but I pressed closer.

"Ma, there are takeout menus in the drawer by the fridge. Find something and order it." Then he turned to his brother. "Keep your trap shut or you're sleeping in the car."

"What—"

"You fucking know what," Trey returned. "Addy and I leave at eight to go to work. You're out by then."

"Eight? Wanted to sleep in. Hotel beds suck. Haven't had a good night's sleep in two nights."

"Not my problem. You're out by the time we leave."

"Adalynn's moved in?" Paige asked.

"Yep."

That was stretching the truth but I decided not to correct him.

"Well, that's wonderful. Cute as a button. I bet she'll have this house in tip-top shape in no time."

Tip-top shape? Trey's house was a showplace, not a frat house. There was nothing to get into shape.

"She's my girlfriend, not my maid."

"Of course, I just meant it will be nice for you to come home and have things done. You know, like dinner and such."

"Addy doesn't cook."

Well, I did cook. I just didn't make my own stir-fry sauce. Mine came out of a packet from the awesome Asian market around the corner from my condo.

"She doesn't?" Paige gasped.

Trey ignored his mother and turned us to the stove, and together, we finished making dinner.

No way in heck Trey grew up with these people.

I took my time washing my face, then I took more time brushing my teeth to the point they were sparkling clean and my gums were near bleeding, then I took even more time and thoroughly lotioned every inch of skin that wasn't covered by my pjs. When I ran out of stuff to do, I had no choice but to exit Trey's bathroom.

I wasn't avoiding him. I actually wanted to get into bed next to him and check on him. My problem was, I was in a state of shock and had been for hours. The Durums were a strange bunch. Paige was nice enough in a weird, downtrodden kind of way. It seemed to me like she knew her husband and son were total jerks and she'd given up. She was nice enough to me, she spoke to Trey like he was a distant relative, not her beloved son. This was different than how she treated her other son. CJ needed a fresh beer, Paige got up and got it. CJ wanted seconds, Paige got up and filled his plate.

Throughout dinner, they mostly ignored Trey. None of them asked him a single question. They just barged into his house, took over, and then talked amongst themselves about a vacation they were taking that Trey had not been invited on.

How freaking weird was that?

In an act of bravery, I put my knee on the bed by

Trey's hip and swung my other one over him. I planted my booty on his lap, straddled him, and looked down at him. Both his hands came up and landed on my thighs. He was not looking at me—his eyes were closed, and not because he was asleep.

My big, rough, brave Trey with his eyes closed, possibly in shame.

Damn those people.

My hand went to his face and his body went solid. I ignored this heartbreaking shift and continued stroking his cheek. My fingertips were met with puckered marks, the proof of what he'd endured. He hadn't shared more than bits and pieces of what had happened that day, and mostly the parts about how he blamed himself. But I knew what happened. My cousin Liberty had told me. Of course, her side of the story was filled with guilt as well, she felt she should've known what was going to happen and warned Trey and Luke sooner to flee. It wasn't anyone's fault but the man who'd been wearing a suicide vest. But none of them would accept the truth. They all went on blaming themselves. Drake would sort Liberty—she was on a path full of love and healing. I would see to Trey.

But who would help Luke?

I shoved those thoughts aside. That was for

another day. Right then, with all that had happened at dinner, I needed to see to my man.

My hand slid up to his temple, then over his forehead as I smoothed the creases between his brows. This was not the first time, not even the tenth time, I'd taken him in. Strong, square jaw, fantastic bone structure, full lips, perfectly set eyes. He was too rugged to be considered pretty, especially with his scars. He was classically handsome, but the marks that dotted one side of his face intensified the rugged and made him look indefatigable.

"What do you need from me?" I whispered.

"Just this."

Just this.

That was the second time that night he'd said those words to me. I still wasn't sure what I was doing, but I'd do it for as long as he needed it.

18

Luke had left me alone at the shooting range when Jason made his approach.

I was in no state of mind to go another round with Addy's brother. My family's unwelcomed sneak attack from the night before still had me simmering. I had not wanted Addy to ever meet them and especially not like that. But as always, my family did whatever the fuck they wanted to do, uncaring I didn't want them to do it.

Now that I had Addy in my life, it was high time I cut them out. I'd never been one of them. As a kid I was different, as a teenager, the distance grew, and when I joined the Navy, a chasm had formed. I didn't want to work beside my father and not for the reasons he claimed. There was nothing wrong with being an electrician, it just wasn't for me. And working for my dad would've sent me over the edge. CJ was of another mind. He couldn't wait to join our father. My brother was twenty-nine and still lived in the apartment above my parents' garage. He was a man-child that needed his mommy to wipe his ass for him. And my mother after years of conditioning happily did it.

Yeah, it was time to cut them off, something I should've done the day I left for boot camp but didn't because I loved my mother. That was, the mom she was when her husband wasn't around.

And Addy was there to witness their bullshit. My family was a far cry from hers.

With all of that on my mind, Jason stopped beside me.

"Not a good time," I warned.

It would become apparent Jason gave zero fucks when he turned fully to me, took in the rifle in my hands, and launched in.

"Have a lot of shit on my mind. Mercy's having a rough pregnancy, still not a reason for me being a dick. Bottom line is, I was way out of line yesterday and I know it."

"This is a conversation you need to have with Adalynn," I returned.

I felt bad that Mercy was having a rough go of it. I'd only met her a few times, but what little I knew about her, I liked.

"Plan on it. But I needed to get straight with you first."

Jesus. I didn't want to rehash his thoughts on me dating his sister.

"Heard you loud and clear, Jason, so there's nothing to get straight."

"I think—"

"Then you're thinking wrong," I cut him off. "The only person you need to talk to is Adalynn. You weren't a dick to me, you were a fucking asshole to her. You embarrassed her and hurt her feelings. As you pointed out, she'll forgive you, so you should see to that."

"Brother—"

"Do not call me that. I'm not your brother. I'm your employee. That's all I am and you made that crystal clear. And as such, I'm asking you as my boss, not to bring my personal life to my workplace."

"Your personal life? You mean my family."

"Yeah, that's what I meant. I didn't miss your disapproval, I didn't miss your dad's. And likely today I won't miss Nick's and Carter's. And when I see them, I won't miss the rest of your family's either.

But what you got to get is, for me, I'm used to the disappointment and censure aimed my way. I know who I am and what kind of man I am, so I don't give a rat's ass what others think of me. However, I do care what Addy thinks, and I really care how she feels. So you all want to give me the cold shoulder, throw shade, give me shit—bring it. But you better learn real quick to hide that in front of Addy. None of this touches her. You wanna fire me because I'm dating your sister—do it. I'll find another job. What I won't do, is give her up."

"You'd walk away from Triple Canopy? From your brothers? Even Matt and Logan who only left the Navy to follow you?"

"In a heartbeat," I returned.

Jason shook his head. He crossed his arms. But what he didn't do was leave.

"I'm not being a dick, but I got work, Jason. Was there something else?"

"Belview's records are on your desk. Ninety percent of it is bullshit. My dad put in some calls and we're waiting to hear back. Nick went to the café and interviewed the manager. There's surveillance footage. It's being sent over this afternoon."

"The record isn't surprising, but it will be interesting what's been left out."

"Send you a text when we have the surveillance."

"'Preciate it."

I dipped my chin to indicate the conversation was over and to punctuate this non-verbal communication, I turned back to the long, open stretch of land that served as the rifle range.

Apparently, Jason didn't catch the hint. Either that or he chose to ignore it. Knowing Jason, it was the latter, which made it more annoying when he said, "We're gonna have to talk about you and Addy."

"There's nothing to say."

"There is, Trey, and you fucking know it."

I set the AR down on the bench and stepped away, both from the rifle and the man.

"Tell me, Jason, in the last twenty-four hours, you suddenly have a change of heart and have decided to welcome me into your family?"

I didn't mask my anger or my sarcasm. Neither did Jason when he returned in kind.

"You suddenly wake up and figure out that my sister isn't strong enough to survive the pain you'll leave?"

That pissed me right the fuck off for so many reasons I was afraid my head was going to explode.

"You don't have the first clue." I snatched my shit off the bench including my rifle, dropped the mag, pointed it downrange, and cleared the chamber. When that was done, I slung it over my shoulder and turned to leave.

"You think *you* know her but you don't."

Jason's statement sent fire through my veins—so much so I didn't take into account he was her brother when I halted and faced him.

"No, Jason. *You* don't know her, and the fact that you see her as some weak little girl is the first clue. The fact that shit has gone on in her life—big shit, bad shit, shit that you don't know about—is a huge, flashing neon sign that you don't know her at all. I get you got a wife with a kid on the way, and before that you had heavy shit going on losing Kayla the way you did. But it's no fucking excuse."

Jason flinched, then full of bravado returned, "Nothing—"

"Keep telling yourself that. Whatever makes you rest easy, man. Keep on lying to yourself that Addy's lived a perfect, charmed life and nothing's touched her. Keep on thinking she's some soft, weak, woman who needs her big brother to step in and protect her. Oh, wait, she *did* need that—twice —and where were you then? Not fucking there, that's where. To end this, you got some brass balls coming at me with this bullshit because if you knew your sister even a little bit, you'd know she's damn well strong enough to survive any damn thing that comes her way."

That time when I turned away I didn't stop, even though Jason called my name. I had shit to do and a class to get ready to teach.

Time would tell how pissed Addy would be when Jason went to her and questioned her about what I'd said. That, I would have to figure out a way to smooth out.

"Got a minute?" Carter called as he walked into the shoot house.

My class had ended and the last officer to leave had barely cleared the door.

No, I didn't have a minute. I didn't have one more second to give to another man who was important to Addy to give me a rash of shit. Most especially not Carter. Jason giving me hell stung, Jasper not wanting me near his daughter was expected but still hurt. Carter? If he warned me off, it would fucking slice to the bone.

But instead, I said, "Sure. What's going on?"

"Got the footage for the café," he started.

Well, fuck, that grabbed my attention.

"Audio and visual?"

"No. Though, I didn't need audio to confirm what you'd laid out—not that I needed confirmation at all. I believed—"

"I get it," I rushed out. "Anything useful?"

"Not in the sense we learned something new. But it might be helpful for Jasper to have when he approaches the general."

"Is he going to Wick?"

General Wick was a close friend of the Walker, Lenox, Clark, and McCoy families. He was also in charge of Liberty McCoy's unit. He was a good ally, however, he was also by-the-book. I couldn't see how he'd be of any use in this scenario.

"No. General Pickett."

"Never heard of him."

"Neither have I. Jasper knows *of* him, but has never had any contact. He has a meeting set up with him today."

It was interesting Jasper would meet with a man he didn't know.

"Is there a reason Jasper's showing his hand? Doesn't seem like something he'd do. I'd keep this close and find someone we can trust. Pickett's gonna hide behind operational security and likely go straight to Belview."

Carter nodded and smiled. "I think that's what he wants."

"Yeah, not tracking that play. It could backfire, piss off Belview, and make him come after Addy thinking she's causing problems for him."

"She'll be covered."

"Damn right, she will be. But I still don't like my woman's ass getting swung out there. I was in this guy's presence for five minutes and I'm telling you, I don't want him having the upper hand. And if he knows we're poking around, especially Jasper, he'll be moved to strike."

"In my opinion, that's what Jasper wants."

It was then I understood Jasper's play. It was also then that I lost my fucking mind.

"Are you fucking serious?" I roared.

"Trey—"

"Fuck that. He's more worried about his daughter living with me than he is about playing this smart and in a way that will actually fucking protect her."

"I think he just wants this done for her." Carter tried for placating but it came out as conciliatory.

Fuck that!

"He wants it done, all right. And his impatience and desire to get Addy out of my fucking house is gonna backfire. And when it does, I'm telling you, Carter, I'm gonna lose my motherfucking shit. She is not happy her life is being disrupted. As in, not at all. She's not pleased she had to rearrange her schedule. But she did it. Belview freaked her out but she's keeping her shit. She and I are just starting out and she was forced to move in because her ex is a nutjob. But when this is over, nothing will change between me and Addy, except I'll be in her bed as much as she is in mine. So there's no purpose in giving Belview a head's up we're looking into him so I can make my approach. Which I won't have to do at all if his time in Georgia is limited and he'll be gone soon."

"I don't think anyone's thinking straight right now," Carter admitted.

I agreed, so I remained silent since there was nothing to say.

"I got your back on this. On both fronts. I'm on your visitor list at the front gate. I'll do drive-bys, Nick and Brady will, too. I also asked Jackson and Brice. They're on board but you need to add them to the list. We'll rotate and keep an eye out. And don't worry about Jason, he'll come around. I'm not making excuses for him, what he said yesterday was jacked, but Mercy's having some issues with her pregnancy and all sorts of bad shit is coming up for him."

"He told me about Mercy. I'm sorry to hear that. I hope everything's okay with the baby. And I hope you don't take this as heartless, but you're right; it doesn't excuse how he made his sister feel."

Carter nodded and then he shared, "You didn't know Jason back in the day when he was with Kayla. The two of them, best friends, they tried to include the relationship stuff and it wasn't a love match, not like he has with Mercy. But he and Kayla, tight until the end. She beat cancer the first time. It came back and Jason stuck to her like glue, fighting right alongside her, all the way to the bitter end. And it was *bitter*, brother. She died in his arms in their bed. Now he's got a woman who is definitely his best friend but also the love of his life, and those old feelings of helplessness are resurfacing. He's being strong for Mercy, shielding her, and in doing that he's tearing into you. It's fucked up. I know it is. And when he pulls himself out he's gonna feel like a dick and he'll struggle with what he's done.

"Now, of course there's a difference between your wife being pregnant but so sick she's in and out of the hospital and you're holding her while she pukes her brains out, and your wife having cancer.

But right now, Jason cannot see that. He's blinded with fear because he's living in the past."

Fucking shit. I didn't think it was possible but all my anger for the guy was wiped clean. And I felt like the asshole for bringing up Kayla.

Fucking *hell*.

Carter went on. "Jasper is...Jasper. He loves his girls fiercely. So fierce, that sometimes he doesn't see reason. When you're on the other side of this, you'll get it."

"I get it now and I take no offense."

"I sure as fuck would," Carter complained.

"No, you wouldn't. You love Delaney enough to take whatever Jasper had to throw your way, eat it, then take the time needed to earn his trust."

"Yeah." Carter smiled. "And you willing to eat his shit proves you'll earn that, too. But just so you know, for me, for Nick, for the rest of us, you've already earned it. You didn't see it, but yesterday, Nick threw down for you. Jason knows he's wrong, he also knows the shit he gave you yesterday is just that—shit. Not a man in that room, except me," Carter stopped to smirk, "can say jackshit about you playing the field. Neither can Jasper and he knows it. But he's holding onto something because Addy's the last one, and I reckon he's feeling that. Don't make it easier for you to swallow, but he'll come around."

My chest started to burn. I hadn't realized until that moment how much I needed to know Carter had my back. It felt good, and the knot that had taken root in my gut started to loosen. In an effort to hide the emotion, I circled back.

"Does she know about that layover we had in Amsterdam?" Carter groaned and shook his head. "Never seen a man pinned against a wall with his hands up and fear in his eyes *without* a gun pressed to his forehead."

"She was damn near naked. Where was I supposed to put my hands?" he grumbled.

The prostitute wasn't *damn near naked*, she was fully clothed—although her ginormous, surgically enhanced tits were on full display.

"You're the one who suggested we hit up De Wallen," I reminded him. "We were game because we thought you were finally lookin' to get laid. Hell, she even offered you a discount."

"Go ahead and talk shit." Carter grinned. "She did have me pinned down, but if memory serves, you're the one who left that night with tears in his eyes."

"Bitch tried to twist my balls off."

In my haste, I'd forgotten that part, or maybe I'd blocked the painful memory of a sex worker literally trying to drag me down a hallway by my balls. By the time I'd freed my bruised testicles, tears had indeed sprung. Carter was being generous leaving out the part where I'd limped the two blocks to our hotel, then proceeded to ice my swollen balls.

"You know, the only good part about being at a bar with you, Trey, was that I didn't have to worry. No one paid me any mind once they caught sight of you."

Carter was full of shit; he'd had women falling over themselves to get a shot at him.

"The *only* good part?"

"Well, it sure as shit wasn't your witty come-backs. And your personality leaves much to be desired. And if it wasn't for Luke taking the top spot for being the most standoffish asshole on the team, the honor would've been yours. And Logan being the most cynical worked in your favor. But, yeah, you taking all the attention worked for me in a big way."

A year ago, I would've asked Carter if he regretted not tasting all that life had to offer. His answer would've been a resounding "fuck no" but I still would've asked. A year ago, I couldn't imagine not living my life the way I had. Now, I understood why Carter didn't regret it, why he'd held out. Why he'd stayed true to a commitment he'd made to himself, even when he was denying Delaney the relationship she'd wanted.

The second my eyes had landed on Addy, all other women ceased to exist. And if I'd met her earlier in life, the same would've happened. Carter was correct, Logan was cynical. He didn't believe in love, and being as his childhood was so fucked up, I didn't blame him. And there was a time I'd subscribed to his way of thinking—but Addy had changed my mind.

I shifted my weight to my good leg. Carter, not one to miss anything, narrowed his eyes.

"When was the last time you went to PT and actually did the work?"

Fucking hell. I didn't want to get into it with him about physical therapy.

"Carter—"

"She's my baby cousin so you gotta know I'm gaggin' as I say this, but now that things have changed between the two of you, I bet you let her work you out, she'll do it in a way that seriously works for you."

I felt my mouth form a smile and muttered, "'Preciate you taking that hit. Think maybe it's time I schedule an appointment with my Addy, see if she can pencil me in for floor exercises tonight."

"That was a fucked way to show your gratitude, friend."

And without another word, Carter left the shoot house. A few minutes later, I grabbed my gear and went in search of my woman.

19

"You both have jobs." I stood in Triple Canopy's gym and looked from Quinn to Hadley.

"Yup," Hadley agreed. "And I'm done for the day."

Awesome. *Not*.

"I'm *at* work." Quinn shrugged.

"Um. I think there's a difference between being at work and actually working," I noted. "I'm sure you have plenty of..." Crap, I didn't know exactly what my sister did. "Stuff to do," I lamely finished.

"Totally. Next month's training schedule is due to Nick by the end of the day and Carter wants the proposals for the new handgun range color-coded before he looks at them. I'm not sure why he needs them color-coded, or what that even means."

"Maybe you should go find him and ask," I supplied, then turned to Hadley. "And I saw Brady earlier. He looked forlorn and lonely, he could probably use some attention. You should go find him."

"No way, sister. Spill." Hadley grabbed a big exercise ball and sat. I watched it wobble and shake as she tried to get her balance. "God. These things are a death trap. Hope the insurance covers broken necks. Who uses these?"

I would never wish my twin to break her neck, but I did wish she'd fall off the ball, hurt her butt, and go search out her fiancé to have him kiss it and make it better.

"By the way, Mom's on her way in." Quinn smirked and I groaned.

"Seriously, you called Mom?"

"Of course I did. Who else is gonna straighten you out?"

"Straighten me out?"

"Help you pull your head out of your ass and give Trey a chance," Hadley explained.

"I don't know what you're talking about. I *am* giving him a chance."

"You are?" Hadley's spine snapped straight, then she pitched to the side, necessitating her arms shooting out to her sides to catch herself. "Seriously. What the hell is up with this ball?"

"If you had any core muscles, you'd have no problems. But you refuse to do yoga with me or even *go to the gym*." I threw my hands up in exasperation. "And I can't *believe* you called Mom."

Quinn didn't look the slightest bit repentant. Completely unfazed. I was irritated she'd called our mom to "straighten me out."

"I have no idea why that'd shock you. The only person you listen to is her."

That was a true statement. My sisters had given me a lot of advice over the years. So had my brother, dad, aunts, and uncles. But it was my mom's advice and opinion I valued the most. However, I was not ready to ask for or hear Emily Walker's wisdom. Part of that was because I was a damn adult and I was bloody tired of being treated like the baby of the family. The other reason was because I was scared to death of what her guidance would be. And I was scared because I knew without having to ask what she'd tell me to do, which was what I was doing— looking beyond all that was Trey's outward appearance into the heart of him. She would not mean his good looks, she'd mean his rough, tough, hardened shell—the man he showed the world—to the center of him. To the parts he'd show only me. Then she'd tell me to heal what ailed him so he could be free to be the man he was meant to be.

I knew this, one-hundred percent, without a doubt. It was what she'd done for my father. It was what she'd preached to me and Hadley.

There was a knock at the gym door and I closed my eyes, not ready to face my mom. But when my lids opened, both Hadley and Quinn had big eyes and worried expressions.

Oh, crap.

I turned, fully prepared for a firing squad. But instead, I saw Bass with a big, wide smile on his face sauntering across the open room.

"Hey," I greeted. "In the neighborhood?"

His smile got bigger and he jerked his chin.

"No, honey. I wanted to check on you," he drawled.

Honey?

Oh, *crap.*

I got it, why my sisters had big eyes and worried expressions. Bass was here out of the blue and Trey was somewhere on the property. No doubt he would've been alerted to Bass's car pulling into the lot.

Crap.

Bass was approaching and I was stuck, rooted, not knowing how to handle the situation. On one hand, Bass was a friend. On the other, Trey had been right that there'd been some mild flirting in the past. Obviously, that was over, and even before I was with Trey I knew nothing would ever become of me and Bass but...damn...what was I supposed to do?

Please don't hug me.

Drat.

As soon as he got close, his arm went around my waist and he pulled me into a bear hug, smooshing me against his wide, muscled chest. My mind drifted to Trey and how much better it felt being held against his. However, that thought was fleeting and I was in the process of breaking the hug when I heard Hadley make a strangled noise from beside me. Then Quinn muttered, "Oh, shit."

And that was right before I heard Trey's voice boom and bounce around the room before the sound hit my ears. "You must be Bass."

Double drat.

Bass's arms tightened around me and my brain came unstuck. But before I could push away, Trey continued. "You mind."

It was not a question. Not even close. He didn't care if Bass minded, it was an order to let me go.

Something that Bass didn't do. Instead, he turned slightly and bent his neck to look down at me.

"Who is that guy?"

My body went unnaturally stiff at Bass's tone and stiffer still at the stern look in his eyes.

"Let go of me, please," I whispered, and Bass's eyes narrowed.

"That Trey?" he asked but didn't let go.

The tremble had started. I knew from experience I had two seconds before it happened. Anger was sliding up my spine. He wasn't listening. He wasn't letting go even though I asked. The helpless feeling was swimming below the surface, trying to break free.

How many times had I asked Keith to let me go, or not hold my hand so tight, or to get off of me? How many times had he ignored my wishes? How many times had I asked and he had not *listened*?

"Let. Go!" I snapped.

His arms released me at the same time I jerked back, causing me to stumble.

"Damn, Addy, you okay?" Bass asked.

Mr. Sweet Guy back in full-force. But it was too late. My heart was pounding and that sick feeling had crept up and taken over.

"When someone asks you to let them go, you *fucking* let them go."

Hadley and Quinn gasped at my outburst.

Then suddenly I was no longer looking at Bass because Trey was filling my vision.

"Baby?"

"Huh?"

"Look at me."

"I am."

"No, baby, you're not."

I blinked and blinked again until some of the haze started to go away. Only, unlike the first time I'd had a freak-out in front of him in his kitchen, I didn't feel embarrassed. I was ticked and I was also lost in my anger.

"I asked him to *let me go*." Trey's gaze went soft and I didn't understand that, so I went on so he'd *understand*. "When someone asks you to let go, *you let go.*"

"Adalynn."

"What?"

"You're not looking at me."

"I damn well am," I told him because I was. I was looking right into his stunning, soft eyes.

"Okay, then, baby, you're not seeing me. I need you to see *me* right now."

"Why?"

"Because you're scaring me."

Scaring him? How was it possible I was scaring Trey?

"What? How?"

"Because I'm sensing that what you're saying doesn't have anything to do with Bass but with something else. And what I'm sensing scares the fuck outta me, Addy. So, please, come back to the room and see me standing in front of you."

That sobered me.

We weren't in his kitchen alone. We were in the gym with my sisters and Bass.

"Trey," I whispered miserably.

"There you are."

Then he wasn't there because he turned to face Bass, which meant I lost his soft eyes and had his t-shirt-covered back.

"Man to man, when a woman asks you to release her, you do it. When that woman is my woman, you do it immediately. I'm guessing you're here because you rightly assumed what Addy was doing in my kitchen first thing in the morning cooking breakfast. What you don't know is it says a fuckuva lot more than you assumed. You two are friends and that's cool. What it means for you from now on is, she takes your class and the two of you go to lunch as *friends*. What it does not mean is you put your hands on my woman—ever."

"Right," Bass muttered and smartly said nothing else.

When no one moved, Trey asked, "You done here?"

"No."

"No?"

"I came here to ask Addy how she was. I haven't done that. So maybe you'd like to step aside so I can do that and apologize for freaking her out when that was not my intention."

God, that was nice of him to offer after I'd made a fool of myself. "Bass, you have nothing to apologize for. I made a big deal—"

The rest of my statement died on my tongue when Trey grunted.

"Don't let me off the hook, Addy. I was shocked and making a point that very obviously didn't need to be made. I scared you, and bottom line, the point I was making was a dick thing to do. And in the process, I might've damaged a friendship. So let me tell you I'm sorry and it won't happen again."

Trey stepped to the side and his arm slid around my waist. Oddly, this wasn't done in a "piss on my patch" sort of way. He was lending me his strength and I appreciated it.

"Thanks," I mumbled.

"I hope you know if you need anything, you can call," Bass went on.

Jeez, that was super nice and it made me feel like even more of a twit. Bass was not Keith.

"I do."

"Hope to see you soon."

And without acknowledging anyone else, Bass turned and left. No one spoke until the front door of the gym clicked shut.

"Uncanny." That came from my mother.

Upon hearing her voice, I turned and shoved my face as deep into Trey's armpit as I could.

"It's a good thing I haven't worked out yet today." Trey chuckled.

"Huh?"

"Babe?"

"Hm?"

I hadn't moved—not that I'd planned to—so I was really happy I stayed put when Trey's body started shaking, causing me to feel the rumble on my cheek, because feeling that for some silly reason made my heart swell.

Last night hadn't been good for him. His parents

and brother had barged into his home and treated him like crap. This morning when they'd left—the same. Not even a "thanks for letting us crash at your house—uninvited," they'd just said bye and left. It was the most bizarre thing I'd ever witnessed. And all of that happened after my brother had been a royal jerk to him. And, though Trey didn't say, I knew my dad had talked to him and *that* couldn't have been pleasant.

So I didn't care he was laughing at my childish attempt to hide from my mother. I was just glad he was laughing the day after he'd had a really crappy day and an equally bad morning.

"Hope he put on deodorant," Quinn muttered.

He had put on deodorant and I knew this because this morning after he got out of the shower I'd watched him do it. I also watched him shave, with a thick navy blue towel wrapped around his narrow hips. He'd tensed when I'd set his cup of coffee on the vanity, then hauled my booty onto the counter to watch. But a few moments later, he relaxed. I knew he'd gone rigid because he was shirtless and I could see the scars on his chest, but more—it was the burns on his back that had his muscles straining. I didn't acknowledge them, because there was nothing to acknowledge. They were just another part of him.

It was on those delicious thoughts of Trey shirtless in his bathroom doing something as normal as
shaving then putting on deodorant I smiled.

"Jeez, Addy, get a room," Hadley teased. "Oh,
wait, the last time you did—"

A throat cleared—the sound very obviously
masculine—but just in case my sister missed the
meaning, my father finished with a "Hadley."

It was a warning not to complete that thought. I
didn't see it because my face was still hidden. And
hearing my dad's voice made me shove deeper.

Kill me now.

Trey was no longer laughing. His body had
gone just as still as mine and we stood locked
together like two teenagers who'd been caught
doing something naughty. No, that wasn't right—
two teenagers would've had the sense to jump
apart. But Trey's arm had tightened, holding me
closer, not letting me go, claiming me in front of
my dad.

So why was I hiding?

"Hey, Dad," Quinn chirped.

"Trey. A word?" my dad clipped, ignoring my
sister, which was odd.

He never snubbed one of his girls. *Never.* But he
just had totally disregarded Quinn in favor of

barking a command. One he'd likely expect Trey to obey.

Um. No.

I pushed back. Trey's arms loosened, his chin dipped, and he caught my eyes.

"Be right back, baby."

I was shaking my head when his lips dropped to mine. Soft, short, but again claiming. If his embrace hadn't communicated his intentions to everyone in the room, that soft, short kiss did. It was sweet, what he was saying to me, reminding me he wasn't going anywhere even though my brother stated plainly his thoughts and undoubtedly my dad had, too, just not in front of me.

Being as it was sweet, I appreciated the gesture. But it ticked me right the eff off Trey had to make the statement.

So when he started to pull away, I returned the favor, only I did it my way.

"Hi, Dad," I greeted, and at the same time, I fisted Trey's shirt, keeping him where I wanted.

"Trey? A word?" my dad once again commanded and didn't spare me a glance.

"Jasper," my mom gently reprimanded.

"Be right back, baby," Trey repeated.

Days later, I would think back on this moment,

and even then after much contemplation, I didn't know what came over me other than I'd had *enough*. Enough of being the baby of the family. Enough of being overlooked. Enough of not being listened to. Enough of my dad—who showed me every day he loved me, who was a good dad, a good man, a good husband, but a man who was so over-the-top in that love it was smothering me.

I wanted to breathe.

"No."

"Addy—"

"I said no."

The creases on Trey's forehead deepened. Wrinkles that just last night I had smoothed while sitting in his lap. This, after he'd sat sentry next to me through dinner with his muscles coiled tight, waiting to pounce on a member of his own blood family should one of them say something to annoy me. This, after he warned he'd show them to the door if they didn't treat me right.

Me.

Not him.

From almost the first minute, CJ had been a total ass to Trey and Trey took it. He hadn't batted a damn eye at CJ talking about the scars on his face. But the second CJ said something mildly offensive to me, he'd flipped and told them they could sleep in the car.

He'd let them be mean to him.

But not to me.

"Adalynn—" he tried again but I pressed deeper and shuffled us so we were facing my dad.

"Let's try again, Dad. Hi. Nice to see you."

"Not now, Adalynn."

"Jasper." This time my mother didn't gently scold, she just did it outright.

"Dad," Quinn gasped.

"Addy, baby," Trey soothed. "I know what you're trying to do. But it's not necessary."

"Yes, it is. Last night you made your point to your family. Today, I'm making mine. I'm a grown-up. I get to make my own choices, and not everyone has to like them but they better darn well respect them."

"Takin' my back," he muttered, and started to say something else but I spoke over him.

"I told Jason I wouldn't stand for him being a giant jerk, and if he couldn't find his way to getting over something that is not his business, then he better find a way to hide it because if he doesn't, I have no problem cutting him—"

"Absolutely not," Trey growled and cupped my face. "Baby, love that you're takin' my back, love what that says about what you feel for me. But you will not cut him out. Whether he learns to hide it or not, *I'll* deal with it—not you. He's your brother and he loves you. I get why he doesn't like me for you. If I had a sister who I adored, I wouldn't like me for her either. Straight up, Addy, we talked about this. I knew going in what I was up against. Just so we're clear, hear this—I eat shit, you don't. I'll deal with Jason, you won't. Your dad wants a word, I'll give him that time. And I'll eat that, too, because, at the end of the day, I'll take any-*fucking*-thing so you don't feel it. But also, because he's your dad, he loves you, he wants what's best for you, and as the man in your life, I owe it to him."

I was too mindless with irritation for Trey's words to penetrate. My mom on the other hand had no such problem.

"It's like looking through a crystal ball back in time," she stated. "Here I stand decades later and yet weirdly I feel like I've heard those very things a time or two."

"Em," my dad grunted.

"Did you think she wouldn't find *you*, Jasper?"

"Emily."

"Addy?" Trey murmured, and my gaze went from watching my mom glare at my dad back to him.

"I'm gonna go out and talk to your dad. Visit with your mom and sisters."

"Fine," I huffed.

"Cute." His lips brushed mine, and I feared with all the anger rolling off my dad, Trey was putting his life in danger. But I figured he didn't care.

The lip touch was meant just for me, and I was finding Trey would go to great lengths to make sure I knew how he felt about me.

20

The burn in my chest grew with every step.

I'd made it a point to exit the gym from the opposite side from where Jasper and Emily had entered. If Jasper wanted a word, I'd give it to him, but I sure as fuck wasn't following him like I was a whipping boy being summoned.

Fuck that.

I'd eat shit. I'd put in the time. But I could only be me. And the man I was rejected the idea of being paged only to receive a dressing down. In front of my woman no less.

"Trey?"

I ignored Jasper's call and continued to walk farther. I didn't want anyone to overhear the conversation we were about to have. I was going to have to swallow whatever Jasper had to say but that didn't mean I'd stand there like some pimple-faced kid and shrink back as Addy's dad force-fed me some bull-shit about how I wasn't good enough for his daughter because I'd enjoyed the field while it was available to me. We both knew he had better things at his disposal to use against me than how many women I'd taken to my bed. The mere fact I'd fucked up so badly on my last mission was reason enough—yet he and Jason had honed in on my sex life.

Total shit.

Once I rounded the corner of the shoot house, I stopped and turned.

Jasper halted and we stood facing each other. Silence ensued and I took the opportunity to tamp down my temper. I also used it to study the other man. Tall. Fit. Even pushing sixty, Jasper still took care of himself. He was an imposing figure. But that wasn't what I focused on.

Jasper didn't look pissed, he looked reflective, and if I didn't know better I'd add beaten down. But that was not Jasper Walker—the warrior I knew didn't let anything best him.

That meant in front of me stood Jasper Walker the father. I was still gauging his intent when he started, and when he did, I was unprepared for what would happen next.

"Fucked up. Saw it, didn't push, but I saw it. Knew something happened but I gave her space to work it out, and in doing so I let that fester."

I had no clue what Jasper was talking about, like I'd been asleep for the first part of the conversation and when I'd woken up we were somewhere in the middle.

"*That*," he seethed. "I let that shit grow in my girl. Dark. Bad shit."

"Jas—"

"You called it straight back there—don't give her space."

I clamped my mouth shut. Pain and worry etched deep. A father's anguish exposed in a moment of honesty.

"I've been blessed. There hasn't been a morning since Em has come into my life I haven't opened my eyes and not known with soul-deep certainty I have everything a man could want. The problem with that; a man who has it all has everything to lose. This is something you cannot understand until you have it. And you might think you have everything when you look at my Adalynn, but I assure you, you're wrong."

I was torn between easing his worry and unleashing my fury at his jab. However, my indecision ended when Jasper took a step closer and started again.

"She is only the beginning. The beam that will light *everything*. You will not know that warmth until she hands you the world and when she does, then you'll feel the weight. The crippling fear a man feels when he knows he has every-*fucking*-thing and he is truly powerless to protect those he loves."

Reading the situation incorrectly I stated, "Belview's not gonna get close enough to hurt her."

"Not worried about that idiot. Again, you called it so you know someone already has hurt her, and he did it in a way that she's hidden for years, keeping it locked inside of her. Twice I've seen it come out and both times it gnawed at my insides. You dig that out, make her face it, fix what's broken, you'll have my eternal gratitude."

His words weren't a ringing endorsement that Jasper approved of me being with Addy. It was more a father who saw the wisdom in a man taking his daughter's back when he'd just been reminded she was vulnerable. Though not what I wanted, I would take it.

"No offense, I'll be digging that out but I won't be doing it for your gratitude."

"You'll have it all the same."

I reckoned I would.

"You need to be worried about Belview," I circled back. "I watched the footage from the café. I was there, but until he raised his voice I was giving them space thinking Addy was on a date. Seems I missed the start of their exchange. Something she said to him made him shut down and from what she told me, I'd guess it was right about the time she mentioned you."

"Me?" A muscle in his cheek jumped. "What about me?"

"Addy wasn't letting him get away with his bull-shit about breaking up with her because he was leaving on deployment. Further, she wasn't buying the excuse he did it because he wasn't in the regular Army. She reminded him she was aware of what deployment would be like and he didn't like the reminder. Told her he remembered who you were and that you were a hard act to follow."

The muscle in Jasper's cheek twitched again and his brows pulled together.

"Last few days I've been thinking on it," he muttered. "Why at the time when he came to talk to me I didn't reassure him Addy was strong enough to handle the separation when I knew damn well she was. And I remembered watching him with her—I didn't like what I saw. So much so when Wick asked my thoughts about possibly pulling Belview into the program, I told him it would be a mistake. There are men who can shoulder the burden and find healthy ways to wash the filth they experience off, some deal with it in not so healthy ways and bury it, but they do it in a way that doesn't hurt the ones they love. Then there are those that are weak of mind and lash out because they're too far gone to see they need help or they were too weak from the beginning. Belview was the latter. Weak of mind and spirit. Saw it on him and didn't want that for my daughter. Or for the program."

One could say I'd been weak and I hadn't dealt with my shit in a healthy way.

Fuck.

"Jasper—"

"If you're tangling that up in your mind, stop. Never once have I thought you were weak. Just the opposite." Jasper suddenly stopped and his stare became seriously fucking frightening. "I know you're not gonna like hearing this, but I didn't want you for my daughter because I wanted her to have easy. And,

Trey, there's nothing easy about you. You've buried yourself under a mountain of guilt that's not yours. Before you protest, I know why you feel it, I know why you let it weigh you down, and I know why you let it bury you. I know because I'd feel the same. And just like your brothers are trying to guide you to the other side, mine would be doing the same, and like you, I'd be fighting it. So I know your brothers are going to fail in their endeavor to make you see the light the same as mine did. I also know who's gonna bring you to the other side. And honest to God, I didn't want that for her. I wanted her to find someone who would see to what's been eatin' at her for the last three fucking years and put a stop to it. Something that kills me because she won't give it to me. I've tried and she pulls away."

Again the veil lifted, and pure, unadulterated pain ripped through Jasper. So much of it, I flinched. Being as Jasper was highly attuned to everyone in his presence, he didn't miss my reaction.

"You getting it now?" he murmured. "I got no power in a situation where a man like me needs not only power but control. My baby girl is hurting and there isn't one fucking thing I can do to stop it. And now, I'm at *your* mercy, praying to God you can make my girl whole. At the same time having to reconcile that you don't give the first fuck I don't want you near my daughter. And in saying that, I have to admit that fucking finally my girl has someone at her back that's worthy of being there."

A fire lit in my chest and scored through me as it burned a path straight to my soul—a burn that hurt so *good* I wasted no time memorizing the feel of it.

Worthy of being there.

Fucking, Christ.

"I hope you know I actually do care what you think," I admitted. "I just love Addy more."

Jasper's eyelids drifted closed and when they opened, there was blatant respect. So I gave him one more thing.

"Belview had one thing right, Jasper. You're a hard act to follow. You taught your girls what it means to be loved, how to accept that love, and how to give it in return. You also taught them not to accept anything less than what you gave them. I'm not stupid, and I have no intention of trying to fill your shoes. Those are yours, they'll always be yours, because you'll always hold that rightful place in Adalynn's heart. But luckily for me, Emily taught her daughter a few things, too, so I don't need to fill a place you'll never vacate—she's already made room for me. And that place is mine and mine alone to fill with all the goodness I can give her. With all of that, I hope you get what I'm saying is, she loves you. So when you're beating yourself up about not being able to fix what's broken in Addy, maybe remember she's yours, and the shield you provided for her goes both ways. And this is Addy's way of protecting you from something she knows is gonna hurt you."

"When you're a father it doesn't work that way. My job is to protect her, not the other way around."

"Right. Trying to explain to a Walker that protection is a one-way street is akin to banging your head on a rock. You didn't raise your family to take, you raised them to give. To protect each other. To be loyal. Just last night I learned what Adalynn's brand of loyalty and protection felt like. Warms you straight to the bone while at the same time chills your blood because it should be *you* shielding *her*. I don't suppose it will make you sleep any easier knowing that, I just hope you understand she thinks she's doing right by protecting you."

"Fuck," he muttered, and dipped his chin so he was staring at his feet.

"You have my word I'm gonna do right by her." His head bobbed but he didn't lift his gaze so I finished what I had to say. "I'll leave you with this.

You also have my word I'll earn your trust, but more —I'll earn hers."

I got another stilted jerk of his chin, then I left him alone to his thoughts.

I didn't go back to the gym to check on Addy. She had her mom and sisters with her. I went straight to my office, needing a moment to process my conversation with Jasper. But also needing to calm down my urge to track down the two men in Adalynn's life that had both caused damage.

My plan was shot to hell when I entered my office and found Luke sitting at Matt's desk. One look told me this wasn't going to be a happy chat. He looked furious.

"What's going on?" I asked when his gaze met mine.

"You tell me," he returned.

Shit.

"Need you to clue me in about what you're asking."

I didn't, but I was hoping I was wrong and he was there to talk about Belview or our upcoming training schedule.

"Known you a long fucking time, never known you to be a liar."

"Come again."

"You don't need me to clue you in, but since this is how you wanna play it, we'll play. This morning something was off. Not the first time I've felt it. I figured I gave you time, you'd sort it out yourself. But it's getting worse, so now I'm seeing I need to help you do that. But just to say, it pissed me right the fuck off I gotta do it."

And there went the kernel of good that Jasper had planted. Seeing Luke, hearing his anger, feeling the vibe in the room shift straight to bone-cold reminded me I'd ruined his life.

"Luke—"

"No. Hell no." He stood and I braced. "Been waiting on you to pull your head out and remember."

"Remember what?"

"Who. Remember *who* the fuck I am. Remember me? Your brother."

Brother.

That one word bounced around and echoed pain-filled memories flooded.

"What?"

"For the life of me, I cannot imagine why we have to have this conversation. And it offends the fuck out of me that we do. You must've bumped your head really goddamn hard. So hard, it knocked all your good sense clean away. You got a problem with me?"

"What the hell are you talking about? Why would I have a problem with you?"

"You blame me for not pulling your ass back when Liberty made her call?"

Oh, fuck.

The twinge of discomfort that was always present started throbbing.

"Hell no, I don't blame you."

"Then why in the actual fuck do think I'd blame you?"

The bone-cold in the room seeped deeper, so deep I was afraid I'd shatter. Guilt pounded, making my head hurt and my chest ache. So many regrets wrapped up in 'what-ifs'. Luke's life upended because of my indecision.

"I should've—"

"You should've done what? Drake was our LPO, he was in charge. Logan was our A-LPO. And I hate to break it to you, but you were not in a position of authority over me. So what in the hell makes you think that your dumb ass could've ordered me to do a damn thing? *Teammates*. Let me repeat that for you, Trey—team...mates. Brothers. You remember what that word means, or has your family been back at you again twisting shit in your head?"

I went solid. *Too damn close to the truth.*

"That "brother" you have, the one that kisses your dad's ass, treats your mom like a nursemaid and will until the day he dies is not a *brother*." Luke kept at me and my lungs seized. "He used you growing up as a scapegoat and you let him in order to shield him from your dad, and I know you felt guilty for leaving him behind when you went into the Navy. But he is not worth that emotion. CJ is a man-child partly because you became the whipping boy and he never had to take responsibility for his actions. Now he's a dick and he blames you that he's near thirty and lives at home with mommy and daddy. News flash, it's not your fault, and no brother—not a real fucking one— would blame his brother for bad shit that happens to him. So with that reminder, I have to ask, did you fucking forget who I am?"

I didn't answer. Instead, I stumbled behind my desk, plopped my ass in my chair, and like a pussy, wouldn't look at the man who'd been more of a brother to me than my blood. A man I called my friend and it was an honor to do so. And lastly, a man whom I admired.

Fuck.

"Yeah, Luke, I forgot who you were," I admitted.

"You remembering now?"

"Yep."

"See you don't forget again."

And that was it. He walked to the door, exited, and the door closed behind him.

That was Luke. My brother. My teammate. Pissed as shit I'd think he blamed me. He pointed it out in true Luke-fashion. Then he'd let it be done and he'd damn well expect you to be done and move on, too. No apology needed. No other words. Just that.

Could it be that easy?

21

"Should we run away?" I asked when Trey drove out of the Triple Canopy parking lot.

"Might not be a bad idea." He chuckled then asked, "How was your visit with your mom?"

"It went," I answered noncommittally.

"It went?"

"Yeah, as in, it went exactly like I knew it would."

"She give you a hard time about me?" he asked, no longer sounding amused.

As a matter of fact, he sounded disappointed.

"No. And I probably shouldn't tell you this but she's all for us. Us being you and me in a relationship and you and me living together."

I turned from the windshield in time to see Trey's brilliant smile.

"Why shouldn't I know that?"

"Because you'll think you have the upper hand," I told him.

"Right."

His smile grew, and after the day we had, I was glad for it. I shelved asking him about what my dad had said even though I really wanted to know. I wanted him smiling more.

"Anyway. My mom was further disappointed when she didn't get to share motherly wisdom, make me see reason, and extol the virtues of a strong man, seeing as I'd already come to my own conclusions."

"What conclusions are those?"

"Well, we're giving this a try. You and me. And that means I'm gonna trust you even if I'm scared as heck. It's only been a couple of days but it feels good so I'm gonna trust that, too. Mom was all fired up to help me see the light and was bummed when I told her I already saw it."

Trey's smile faded and my worry hit my stomach. He'd endured two days of my dad and brother giving him shit; maybe they'd made *him* see the light —that being I wasn't worth all the crap they were giving him.

"Means a lot to me," he said, his voice thick, and that worry slid clean away.

Trust. I'd promised myself I was going to trust him.

"The better part of the visit was when Mom started bossin' Quinn about her wedding. Mom's still salty Quinn and Brice are getting married at Uncle Clark and Aunt Reagan's."

"Why would your mom be mad about that? I've been to the house—it's beautiful and one of the few places where all five thousand of you can get together and not have the neighbors complain about taking over the street with cars."

He was correct. My aunt and uncle lived outside of town with no close neighbors. The only other person in the family who could host a get-together and not have people complain was Jackson and Tuesday. Tuesday had inherited her family's sprawling mansion. It wasn't a mini-mansion like Trey had. It was a real Southern mansion, real in the sense it had a music room, a parlor, a library, a beautiful orchard, and it even had a name, The Manor. No one complained when we got together there, mainly because the huge circular driveway had enough room for everyone to park.

"Five thousand's a slight exaggeration, don't you think?"

"Only a slight one, Addy. When I first met everyone, I almost asked if y'all would wear name tags."

I felt myself smile at that. He wasn't wrong. There were a lot of us.

"So, Mom's not mad Quinn and Brice are getting married there. She's mad about why and the timing of the wedding. Have you heard the story about Delaney and Carter's wedding?"

"Just that Delaney surprised Carter."

"Yeah, she surprised him all right." I laughed as the memories of that day hit. "But more, Hudson surprised us."

"Hudson? Ethan's son?"

"Oh, yeah." I couldn't contain my laughter when visions of my cousin Ethan's face came to my mind. "Get this..."

I spent the rest of the drive home telling Trey the story of how Delaney had arranged a surprise wedding for Carter on Ethan's birthday. Then right after they exchanged their vows and Carter kissed his wife, Honor had screamed and doubled over in pain. Not wanting to miss the wedding, she hadn't told anyone she'd gone into labor hours before. And being that her labor had started hours before when her water broke right there in the backyard, Hudson was impatient to make his appearance, and Honor had given birth in my aunt and uncle's house, on the kitchen floor with Ethan delivering his son.

Trey gave a wave to Lenny as he drove through the gates then turned his horror-filled eyes toward me.

"Jesus."

"Yeah," I agreed. "At the time it wasn't funny. Now it's hilarious. Quinn being the troublemaker of the family has set her wedding date close to Delaney's due date hoping for a repeat performance. Mom's not impressed. Delaney thinks it's amusing. I don't know how Carter feels about this, but considering his wedding day ended with him sitting behind his sister-in-law helping her push while he watched his brother out-of-his-mind with worry, I don't think he'll be all that fired up for what Quinn is calling Lenox V2."

That made Trey smile.

"Never seen Carter Lenox off his game. Never seen him break a sweat. If there's a possibility of either of those happening, I'm not missing your sister's wedding."

Quinn's wedding wasn't for seven months. Seven. That was a lot of months for Trey to be planning ahead. Of course, I hoped I got to attend my sister's wedding on Trey's arm, but I decided to keep that part to myself, and instead, I told him, "After Mom got done with Quinn, she turned her attention to Hadley, and get this..." I didn't wait for him to respond, I was so excited I barely contained my urge to clap. "Hadley and Brady are getting married in two weeks."

"Two weeks?" Trey choked out, laughing. "Not wasting any time. Good for him."

No, Brady wasn't wasting any more time; he'd already waited four years for my sister.

"Well, she wants seven kids and she's not joking. It's best they hurry up and get on that before she's still popping them out when she's ninety."

"Seven?" he sputtered. "She wants seven kids?"

"Well, between you and me *she* doesn't want seven kids, she wants *Brady* to have seven kids. The way he grew up with no family, she's determined to give him one."

"Taking care of her man," Trey muttered, and it took me a moment to understand his gruff tone. But when I did, my heart clenched.

Had anyone ever taken care of Trey?

His mom? A girlfriend? Anyone? Judging by his reaction last night, the answer to that was a big fat no. Knowing that, remembering how his family behaved, what little he'd told me about them, my anger grew and grew and kept growing until he pulled into his garage. And then it didn't stop growing—it just boiled over.

"Babe?"

"Hm?"

"Not sure what my dashboard did to you, but I'm fairly certain it's gonna catch fire any moment."

"What?"

I blinked and looked over at him.

"What's with the look?"

"The look?"

"Yeah, the death rays that were shooting from your eyes and the scowl."

Okay, that was funny, but I didn't feel like smiling nor did I feel like participating in banter.

"I'm fine."

"And I'm not dumb."

"Please let me have this," I whispered.

Trey waited a beat and nodded. "For now. But at some point, we're gonna have to stop putting off these conversations."

Gah. He was right. There was a lot we needed to talk about, but right then, I had something more important I had to do.

"I know."

"Tonight I'm cooking," he decreed. "No phones. No answering the door. Just you and me."

That sounded perfect. Only, I had one call I had to make before it was just me and Trey. And as I didn't get to taste any of the dinner he prepared last night, I was also looking forward to him cooking again.

TREY WAS downstairs in his kitchen. Steaks were on the grill, red potatoes in the oven, and he was roasting green beans. I'd snuck up to his bedroom to make a call.

"You okay?"

I rolled my eyes to the ceiling and prayed for patience.

"No," I answered.

"Where are you?"

I sighed at the worry in my brother's voice.

"We need to talk."

"Are you at Trey's? I'll come get you."

Praying wasn't working. My patience had slipped and so had my sympathy.

"Actually, you won't come get me. And I'm not okay because you're acting like an asshole."

"Addy—"

"No, big brother. It's your turn to listen and listen good. I know Mercy's having a rough pregnancy. I can imagine that's not doing good things for your peace of mind. I can also imagine how hard it is on her and that's stressing you out. But you do not get to lash out at those around you. You don't get to behave like an extreme prick to Trey. You don't get to hurt my feelings and embarrass me."

"Adalynn, you have no idea who Trey is."

That ticked me off to a dangerous level.

"How dare you. I love you, Jason. But right now I'm so ashamed of you and Dad. So freaking ashamed, I don't know what to do with how mad I am. You...you of all people are judging Trey. I assume you're still talking about how many women he's slept with. Which is none of your damn business—"

"It is when my baby sister is the latest in a long line of women who have warmed his bed."

"So if Mercy's dad was alive, would it be his business to judge you on all the women *you've* slept with?"

"Ad—"

"Just stop. I am not your *baby* sister. I'm just your sister. And I'm not some stupid twit who doesn't know the way of the world. I do not care about Trey's past and the longer you hold on to this and behave like you're behaving, which to say is not like my loving brother, the more you're gonna drive a wedge between us. And it bears repeating I'm absolutely ashamed of my family, something I never thought I'd be. Get. Over. It. And be the man I know you to be, not this jerk who's stuck in his own past so he's taking it out on those around him."

That might have been too far, but in my anger, I didn't care. "It's crap, Jay. And you're hurting me because you're hurting Trey. His family treats him like he's an outsider, his brother is horrible, and when I say that I can't stress that enough. His dad is...I have no words for him, he's just mean. And his mom is sweet but beaten down. He does not need this from you or Dad and I will not stand for it. This is your last warning. Get the *fuck* over it or stay the hell away from me."

"Addy," he scolded, and I knew why. I rarely cursed but I was so irate I didn't care. "We're your family."

"You are. Though remember the part where I told you I was ashamed of you?"

"You're seriously calling me to tell me you'll pick him over me?"

Well, I hadn't intended for the call to take that turn, though it seemed to.

"If you don't stop, then yes. I'll take his back over you and Dad."

There was a long stretch of silence. I needed this conversation to be done so I could get back downstairs before Trey came looking for me. I also needed this done because my heart was breaking.

"Fuck," he clipped.

"I see you get me. So we're done."

"We're not," he disagreed.

"We are, Jay. This isn't a two-way chat so much as it's me telling you, you're gonna cut the crap or I'm gonna cut you out. That's it. Please give Mercy my love."

I ended the call, turned my phone on silent, tossed it on Trey's dresser, and went in search of my man.

Either Jason would listen or he wouldn't. If he didn't, my heart would shatter but I wouldn't back down.

Taking care of her man.

Yes, Hadley was taking care of Brady.

Takin' my back.

Yes, I was taking my man's back the same way he'd taken mine.

———

"ADALYNN," Trey groaned.

I was on a downward glide.

"Almost," I panted.

His hand left my hip, slid up my side, his thumb swiped my nipple before he went back and rolled it between his fingers.

A shiver skated down my spine and I tipped over the edge.

Heaven.

Trey cocked his legs and powered up into me, seeking his pleasure while my climax seared through me.

So *good*.

"Mouth," he grunted and I fell forward to happily carry out his command.

His arms went around me, he drove down, filling me completely. At the same time, his tongue tangled with mine, and he filled me a different way.

My orgasm was sublime. His tasted better.

22

There was nothing better in this world than my cock buried deep and Adalynn's weight on my chest. Nothing compared. Only thing that came close was when I was on top and all four of her limbs were wrapped tight and she was holding on.

But there was something about the feel of her on top of me, with her face shoved in my neck, her breath fanning over my skin, her heart pounding against my chest, the smell of her hair, my arms wrapped around her, and her melting into me.

The best.

Both ways good, one way her claiming me, the other me claiming her.

"Trey?" Addy muttered, then pressed her lips to my throat.

"Yeah, baby?"

"Can't breathe."

My arms loosened but I didn't move them.

"Better?"

"Yeah."

I took a few more moments committing the feel of her to memory before I rolled us to the side. Addy being Addy, not wanting to lose our connection, arched into me. This was something I fucking loved. Didn't know I needed it until she gave it to me. Though, likely, I'd never needed it before. It was her, the way she sought closeness, the way she reached for more, sparked something inside of me to life. A feeling that warmed me straight to my soul—raw, relentless, and ruthless in its invasion. I wanted it just as badly as I feared it.

A man who has it all has everything to lose.

I wanted it all—everything. Jasper was right, the promise of Addy was just the beginning. The depth of her character, her loyalty, her sweet brand of protection. I wanted her to give all of that to the horde of kids I'd never wanted before I met her. In my opinion, Hadley had the right idea—the more the better.

I wanted to be a man who had it all and worried every day about all the precious he had in his life, all the beauty his wife had given him. I'd take the worry and fear if I had Addy by my side.

"Where'd you go?" Addy whispered and trailed her fingertip over my forehead, down my temple, and traced the line of my jaw.

I didn't tell her my thoughts. Instead, I asked, "You don't see them, do you?"

"See what?"

Jesus, fuck.

Every damn time she reminded me, it's like a kick to the gut leaving me breathless.

"My scars."

Her gaze darted from mine to the side of my face and her eyes roamed.

"They're just you." She shrugged one shoulder and resumed scanning. "I can't say I don't care about them, because I care deeply about *how* you got them, but beyond that there's...I don't know, not much to say about them. Same for the burns on your back. I see them and think about how painful it must've been while the injury was healing, but it's just another part of you."

I swallowed the lump in my throat and knew she meant every word she said.

"May I ask you something, Trey?"

"Of course."

"Why does your brother dislike you?"

Leave it to Adalynn to get straight to the point. She was shy and quiet with most everyone, but she didn't mince words. And as I was learning, she wasn't shy with the people she trusted, she was open and honest.

Except she had a secret. One I intended to learn, only I couldn't dig it out like Jasper had suggested. I needed her to give it to me. Not because I'd coaxed it out of her, but because she trusted me enough to give it freely.

"Have you ever dealt with a narcissist?" I asked her.

"No, I don't think so." She scrunched her face and looked so fucking cute doing it I bent and pressed a hard kiss to her pinched lips, then pulled back and settled in.

"My dad's a narcissist. For as long as I can remember, he also has a nasty temper—each on their own isn't easy to deal with—combined torture. When I was a kid, I could sense how bad the night was going to be as soon my dad got home. We had three options; he'd come home all smiles and praise my mom and brother, he'd come in and immediately start belittling, or he'd come in and sheer evil would roll off his tongue. The first I ignored, the last two I tried to shield CJ from.

"The problem with that was CJ wasn't stupid, he found a way to play my dad. It's like the two of them are co-dependent in their dysfunction. My dad is a textbook narcissist. He's never wrong, he believes he is more important than anyone else, therefore the smartest, the best, and everyone around him should stroke his ego and give him proper credit. And when CJ was a teenager, he learned if he stroked Dad's need and kissed his ass, Dad would mostly leave him alone. But if CJ *idolized* him, worshiped him, and crawled up Dad's ass, then Dad not only stopped ripping into him, but returned the worship.

"So the cycle began and they became a team. I don't know if it was something that CJ was born with, therefore destined to become a narcissist as well, or in a desperate attempt at self-preservation, CJ learned it. I don't know if CJ truly hates me or if he says and does things he knows will impress my dad, even inwardly, so he stays in his good graces. There's no way CJ could forget how bad it was when we were growing up. So part of me, albeit a tiny sliver, understands why my brother cuts me down."

"Did he hit you?"

There was a wobble in Addy's voice that made

my muscles tighten and I forced them to relax before I answered, "No, baby, he didn't use his fists. He found other ways to strike."

"Your mom?"

The wobble turned into a tremble and I really didn't fucking like what that tremor was saying. So I went gently but I still went for it.

"Did Keith take his hands to you?"

I watched her flinch, and the shutters slammed down before she responded.

"Why are you asking about him?"

Why? Christ, how could she ask that?

"Twice, I saw it. Once, when you thought I was telling you who you could be friends with and once when Bass wouldn't let you go. While it's uncool any man has a hold of you and you ask him to let you go and he doesn't. But I was there—that time, I didn't only see your reaction, baby, I felt it. And your reaction didn't say uncool, it said scared as fuck. Now, you being in a room with your sisters close—me close —no way should you be scared. So, to me, what I felt coming from you, it screamed flashback."

The shutters locked and her face closed down at the same time her body got tight.

Fucking, fucking, shit.

Motherfucker put his hands on her.

White-hot rage scored through me.

"Baby," I whispered, uncaring it sounded as tortured as it did. Not giving two shits I wasn't hiding my anger.

"He didn't. Um. Not really. Not, um, like, punch me."

Punch?

"Adalynn, I'm gonna say this as plain as I can—a man puts his hands on you in anger, no matter he balls up his fists, kicks, slaps, holds you down, grabs you, or any other matter it can happen, he's wrong. Flat-out wrong."

We were on our sides, lying close—so close, I couldn't miss it but even if we were miles apart, I was looking for it so I wouldn't have missed it. It was just that up close when it happened I didn't just see it, I didn't feel it, I *absorbed* it.

The lock she'd turned wasn't strong enough to keep back what had been piling up behind it. Her green eyes flared, fear flashed, then wet pooled before it spilled over and ran down her cheek.

Then she delivered her blow.

"I can't talk about it. Not that I don't trust you to take it, I don't trust myself to give it. I shoved it down into a dark place, so dark I can't feel it. I'm afraid if I open the door it will explode all over the place and

I'll never get it back. It's not that I don't want to talk about it, Trey, it's that I can't."

During this time, my muscles coiled tighter and tighter until I felt like I was going to snap.

"Baby, once you give it, you're not supposed to take it back."

"Can't."

Addy closed her eyes, shutting me out, and the pressure in my chest grew.

The motherfucker had taken his hands to her.

And no one intervened. Which meant she'd hid it. A week ago, I would've said Addy couldn't pull anything over on Jasper, most especially something like this. Yet, there it was.

I shoved it down into a dark place, so dark I can't feel it.

"Okay, baby."

I felt her body relax and I knew I made the right decision not to push. Without opening her eyes, she dropped her forehead to my shoulder and scooted closer, and I gave her the only thing I could give her —silence.

It took a while, but her breath evened out and she melted into me. Only then did I exhale.

That night, Adalynn Walker found sleep. I, however, did not.

23

"Really? I can?" I excitedly asked and flipped Trey's omelet.

When I was done with that, I craned my neck to look at him sitting at the bar with a cup of coffee in front of him. Incidentally, Trey made great coffee. Or I should say, Trey bought expensive, Jamaican coffee beans he ground fresh every morning.

"Yeah. I called Bass yesterday, asked him if I dropped you off if he'd bring you back to the compound after you were done."

Unease choked out the happiness I'd felt moments before when Trey told me I could go to my kickboxing class. It had been a week. A great week of living and getting to know Trey. He'd made it so great I'd forgotten I was there because I was on lockdown.

"You called Bass?"

"Babe, the eggs."

I turned back to the stove, slid the omelet on the plate that already had three rashers of crispy-nearly-burnt bacon on it. Something I learned about Trey while living with him, he liked his bacon nearly burnt, his eggs still runny—if you could believe that, gross—and his toast lightly browned.

We'd fallen into an awesome routine. I cooked breakfast—but he made the coffee—we ate lunch at work, and he cooked dinner. After dinner, we'd lounge. Sometimes we watched TV in the living room on his big comfy couches and I'd been right, they were warm and inviting and when you sat on them you wanted to snuggle under a blanket and not move. But the best part about those couches, they came with Trey. And once we sat down and he arranged me where he wanted me, which was as close as he could get me, I never, ever wanted to leave.

Some nights after dinner and clean up, we'd relax in his Jacuzzi and he told me more about his family. None of it good. He hadn't shared a single good memory and I couldn't fathom growing up the way he had. I had a good, loving, tightknit family. That drove me around the bend with their in-your-face nosiness, but it was always done out of love. Even my brother being a monumental jerk was shrouded in adoration, even if I had to dig deep to find it.

But I could've dug to China and not found a shred of evidence to suggest Carl, CJ, or Paige loved Trey. Carl and CJ were obvious. They were jerks. But Paige was a puzzle I couldn't figure out. I'd spent one evening with the woman, and while she was nice...*ish*...it was clear she didn't attempt to protect Trey from her husband's venom. Nor had she corrected or reprimanded her other son for being downright cruel to Trey. She was no help whatsoever. I couldn't wrap my head around how a mother could stand by and meekly watch one of her children get verbally attacked.

Emily Walker would rain hellfire and scorch the earth before someone would abuse one of her children.

Shame coiled in my stomach and I rushed to put Trey's plate in front of him.

"Bass?" I asked, needing desperately to clear my mind of the past.

"What about him? He said he had time after class to bring you back."

"You called him," I reminded him.

"Yeah, baby, just told you I did."

"Why'd you call him?" I snapped and Trey slowly sat up straight.

Then suddenly everything about him gentled.

What in the world?

"We've made some headway, but not enough. Your dad talked to a few of his old contacts as well as Belview's commanding officer. He's still in town, but we haven't been able to track him down. There wasn't much for Dylan to find—his service record is mostly bogus, so we know he was telling the truth about being Special Forces. Only problem with that is even being SF there should've been more in those files. That's concerning. But more, Dylan found an assault charge filed against Belview that'd been buried. So we're moving forward cautiously."

I knew nothing about service records or files. I knew *what* they were of course, but even working at the VA I still didn't know what should or shouldn't be in them. But Trey would and my dad absolutely would. So I wasn't concerning myself with that; what I was honing in on was the assault charge.

"Assault?"

"Wasn't pretty. He nearly beat a man to death outside a bar in Tucson."

I was stunned into silence. Not because Jake beat a man outside a bar, which freaked me the freak out. But I was shocked at Trey's forthcomingness. Sure, he'd told me as gently as he could and he did it softly to cushion my response, but he'd still told me.

"Was he arrested?"

"No. Whole thing swept under the rug. No police report."

How in the world was that possible?

"Then how'd Dylan find it?"

"He found a notation in Belview's file. Just enough to ping Dylan's interest. He dug around and found the police report—unsolved. Belview's name not listed. But the dates match; Belview and his team were in Tucson on a training exercise. Description matches Belview. Witnesses' statements all the same. The victim stumbled, knocked into Belview, tried to apologize. Even offered to buy Belview a beer. Belview got in the victim's face, an argument ensued, and Belview dragged the victim outside.

"Question is, if someone in Belview's chain of command knew there'd been an assault, why wasn't disciplinary action taken, and why wasn't he turned over to local authorities? Hospital records show the victim wasn't just fucked up, he was *fucked up*. Left on the street barely breathing, laid up in a coma for weeks. Someone covered that shit up. Don't give a fuck why. But knowing what we know—what we know he's capable of, the training he has, and the fact he's got zero self-control—we're going forward cautiously and not taking any chances."

More honesty I couldn't believe he gave me.

There was a long stretch of silence, so long Trey called my name. I didn't answer; I was too busy sifting through my feelings. I didn't know what to make of this, any of it. I was creeped out that my ex-boyfriend, a guy I'd convinced myself I'd loved, *the* guy I'd given my virginity to, had it in him to beat a man almost to death outside of a bar in Tucson.

Tucson, Arizona. I didn't understand why that mattered to me, but it did. Jake hadn't been overseas when this occurred, he hadn't been fighting for his country, protecting his unit, protecting innocent civilian lives in whatever foreign country he'd been sent to. Jake had been on U.S. soil, in a bar, in Tucson, Arizona, and he'd lost control; using his fists, he'd almost killed someone.

"Baby?" Trey called again and I lifted my gaze from the counter to his concerned stare.

Something struck me—he hadn't moved. He'd

stayed in his seat. And I searched back over the last week to one other time I'd gotten irritated with him and he'd stayed feet away from me then, too. As a matter of fact, he'd backed up, putting more distance between us. *And* he'd gentled his voice then, too. *And* he'd softened his features.

"What's going on?"

"What's going on is, a few days ago you told me you were antsy not being able to go out and do things. You didn't mention it specifically, but I know you like your kickboxing class. It's today, I made a call last night so you wouldn't miss it. Bass was happy to help so it worked out."

That was sweet, made sweeter by him calling Bass, who I didn't think was his favorite person. After what happened at the gym, I figured Trey had a few things to say to Bass that would probably freak me out and tick me off so I wasn't going to think about it. But that was not what I was asking about.

"Why are you sitting over there?"

"Not tracking, Addy."

His response made me second-guess my sanity. Perhaps I was imagining him acting strange when I showed the barest hint of annoyance. But I wasn't, this was not Trey. I'd known him for months, and in those months we'd argued, a lot. And he'd always gone head-to-head with me, he'd never gentled his tone, he'd shown me his frustration. It was one of the things I loved about him. His honesty, he didn't hide from me. But now he was.

"Why are you treating me like I'm fragile?"

"Babe, I just told you your ex beat a man half to death." Gently. Softly. Carefully.

"What's with your face?"

"Come again?" He jerked back.

"Your face." I leaned in. "Why is it so gentle? Why are you talking softly?"

"Adalynn—"

"Why are you hiding from me?" I asked the real question.

His eyes narrowed and all the softness fled. "Let me get this straight, you're pissed at me because I'm breaking some shit news to you as gently as I can?"

"Yes."

Okay. That made me sound crazy.

"I got nowhere to go with that."

"A few days ago, we were in your bathroom having words about me going back to the VA. You took a step away from me. Actually, as I think on it, you moved so you weren't blocking the door. Tell me what that was about?"

He changed again. Right before my very own

eyes, I watched the transformation. Soft to hard. Hard to soft. Then soft to guarded.

What was that?

"A man has a woman cornered in a room while they're exchanging—"

"Bullshit!" I shouted. "Maybe some men do that, but you don't."

"Not sure you can make that call, Addy, seeing as that was the first time we'd had a discussion in the bathroom, where I didn't like the direction it was turning, so I knew it was going to get heated."

"That's crap and you know it. We've argued plenty. You've never stepped away from me."

"Never been in a tight space with you when it happened. And just to point out, Addy, you've made it clear you don't..."

I didn't hear the rest. Humiliation ricocheted through my insides. Bitterness and shame and guilt. Old guilt and new guilt. I'd made Trey wary. And in my musing, thinking about everything Trey had told me about his upbringing, how his mother was, I'd judged her harshly. I compared her to my mother when I should've seen myself in Paige Durum. To a lesser degree, I'd been her. I'd cowered. I'd ignored things I shouldn't have. I'd blamed myself. And I'd taken it.

"Adalynn."

A whisper. Back to gentle.

That was why I'd kept my secret.

If they knew, they'd treat me worse than Trey was now. They already treated me like I was a baby. Naïve and stupid. If any of them knew, it would be horrible. I couldn't live with the way they'd look at me.

"Please don't do this to me."

"You're going to have to explain how I'm treating you. I'm totally lost, baby."

"You know."

"I don't."

I took in his confused stare, his beautiful soft eyes, and hated seeing both. Hated that I exposed too much. He'd seen it. And now everything was ruined.

"If you don't, then you're just as bad as the rest of them."

With that, I left the kitchen, abandoning my breakfast.

Trey didn't follow.

He didn't get in my face and argue.

He didn't demand me to explain myself.

He just let me go.

"You're in a mood," Bass said after class.

"I've been cooped up," I huffed, and my fist connected with the heavy bag. "Pent-up energy."

"Honey, I've met your man." He laughed.

"So?" I snapped and threw another jab.

"Right. Not just a mood. A bad mood. We'll talk after class. And dip your shoulder. You're too stiff."

"Whatever," I grumbled.

I *was* in a bad mood. A very bad mood. After our argument in the kitchen, Trey left me alone to get ready in his room. And only went up to do the same when I came down.

He didn't broach the subject, nor had I.

And he was silent on the drive to the gym. Only speaking after he'd walked me in and that was to demand I didn't leave the premises without Bass or calling him for a ride. I agreed because I wasn't stupid, contrary to my family's—and now his— beliefs. I still thought everyone was making a big deal out of nothing, but I didn't want to run into Jake knowing what I knew now. I never wanted to see him again and he had made it clear he wasn't done.

I agreed. Trey left. And that was it.

No kiss. No goodbye. No have a good day.

Nada. Zilch. Zero.

Whatever.

So now I was working my frustrations out on a heavy bag, the same way I did anytime someone in my family irked me.

It was better than the alternative, which would be an altercation that I would undoubtedly lose because I always lost.

24

"Here's your schedule." I glanced up from the photographs I was studying and quickly closed the file.

The look on Quinn's face said it all—she'd seen them.

Damn.

"Thanks." I held out my hand but she dropped the papers on my desk and shook her head.

I lowered my hand and shifted the paper so I could read the printout. Seeing no surprises, I looked back up at Quinn.

"Looks good. Anything special I need to know about?"

"Nope."

Normally, this was where she'd smile, wave, and flounce out of my office. But she wasn't moving, which meant she had something on her mind. Before I was dating her sister, I would've sat back and waited for it. Quinn was a riot, you never knew what crazy shit was going to come out of her mouth.

Like all the Walker women, Quinn was stunning —shiny black hair and green eyes, Delaney being the exception and inheriting her mother's blue eyes. All four women could be in a crowd of thousands and you'd still be able to put them together as sisters. But their looks were where the similarities ended. All of them had quick smiles, each was funny in her own way. Smart, thoughtful. But their personalities were very different.

Adalynn and Quinn were probably the most different. Quinn was high-maintenance and high-drama. Not my scene. I avoided both of those the same way I avoided blondes, which in and of itself was *why* I avoided blondes. Brice on the other hand, didn't mind Quinn's drama. He got off on it, which was good since their wedding day was fast approaching.

Knowing all I knew about Quinn, the way she was looking at me, I braced. And it was a damn good thing I did.

"Something happened to my sister."

Fuck.

No lead-in.

No finesse.

My jaw clenched and I said nothing.

"She's never said, but I saw the change. It was so slow that at first, I thought I was imagining it. I saw a bruise." Those last four words were spoken so quietly I barely heard. But I damn well fucking heard.

"What'd she say about it?"

"I've thought about it. That was the first time my sister ever lied to me, but it wasn't the last."

Shit.

"She told me she tripped and Keith caught her right before she took a header and jerked her up. It was a good lie, a plausible lie, since the bruise was very clearly a handprint on her bicep. You know what's most surprising?"

"What?" I asked, even though I didn't want to know the answer.

"How smooth she lied. And the second time, too. That lie was worse. We were shopping and I squeezed into the dressing room to give her a shirt to try on and she had bruises on her back. I freaked the fuck out, and to my face, blushing, she lied and told me she'd had sex on the floor at Keith's and he had wood floors and she was on her back."

Jesus, fuck.

"After that, Addy's pulling away from us wasn't slow, it was immediate. She even pulled away from Hadley. When anyone asked, she blamed school, said her course load was heavy and she was studying. There was so much going on—Delaney was not herself, Mom and Dad trying to drag it out of her, then Carter came back. Before that, when it started, Tuesday had a stalker and she and Jackson were battling it out.

"But then suddenly, Addy was back. Not the old, shy-but-still-bubbly-and-fun Addy. This new shy-but-watchful, secretive Addy. But she was around all the time like she used to be and things seemed to settle. I know Dad tried to talk to her. Mom did. I did. And she'd lie and tell us that she was fine. Nothing was wrong, nothing was *ever* wrong, and we were all making a big deal out of nothing."

Big deal out of nothing.

Fucking hell, I'd heard that before.

Quinn wasn't done. "The gym. I know you saw it."

"Yeah, Quinn, I saw it. Not the first time something like that happened."

"What happened?" Quinn's green eyes flashed, and fuck me, they were almost as pretty as her sister's. High-maintenance wasn't my thing but I could see how it would be Brice's.

"I'm walking a tightrope here. I won't break Addy's trust."

Quinn's hands went to her hips. She leaned in and spat out, "Fuck that, Trey. She needs to be sorted."

"She will be."

"Trey—"

"I get it, you love your sister. What I'm asking from you is that you get *me*. We're feeling each other out, learning each other. Luckily for me, we're doing that while she's living with me so it's going faster than it normally would. But bottom line is, I need to go gentle with this. She needs to trust me before she gives it."

"She won't give it. And you going gentle with Addy is the wrong thing to do."

Just like last night, my muscles clenched and I felt like I was walking through a minefield.

"Mom tried gentle, Dad tried it, I did, Jason did, and gentle doesn't work with Addy. Besides, she's been treated gently her whole life, being the youngest. God love my brother, but someone needs to find the Protect my Sisters gene and cut his in half. He loves us all, but Addy's his favorite. I was young but I still remember if Mom was feeding or changing Hadley, Jason had Addy. I don't know how to explain it beyond when the twins were born, Jason being the eldest kicked in a lot, and he formed a bond with Adalynn that cannot be denied, and because of that, he is crazy-protective over her. And the unfortunate side effect is, he babys her. She loved it when she was little. Didn't like it when she was a teenager, but hates it as an adult."

Well, that explained some of why Jason was being over the top.

Please don't do this to me.

That morning's argument rushed back and I understood. I hadn't meant to, but I had done exactly what she'd accused. I was being gentle, not wanting to set her off or make her feel trapped. I was big, and while I wouldn't call Addy tiny, she was damn smaller than me.

"Fuck."

"What's wrong?"

"Gentle's not gonna work."

"No," she softly agreed.

"Fuck."

I'd been so caught up thinking about what Jasper

had said about wanting his girl to have easy, I was hellbent to give it to her, and inadvertently, I'd done the very thing she told me she hated and treated her like she needed to be coddled and shielded. When she absolutely didn't.

I'd forgotten how strong she was.

"Fuck."

"Thank you." Quinn smiled.

It wasn't her pretty eyes, it wasn't her shiny black hair, or her drama that had hooked Brice deep. It was that smile.

Goddamn, Walker women.

Lethal.

Every last one of them.

TWENTY MINUTES LATER, I went in search of Jason. Bass had texted that he was taking Addy to lunch then he'd bring her back.

Had yesterday's conversation with Bass gone any other way, the thought of him having lunch with my woman would've sent me zero to sixty. I was not a man prone to jealousy, then again I'd never had a woman who I cared enough about to contemplate the emotion. Since my feelings for

Addy ran deeper than care, and straight to where she'd be the mother of my children, I figured I could cut myself some slack on my need to be possessive.

But Bass got who Addy was to me, admitted he knew he was never going to break through, and didn't want to lose the friendship. He was also fully on board with having Addy's back should the need arise. So I knew she was in good hands and wouldn't be back for at least an hour.

Hopefully what I had to say to Jason wouldn't take an hour.

I found him in his office. Blueprints to the new building opened, taking up the surface of his desk. His head came up when I entered but other than that, he gave me nothing.

"I know you're busy. But I'd appreciate it if you'd give me some time."

Jason folded the blueprints and dipped his chin toward the chair in front of his desk. Not the most welcoming invitation, but I'd take it.

"How's Mercy?" I started.

"Feeling better."

"Good. Addy said she called to check on her and Mercy reported feeling fat, human, and hungry. Never been around a pregnant woman so I didn't know, but Addy says that means she's feeling good. Glad that's the case."

Jason's lips twitched and he said, "Yeah, few days ago, it's like a switch flipped and she stopped throwing up. Thought that shit was supposed to end sooner. I'm just happy we've moved on to the hungry part. That I can handle. Waking up in the middle of the night to make her a cheeseburger is a helluva lot better than waking up to carry her to the bathroom."

I wasn't there to discuss Mercy's pregnancy cravings though I did file that away for future use. Middle of the night cheeseburgers did indeed sound better than puke.

"Happy for you but happier for Mercy," I told him, then instead of wasting a bunch of time with small talk, I went for it. "I'm gonna marry your sister."

Jason jerked in his chair. Surprise registered, then it turned into something ugly.

I didn't have time for any more games, so this ended today.

"Straight up, no bullshit, I'm gonna marry her. So I'm sitting here across from you out of respect—"

"Doesn't—"

"No bullshit, out of respect, even though you haven't shown me any," I spoke over him. "You know me but not well, so I'm gonna put this shit to bed once and for all. So I can move on to what's important—and that's making Adalynn happy. You're all fired up to hold to and call me out on my past, specifically who I've fucked. It's not your business but I'm gonna give it to you. I've been with a lot of women, all of them shallow, all of them users, all of them after one thing, not one of them looking at anything beyond my face, my body, my job. There has not been a single fucking time I've entered a bar since I was twenty-one that I didn't have a woman at my side within five minutes.

"In the beginning, I took advantage of that. Later, it was tiresome and I'd fend 'em off. Then I became more discerning, but only in that I only took home what I liked when she didn't fall all over me. Shallow women who wanted my dick and couldn't care less *who* I was. Users. Bitches. Drama queens. So, yeah, I've run through them all. Can't go back and change it, and really, I don't think I would.

"All of that taught me something, and that's what I wanted when it came time to find a woman. Something else it taught me—there are women you fuck, then there's Adalynn Walker. There's a big fucking difference. Told you once I knew the difference and I don't like having to repeat myself, but out of respect for you, I will. I am not *fucking* your sister.

"Now that's done, Jason. Serious as shit, I won't allow you to continue to hurt her. This ends now."

I paused to catch my breath and stared at the man who would one day be my brother-in-law. I had one more thing to say, then this could be done.

"I need to apologize to you."

Jason shifted in his chair and held my gaze but remained quiet.

"Last time we spoke, I was a dick. I said a lot of shit I shouldn't have. I brought up Kayla and that was a dick thing to do. I'm sorry for that. You told me Mercy was having a tough time and I should've had a mind to that and I didn't. Again, I was a dick about that, too, and I'm sorry. There's never a good enough reason to gut a good man the way I did. All I can tell you is my head wasn't in a good place. The night before, my parents and brother had shown up out of the blue, and Addy was treated to the Durum dysfunction. Before you ask, no one said jack to her and I made it clear I'd kick them out if they so much as looked at her funny. But she still saw, something I wanted to prepare her for and hadn't yet."

"Durum dysfunction."

"Not lucky like you, Jason. I didn't grow up with

good parents and siblings that I was close to. I grew up dodging insults, and when I wasn't dodging them, I was stepping in front of them so CJ wouldn't feel 'em."

Jason's face screwed up in disgust and he asked, "Your mom didn't step in?"

That was hilarious in the sense that it was so fucking sad, my heart clenched.

"Paige Durum is not Emily Walker. I can't remember a time when my mom tried to shield me from my dad. But I do remember her hiding behind me to get herself clear. Like I said, dysfunction. I've put up with a lot of my family's shit out of what I thought was duty. And that's what I was dealing with when you approached—knowing that I have a shit family but I still have one. After the bullshit they pulled in front of Addy, that's done—long overdue. I will not have her around that poison and I sure as shit will not have my children around it."

"Unfortunate timing," Jason mumbled. "Addy called last week and handed me my ass. Told me to cut my shit or she cut me out. Told me she'd take your back against me and Dad. My sister's smart, always has been. She also feels the deepest. She's pure down to her soul, trusting, giving, so much like my mom it scares me. I knew it was a weak excuse, but it was the only thing I had to latch onto. There's nothing else I could've used to warn her off."

Fucking hell. Even when I didn't know she was doing it, she was taking my back. *Christ.* I was still reeling, trying to sort through the knowledge that Adalynn had called her brother and told him she'd cut him out, when Jason continued.

"After Kayla died, my head was so jacked I completely disconnected from my family, and in doing so, I let my sister down. She was hurting after that asshole Belview broke up with her and I missed how much pain she was in. But what's more, in the years to come, trying to sort myself, finding Mercy, I was so wrapped up in my life I let Addy down in the worst way. I told myself I was giving her her head. Stepping back a little so I wasn't the overbearing big brother she always accused me of being. But really, I dropped the ball, and because of that Adalynn got hurt.

"So now after years of keeping herself to herself, never dating, not even looking at a man, you show up and she's gone for you. A man who's got some serious experience, and I got nothing else, no other objections, since I like you. So I held on to that experience because I'm scared as fuck and determined to make sure that my sister never feels another moment of hurt."

"I'm not gonna hurt Addy."

"I know you won't."

Fucking hell, that felt good.

"I'm gonna heal those hurts. But, Jason, while I'm doing it, I need you to have my back. She's locked them down tight. Told me she can't give me those secrets because she's afraid once she does they'll explode all over the place and she won't be able to take them back. I tried going gentle, knowing what I know about what happened, and she accused me of treating her like she was fragile. So that means the next opening I get, I'm going hard and I'm gonna start digging. Problem with that is, she's gonna fight me, and when she does, I need all of you to have my back."

"I'll have your back."

Jesus fuck.

There it was.

Fucking *finally*.

"Guts me to tell you this, but you gotta know and there's no way to cushion this for you. Keith took his hands to her, brother. Twice, Quinn saw bruises. And we both know any motherfucker who thinks to use his fists on a woman doesn't suddenly see the light after he fucks her up and just stops. Which means the shit she's buried is so dark, it's gonna rock your family. And when it does, Adalynn cannot feel the ground moving under her feet. You gotta use this time to sort your head because when it all comes out, you gotta be solid."

Jason's head lulled and his shoulders slumped forward and I waited for him to gather his composure. It took a long while, and during this time, Jason intermittently muttered his anger. On a deep exhale, Jason lifted his chin and I was met head-on with a Jason Walker I'd never seen, though I should've expected it the way he loved his sister. The man was undone and whether he meant to hide it, tried his best to do that, and failed, or simply didn't care if I saw the tears in his eyes, they were there.

"Whatever it takes, we got your back."

"'Preciate it."

"Trey—"

"Nothing left to be said, brother," I cut him off.

It took a moment, but Jason pulled himself together and stood. Once he was on his feet he extended his hand. Christ. That felt good, too. I followed and got to my feet. We shook hands and with no further words needed when we broke apart,

I turned to leave his office. Jason called my name, stopping me from exiting.

Before I could turn, he delivered his kill shot.

"Welcome to the family."

Jesus fuck.

I took a moment and let the golden warmth of his words burn through me. Then I wordlessly left.

25

"Thanks for lunch," I said to Bass as soon as he pulled into a parking spot.

This was not me being rude, it was self-preservation. Bass had been cool throughout class and lunch because Bass was cool. He'd apologized again for freaking me out and thanked me for not holding a grudge. I let him do this and didn't tell him I agreed because I needed to face the fear head-on. If I didn't, I knew from experience it would fester until I couldn't face it. So now, through small things, I faced my fear, and that meant having lunch with Bass even though I was embarrassed he'd witnessed a mini-meltdown.

But I sensed the cool was wearing off, and he'd

used the drive to Triple Canopy to figure out how to broach a topic I didn't want to talk about.

"Before I walk you in," Bass started, and I felt the air turn heavy.

No way.

"Please don't. Whatever you have to say, please don't say it."

"Sorry, honey, needs to be said," he told me and I gritted my teeth. "I had a talk with your man so I know you have a lot on your mind. And I hope you know, I wouldn't heap more on if I didn't think it was important. I didn't keep it a secret I wanted more with you, thought that's where we were headed—"

Oh, crap.

"Bass—"

"Addy, as I said I talked to *your man*. I got it the day I came to see you, but if I'd missed it then, I didn't miss it when we talked. I know where things are headed for the two of you and that's why I need to say this."

"Where do you think we're headed?"

For someone who didn't want to participate in this conversation, it was a mighty stupid question, but still, I couldn't stop myself from asking. And when Bass smiled huge, I regretted my participation even more.

"To the finish line."

Finish line?

Having learned my lesson, I didn't verbalize my thoughts and remained quiet.

"Open up, Addy."

I felt the heavy air press on my chest and was suddenly finding it hard to breathe.

"Bass—"

"Not to me. To Trey. Open up. Whatever it is you're holding back, let it go, and open yourself to him."

Oh, crap.

My eyes darted around the interior of his car, needing something, anything to ground me. I pushed the fear down where it belonged, deep down where it had to stay so I could escape it.

"I appreciate you—"

"No, you don't. You're sitting there quaking in your seat. Something's eating at you. I've known for a long time and I hoped one day you'd give it to me. I know now, you never would have. But, honey, you have to open up."

Fuck.

I had to get out of the car. It was clawing its way up my belly, fighting to get out.

Never. I never wanted it to break free. If it did, it would ruin everything in its wake.

"I have to go."

"Shit," he muttered. "I didn't mean to upset you."

"You didn't," I lied.

Without another word, Bass got out and I watched him disappear around the back of his car. I used these moments to get control of my ravaging thoughts. But when my door opened, I was no closer to getting myself under control.

Bass tipped his head down to look at me and the spark in his eyes said it all. However, I was too raw to fortify my defenses, therefore Bass tore a pound of flesh clean away.

"You're the best woman I know, Adalynn Walker. Sucks thinking I won't be the man at your side. But it will not suck quite as bad living with it if you open the fuck up and let Trey take that fear out of your eyes."

That was a nice thing to say, the part about me being the best woman he knew, but the rest scared me to death. Bass saw it and I'd tried my best to hide it from the world. Yet again, I was reminded my best wasn't good enough.

Instead of arguing, because really, I had to get

someplace quiet where I could be alone before my insides split in two, I lied.

"I'll think about it."

Bass knew I wasn't being honest, but being as he was a nice guy and back to being cool, he didn't press the issue further.

But the sad, forced smile on his face said it all.

Crap.

"Hey, Momma," I greeted.

"Was that Bass?" she asked, and settled onto one of the two chairs Trey had brought into the gym. He'd also wrangled Carter and they'd set up a mini-office for me in the corner. A desk, a super comfy high-back leather chair, and a small table where I stacked my files.

"Yeah. I took a class today, then he took me to lunch," I explained, and my mom lifted a perfectly manicured brow.

"Trey know you went to lunch with Bass?"

"He set it up."

My mom settled into the chair and held my eyes before she smiled huge.

"Knew I liked that boy."

I couldn't stop myself from laughing at my mom's absurd comment. There were a lot of ways to describe Trey. "Boy" was not one of them.

"What are you doing here?" I asked through waning amusement.

"Meeting your dad here so we can get the RV situated."

It was my turn to smile huge.

"Seriously? You and Dad finally going cross-country?"

"Quinn's being stubborn," she mumbled and busted out laughing again.

Quinn wasn't being stubborn, she was being Quinn. When she first mentioned having her wedding at Uncle Clark and Aunt Reagan's house, my mom made the mistake of grumbling about this. Then when Quinn jokingly declared the ceremony would be held the week before Delaney's due date, Mom actually growled. Quinn being Quinn thought it was outrageously funny and what had started as a joke had turned to stone.

"Well, Momma, she's Dad's daughter. I'm unclear how you fell into the trap. All you had to do was play along and tell her that was the best idea she'd ever had and she would've laughed, then planned something else. Besides, Aunt Reagan's yard is beautiful. And Quinn's idea to fill the pond with floating tea lights sounds amazing. Everything's going to be perfect and Delaney will keep her legs crossed so she doesn't pop out the baby on the kitchen floor. It's gonna be perfect."

"Hadley's getting married in Tuesday's orchard." She told me something I knew and had helped plan.

I also didn't have anything to say about it because I loved Tuesday's orchard and couldn't wait for Hadley to get married there. But something was obviously bugging my mom so I waited her out.

"A church wedding would've been nice."

"What do you mean?"

"I know it's silly, but just once, I wanted to watch your father walk one of you girls down the aisle. Delaney and Quinn at Reagan's. Hadley at the orchard, and you already said that's where you wanted to get married. That means no church wedding. No watching your dad."

After Jackson and Tuesday got married in the orchard, I had told my mom that's where I wanted to get married one day. But it wasn't the orchard, though it was beautiful, it was the intimacy of the wedding. Family only. Just like at Delaney and Carter's, everyone stood gathered around the couple. Circling them, surrounding them, the very essence of my family. That was what I wanted. But I wanted my mom to have what she wanted more than I wanted to get married in the orchard.

I wondered what Trey thought of a big church wedding.

My lungs seized at my wayward thoughts.

Why was I thinking about what Trey thought of a church wedding?

Because you're headed to the finish line and you know it, so stop denying it.

Was I in denial?

Heck, yeah I was. The finish line meant forever. And forever meant I'd have to share my secrets.

My mom was staring at me with big eyes and I wondered if I'd asked and answered myself out loud.

I was officially going crazy. All this Jake business had creeped me out. Trey was pushing me around the bend. And thinking about Keith had sent me careening straight back to hell.

"You know, I'm really happy you and Dad are gonna—"

"Adalynn," my mom warned.

Crap. She knew my thoughts. She knew *everything*. Emily Walker had superpowers, all my life she'd had them. Perfectly in tune with her children. She might not know the details but she *knew*. The rule in our house was, if you didn't want Mom to know, you avoided her. Seeing as she was our mom we couldn't avoid her forever, so you did your best, praying whatever you'd done that you didn't want her to know dissolved before she cornered you.

It was a rule, but it never worked. My father could spot trouble a mile away. My mom didn't spot it, she felt it in her soul, and if one of her cubs was hurting, she didn't just feel it, she experienced it right alongside you.

Darn.

Knowing that avoiding her was fruitless, I gave her the truth.

"I'm terrified."

"Of what?" Her brows shot to her hairline and her blue eyes glittered with a fierceness I'd seen hundreds of times.

Momma Bear was out in full force, ready and willing to attack. Conquer all my demons. Hoping I'd hand them to her so she could slay them for me.

"Life. Trey. Everything."

The glitter turned watery and I swallowed the lump in my throat. I didn't want to see my mom teary-eyed ever, but especially not because of me.

"Momma—"

"Adalynn, I want you to listen to me carefully." I

nodded and pinched my lips, afraid of what she wanted me to hear.

Afraid of what would happen if Trey and I went the distance. Afraid of my secret coming out. Afraid of making another bad decision. Afraid of what my dad would do if he knew the truth. Afraid my mom would think I was a weak coward. Afraid my sisters would wonder what was wrong with me that I allowed myself to be abused.

Afraid.

Afraid I'd live the rest of my life lonely in a room full of people because I was the biggest liar on the planet.

Just afraid of everything.

"In life, you have three choices; you let the obstacles you face define, destroy, or strengthen you. That's it, my sweet girl, those are your choices. Your father's been fighting a losing battle for about three decades now, and I figure he'll be fighting it for three more. He cannot shield you from these obstacles and I cannot fight them for you. That's not our job. My job is to listen, watch, and guide you. Sometimes, sweets, a mother has to stand back and watch her children claw their way out. Sometimes she must watch them struggle and cry and be afraid. And one day you'll get this—it cuts to the quick having to watch that knowing you can't step in, all you can do is wait while at the same time wanting so bad to heal the hurts. Waiting for your daughter to reach out and needing her to desperately. I can't right a wrong when that wrong is being kept from me."

My spine snapped straight and my stomach roiled and the grilled cheese I had for lunch threatened to make a reappearance.

"So, here's your chance, Adalynn. Define, destroy, or strengthen. This is the moment you decide if you're gonna let what happened to you define you. If you're going to keep looking back and continue to be afraid, or if you're gonna move forward."

"Momma," I muttered then stopped.

It was right there on the tip of my tongue to tell her, give her what she wanted, spill my secrets, and let her guide me. I was so close, I could taste it—the ugly, bitter taste that I'd swallowed so many times.

In the end, I couldn't do it. I couldn't tell her. I had to beat it back. Telling her wouldn't strengthen me, it would destroy me.

"It's right in front of you," she whispered. "Do you hear me? In. Front. Not behind. Reach out and take it, Adalynn. None of us can get through this life alone. Trey is standing right *in front* of you, his hand is out, his shoulders are broad, his heart true—give him your pain. He's ready for it. You took his, he'll—"

"I didn't take his," I denied.

"Sweets, open your eyes and pay attention. A man like him, like your dad, so strong they think they can take on the world, and when they're reminded they're flesh and bone, they're not keen on the reminder. What happened to Trey, horrible. But it was never the external scars that burdened his soul. It's not my business to know what was tearing him up on the inside. I'm just proud it was my daughter that soothed that ache. Proud that you gave that to him so now he's ready for you. Let him."

"I didn't do anything."

My mom smiled. It was shaky, it was sad, it didn't light her eyes, but she gave it nonetheless.

"That's the beauty of it, sweets, you didn't have to do anything to give him everything. That's what love's all about."

What do you need from me?

Just this.

That was all Trey needed. Just me.

"Thank you, Momma."

"I love you, my sweet Adalynn." She gave me another wobbly smile, then to cut the heavy and bring me back to the light, she joked. "Now, if your dad doesn't hurry up so we can pull out the RV, air it out, and fix the kitchen sink, I'm gonna do it my damn self."

"Not a good idea," I reminded her.

"One time." She waved her hand in front of her, this time her smile bright and cheery. "And there was barely any damage."

"Barely?" I sputtered a laugh. "Maybe not to the RV but you took out a cinderblock wall."

"Whatever." My mom's lips twitched and I knew she was holding back her laugh. "Who put a wall up in an RV park anyway?"

"Um. Maybe because behind that wall was the national forest's welcome center. And someone had the good sense to put up a wall so some crazy woman didn't mow it down."

"I'm not a crazy woman!"

"Ma. Seriously, Dad said he'd be back, he told you not to move the RV."

"Learn this, too, daughter—when they get bossy, you have to push back. Don't ever stop pushing back. That was where I went wrong in the beginning. Your dad and his green eyes dazzled me, and I gave in too much. Now he thinks he's the boss. The RV was my idea. I'm the boss of the RV and I'll move it if I want to."

"Right."

I tamped down my amusement until my mom finally admitted, "Next time, maybe I'll check the mirrors first." Then I lost it and busted out laughing. "Or maybe do a walk-around."

There it was—my momma giving me something good to make me laugh.

I had the best mom in the whole world.

Which in turn, made me the crappiest daughter for holding out on her.

26

I heard it before I opened the door. I froze, then I looked at my feet.

Thank fuck.

Addy laughing.

Our day had started good, then slid straight to beautiful when her pretty eyes had locked with mine as I moved inside of her. We'd showered together, I'd made coffee, she'd made breakfast, and after that everything went down the toilet. She'd been nursing a snit and I'd been weaving through mines I didn't want to blow up in my face.

Now she was laughing.

I felt a bone-jarring clap on my shoulder and looked up to find Nick. There was a second thud, then he wordlessly continued down the hall. His silent support hit me square in the chest, reminding me I'd need him, too, in the days to come. I was going to need everybody. I figured while I had Addy sequestered at my house, I was going to use it to my advantage and push. I wasn't going to give her an option, neither was I going to allow her to run.

I heard another burst of laughter then I moved down the hall to the back door thinking about how much I loved that sound. I stepped into the Georgia sunshine, stopped, tipped my head back, and prayed when this was over Addy didn't hate me.

"Where'd you learn to cook?" Addy asked.

It was after dinner and we were in the hot tub. Addy was in a sports bra and panties since we'd yet to go by her place to pick up her yellow bikini. I scratched that on my mental to-do list for tomorrow and smiled. To cover up the turn my thoughts had taken, I answered.

"When I was in the Navy." Her brows scrunched so I went on to explain, "There's only so much fast food a man can take, and eating out's a pain in the ass so I learned to cook."

"You're good at it."

"Glad you think so."

"Do you miss the Navy?"

I waited for the unease to twist my gut—the ugly ball of regret to knot before the familiar guilt burned my chest. But it never came. Not even a twinge of bitter that I'd been discharged and cast aside. The burden no longer weighted until I couldn't breathe.

"No."

"No?"

"If you would've asked me that two weeks ago, the very mention of the Navy would've set me on edge. Likely I wouldn't have answered, or I would've given some bullshit answer."

"Like what?" she asked.

"Like what bullshit answer would I have given?" She nodded and I searched my thoughts. "Likely I would've said no." I grinned.

"Right." She shook her head in amusement and dropped her gaze to the water. "But it's not bullshit now?"

I watched her hands as they skimmed the bubbling water in front of her, and having no other way to explain why I no longer missed being in the Navy, I went with the obvious.

"If I was still in, I wouldn't be here with you."

"Trey—"

"I wouldn't have met your dad and your uncles. I wouldn't have been given the opportunity to watch how a nosy, healthy family interacts. I wouldn't have a job I enjoy."

"You didn't enjoy being a SEAL?"

"Enjoy is not a word I would use to describe being shot at." I smiled. "Proud of, hell yes. But enjoyed? Not even a little bit. Two weeks ago, I would've given a bullshit answer because I was hung up on my mistake. I couldn't see past it even though everyone, including you, called me out on it. A week ago, Luke was waiting for me in my office and laid into me. He's got a way with words. Being as such, he's effective when he cuts you down to size."

Addy's eyes flared before they narrowed.

"What did he say?"

One more reminder of Addy's protection. I figured my answer would be the difference between her being pissed at Luke if she didn't like what he had to say, or seriously pissed if she felt he was out of line.

"Nothing I didn't need to hear. But mostly he reminded me he was my brother, and as such, he'd never blame me for what happened. He called me a few names, got in my face about my attitude, and when he felt his message had been received and I harbored no guilt, he left."

"Called you names?"

Admittedly, I'd thrown that part in there, testing my theory, and I'd been proven correct. Addy's brand of protection—when that burned down my chest it felt a fuckuva lot better than guilt, so I let it settle before I smiled and hopefully got Luke off the hook.

"It's a guy thing," I told her. Then she needed to know one last thing so I told her that, too, "That wasn't the first time one of the guys had cornered me to give me a dressing down. Though it was the first time Luke had come straight out and tackled the issue. But if he would've come at me two weeks ago, I wouldn't have been ready to hear it. I would've listened but nothing he said would've penetrated."

"What changed?"

My smile grew at her question.

"You've asked me that before and my answer hasn't changed. You. I needed *you*. I have good friends. My brothers, they have my back. But other than that, I had no one. You've met my family so it won't come as a surprise none of them have ever taken care of me. Even after I was hurt. Dad used that opportunity to remind me I wasn't good enough, and me laid up in a hospital bed facing a medical discharge was proof. CJ was all too happy to take jabs at the military and joke about their shitty training when the doctor had told me I might lose my leg. My mom was crying, carrying on about my face and how her beautiful boy was ruined.

"Before I met you, never thought I'd find a woman to marry. Didn't believe I'd find one that wasn't a shallow, manipulating bitch. That's all I'd known.

"Then you walked into my life when I was at my lowest, when I felt like my world had ended. I lost the Navy. I lost the opportunity to do work I was proud of. Beautiful, sweet, shy Adalynn Walker."

I took her beauty in as she listened. "But I soon found out she's not shy, not when she's trying to break through and not when something means something to her. And the sweet I thought you were only gets sweeter when that fierce loyalty comes out. So it started the day I met you, it grew when you came into my office and got in my face about missing PT, it was near-consuming when you called me a quitter and told me to find a new therapist. But it was undeniable after the first time we made love and I asked you what you felt. You were so confused it tore away all the ugly that had been filling my head. When all you felt was me—not my scars—just me. That was all I needed to start letting go. And every day since then, it's just drifted away without me knowing it was going."

Addy was staring at me but she wasn't seeing me, and wherever she'd gone in her head wasn't a good place to be. Before I could ask what was wrong, she was blinking, seemingly coming back to the conversation. But what she said next made no sense.

"Define, destroy, or strengthen," she whispered.

"What, baby?"

"You didn't like the reminder of it."

"Reminder of what?"

"Flesh and bone. A man like you wouldn't like the reminder."

What the fuck?

"That's what Mom says," she finished, and I still didn't have the first clue what she was talking about.

But I didn't get a chance to ask because she kept going.

"I didn't have to do anything. You gave it to me and I didn't have to ask."

"What—"

"That's what love is. Not having to ask. Not knowing you're doing it, just giving because that's what feels good. And giving means everything."

I shifted to turn down the bubbles so I could hear her better, then stood to move but halted when Addy's hands came out in front of her.

"Don't move."

"Baby?"

"Please don't move." Her pain-filled voice hit my ears right before they hit my heart and I froze.

I'd stand statue-still for the rest of my life if I never had to hear Addy sound like that again.

"I made you ask," she declared.

"Ask what?"

"About Keith," she spat and my lungs seized.

Oh, fuck.

"Addy, baby, let me come over there."

"No. No. I made you ask. You didn't make me ask, you gave it. I can't stop looking back. If I stop, then I won't be strong enough to keep it inside. If I go forward, it will come out and everyone will know how stupid I am. Weak and stupid."

"There's not a damn thing weak or stupid about you."

"You don't know," she fumed.

I'd wanted my opportunity to push and there it was right in front of me. She'd opened the door, but seeing her ravaged face and wild eyes, I was having second thoughts.

"I do know, Addy."

"You don't."

Christ.

Toughen up, Durum.

"I know he hit you. I know he left bruises. I know—"

Addy's swift inhale left me without oxygen. But when her face paled, my heart constricted.

"So then you know I'm stupid."

The heat pressing in had nothing to do with the hot tub. Thick caustic air surrounded us—a warning for me to stay calm and see her through. Her grief-stricken face should've been enough for me to check my temper, but it wasn't.

"Goddamn it, Addy, stop saying that!"

"Why? It's true. He *hit* me and I stayed after the first time. I stayed and he did it again and *again* and I still stayed because I was weak and scared. That's stupid."

Jesus fuck.

I'd known what that motherfucker did—she'd given enough signs—but hearing her finally admit it hollowed me out. Fury and fear mixed together. So much anger, I was afraid of it. And when her sobs came, hearing the hideous sound, cut straight through my fear. And in its wake, I was left with the putrid knowledge my sweet, shy, beautiful Adalynn had been physically assaulted by a man she trusted.

I'd had enough.

I surged forward, scooped her up, and hoped to God my bad leg didn't give out as I climbed out of the Jacuzzi with Addy in my arms. She shoved her face in my neck, her body shook, and pain radiated from my thigh to my groin. So much fucking pain I had to bite back my groan as I walked to the back door.

By the time I made it to the stairs, I had to stop to breathe through the agony.

"Trey."

"Shh, baby."

Addy. This was about Addy. Not the garbage in my head, not my leg. I shoved the feeling of inadequacy down and ascended the stairs, and on shaky legs, I walked to my bed. There was no hiding my limp, and I wondered why in the fuck I'd tried to hide it from her in the first place.

Once I had us settled—me on my back, Addy tucked to my side, her head on my shoulder, my arm wrapped around her tight, I said, "Tell me."

"We're soaking—"

"You cold?"

"No."

"Then I don't give a fuck. Tell me."

The silence stretched a good long while. And finally, she whimpered, "He hit me."

My arm tightened and I waited for more.

"At first he didn't. He'd just grab me to get my attention."

I gritted my teeth in an effort not to tell her there is no "just" when a man grabs a woman with the intention of causing harm.

"That bruise Quinn saw, I lied to her. I lied to everyone."

Again I waited for her to give me more, needing her to get it all out, yet dreading hearing any more.

"We were arguing. I was meeting my friends. He didn't want me to go. I decided I didn't like being told I couldn't have dinner with friends so I walked away and he grabbed my arm, then twisted it behind my back. I missed dinner. Later that night, he explained it, how he'd lost his temper, how it would never happen again. With tears in his eyes, he kissed the mark on my arm and told me how sorry he was. Begged me to forgive him. So stupid," she mumbled and I fought the need to remind not to fucking call herself that. "He didn't do that again for a while, grab me, that is. But he found other ways to control me, ways that I didn't understand he was doing. At the time I thought they were sweet, him wanting me to spend all my time with him. It was slow, so slow, I missed it. I was calling my friends less and less, not seeing my family because he was always taking me somewhere or had plans for us. Then one day it dawned on me my phone hardly ever rang anymore. I figured my friends got tired of me blowing them off. But that wasn't it."

The bastard was textbook—alienating Addy from her friends and family. Taking away her support system. Keeping her from the very people who would see the change and make moves to end it.

"After class one day I ran into my friend Jackie. She was cool about it but I could see her feelings were hurt I hadn't answered her calls or returned her text messages. The thing was, I hadn't missed any calls from her and I hadn't seen any text messages, but I lied and apologized, blaming it on school and my busy schedule. So stupid. She would've helped me, Jackie was a good friend. Instead, I went to my car, checked my phone, and saw that all my friends' numbers were blocked. He was smart enough not to block my family, but none of my friends could call me."

Jesus.

"Then I did something really stupid and I went

to Keith's place to confront him. I was so pissed, I didn't think."

The bile in my throat turned sour, swelling, threatening to choke me, yet I laid there perfectly still, giving her the only thing I could—making it safe for her to give me her hurt.

"He ended up being more pissed I'd confronted him. I was so mad I didn't see it coming, I don't even know how it happened, but we ended up on the floor. He was on top of me and I was struggling to get him off, and when I finally did and got to my feet, he punched me in the back, taking me to my knees. I was in so much pain the second and third punches didn't register. Not until later when it hurt so bad I couldn't breathe."

Throughout this, my muscles were clenching tighter and tighter, but not Addy's. Her voice was even, no emotion, completely detached like she was telling a story, not the abuse she'd experienced. And that scared the fuck out of me.

"That was it. I was done. I needed help. The next day, I was out with Quinn and I was going to tell her, make a plan to get Keith out of my life. But then she brought up how upset Mom and Dad were because something was going on with Delaney. And how Jason had finally pulled himself together and was happy with Mercy but Mom and Dad didn't get a chance to enjoy that before a new crisis hit. I knew I couldn't tell them," she finished on a whisper.

Jesus fuck.

Jasper would lose his ever-loving mind if he knew that his daughter didn't reach out for help because she didn't want to add to his stress. Delaney would feel guilty and Hadley would...Christ, I couldn't even think about what Hadley would feel if she ever knew Addy was on the verge of asking for help but didn't because of their conversation.

"Baby—"

"So I lied to my sister, *again*. She saw my back and I continued to lie. But I couldn't do it. Quinn was right, Mom and Dad were beside themselves with worry. I couldn't add to it. And the more I thought about it, I knew I was doing the right thing by not telling. You know my dad, my family. They would've gone ballistic, and one of them would've ended up in trouble because of my stupidity. I couldn't do it. I had to figure it out myself."

The thought of my sweet Addy going at it alone ripped me to shreds.

"Then it happened. The worst of it. The very worst."

The worst?

It got fucking worse?

"What happened?"

"It had been too easy. I should've known better. He'd said over and over he'd never let me go, he loved me, he'd never do it again, never yell at me, scare me. So many promises, all of them broken. So I should've known he wouldn't have given up. But I thought after a week of me hiding out, dodging him, not going to campus for classes, I thought maybe he'd moved on. *So stupid.*

"I was getting out of the shower and he was there standing in my bathroom. And I knew, it was going to be the worst, and it was. When he was done, I was on my bathroom floor in a puddle of my own blood. I couldn't move I hurt so bad, everywhere hurt. I finally crawled to the vanity and got my phone. I called Jackie, her dad's a doctor. She was the only person I could trust."

Visions of Addy beaten and bloody tortured my brain, my hands itched to wrap them around Keith's throat and choke the life out of him. But not before I did to him what he'd done to Adalynn.

Her flat, emotionless voice pulled me from my plotting and filled me with more outrage.

"Jackie came over, helped me get dressed, and took me to her parents' house. I begged them not to call the police, not to take me to the hospital. I think Jackie's dad was afraid I'd bolt so he agreed to look me over at his house.

"He took pictures," she whispered. "So many pictures. I was like...it was like a movie...it wasn't happening to me. How could something like that happen to me?" Addy's body started trembling. My eyes drifted closed and I held her tighter. *Thank fuck. A response.* "I couldn't understand how I let it happen."

"You didn't *let* anything happen."

"I did. I should've left the very first time he touched me. I knew better. I trusted him. He promised he wouldn't do it again. I ignored all the red flags. I saw them and ignored them. And now I have to live with it. My stupidity. I'm exactly what my family thinks I am, stupid and naïve."

"Serious as fuck, stop calling yourself stupid. You are not that and you are not naïve. And not a single person in your family thinks that."

"Jason—"

"Jason was acting like a dick, lashing out because his head was fucked up. Mercy was sick, he was having flashbacks about Kayla, and he took it out on you. It doesn't make it right, but it's the truth. You're his favorite and you have to know that. He knows something went on with you and he knows he missed it. He feels guilty for that and he took that out on you, too. He fucked up and he knows it. Then and now. But the bottom line is, he doesn't think you're anything but what you are—smart and strong."

"But—"

"Listen to me, Addy. I know weak. I've lived with it my whole life. I watched my mom take my dad's shit since I can remember. Never protecting her boys or herself. Using me to hide behind so I'd get the brunt of my dad's abuse. My brother learning to be like my dad as a tool to get himself clear. Now they both give my mom shit and she takes it. I will never understand why. She had the resources to leave him when I was a kid, and she certainly does now. I don't know why she is the way she is and I've never asked, but I have offered to get her out and she was appalled I'd suggest such a thing. Making excuses for my dad, bullshitting herself into believing he loves her.

"Love does not hurt. Not fucking ever. And it sure as fuck doesn't break you. She lives in denial— that's weak, Adalynn. Not only did you get out, you did it on your own when in reality you had an army at your back."

"I didn't get myself out."

"You damn well did."

"No," she denied. "Keith was tracking my phone and showed up at Jackie's house. Her dad answered the door, showed Keith the pictures, and told him if he ever contacted me again they'd go public. Keith worked as a programmer on government contracts. He'd lose his security clearance if he had a police record. But in the end it didn't matter—he lost it anyway."

"How'd he lose it?"

The trembling turned into racking shakes, vicious jerky movements like she was trying to get out of her own skin.

"He killed someone," she whispered, and my stomach started to tighten.

"What?"

"Ethan called me the next afternoon to tell me Keith had been arrested, vehicular manslaughter. He left Jackie's, got drunk, and killed someone driving home."

"That's not your fault."

Addy flinched and I realized in my haste, I'd shouted.

"It is. All of it is. I was too weak to stop it, too weak to report it to the police that night. Too stupid to see the lies. Jason's right—"

"The hell he is," I cut her off. "That is not weak or naïve. That is the very fucking definition of strong. And your brother and dad will think so, too."

"I CAN'T. You can't. He can't," she stammered and I realized my mistake.

I shouldn't have brought Jasper into the mix. Not yet. Not until I understood why she'd never told him. I had my suspicions and I figured they were good ones. She'd said she didn't want him to get into trouble but it had to be more.

"Why not?"

"Why not?" she breathed.

The shaking stopped and her body grew taut.

I would find that was my second mistake. And the stillness was the calm before the storm.

Because seconds later, all hell broke loose.

27

It was out.

And just like I knew would happen, I couldn't shove it back down.

"Adalynn."

"No."

My hands came up and I vaguely noted I was out of bed and I didn't understand how that came to be.

I'd been safely tucked next to Trey, now I wasn't.

I was cold and alone.

Terrified I couldn't shove it back down.

Say it, Adalynn. Keith's harsh voice assaulted my mind. *Say it. Tell me how much you want it.*

"Addy, baby, you're scaring the fuck outta me. Please come here."

"No."

Say it, bitch.

I didn't want to say it. I couldn't say it through the pain that had exploded after Keith had back-handed me. So I didn't say it.

But he didn't care.

He never cared.

He just took it.

And my mind drifted.

"Jesus Christ." Trey's voice cut through my memory.

Escape. Run.

I turned to do just that but strong arms wrapped around my middle.

Don't walk away from me. You don't ever get to walk away from me.

My foot connected with his but he didn't release me. He never did. Keith always got what he wanted. Always.

"Let me go."

"Baby, I can't. I'm afraid you're gonna hurt your-self. Please calm down and tell me what's happening."

Tell me how much you want it.

Tell me.

"I won't tell you. I'll never tell you."

The arm around my middle got tighter and I

twisted and fought until I broke free. I dashed to the door but Trey was faster and blocked my only way out.

No escape.

"Come back to the room, Addy. It's me and you, honey. Just me and you. I'm not gonna hurt you. I'd never hurt you, I love you, honey. Please let me help you."

You know I love you, Adalynn. I love you so much you drive me crazy. I love you so much you make me lose my temper.

"You don't love me."

Suddenly, I couldn't breathe.

I had to shove it back in. It was too close, clawing up my throat, almost there.

This was all wrong. Everything was wrong. I had to beat it back before it was too late. Everything would be ruined.

I was ruined.

You think you can leave me? You think I'd let you walk away from me?

Another slap. More pain.

I'll ruin you before I let you leave me.

"No!" I screamed.

But I didn't scream then. I didn't fight because I knew it would hurt worse if I did. I was weak.

My vision cleared and my gaze landed on Trey, still in front of the door but with his phone to his ear. "Yeah, Emily, it's Trey."

Oh, no!

No. No. No.

"Don't!" I shouted.

"Yeah, that was Addy. I need you at my place."

There was a pause and his pain-filled stare held mine. I ignored the fear I saw, I ignored the worry, I ignored everything.

"Please, don't."

"Jasper's on the visitor list at the guard gate and the back door is unlocked. I know he's coming with you but he doesn't come upstairs. Only you."

My dad.

No.

"I hate you!" I screeched.

"One more thing, and I want this crystal clear. This ends for Addy tonight. And when it does, she's not leaving my sight. Right now, she needs her mom, probably needs her sisters, too. And, Emily, brace."

"It was over," I told him. "It was over and now it will never be. You ruined everything. Everything."

How could he be so calm?

My life was over.

Everything was ruined.

"Thanks. See you soon."

Trey tossed his phone on the dresser and just stared.

"I fucking hate you."

"No, baby, you don't. We're gonna get it all out and when we do, it won't be able to hurt you anymore."

"My dad will kill him."

Trey's face turned to granite and he squared his shoulders when in a low, terrifying growl he said, "And he goddamn well should. That motherfucker took his hands to you. Hit you. Hurt you. And, Addy, I'm scared as fuck, because you're leaving something out. Something big. And you have to give it to me. What else did Keith do to you in your bathroom?"

Tell me how much you want it.

I screwed my eyes closed to block out that horrible voice in my head. The sight of Keith above me.

Down.

I had to shove it down, but the problem was it was coming up fast. It was gagging me. I couldn't breathe.

Then I wasn't standing. I was moving. My feet hit the cold tile, then my knees didn't, and my hair was pulled away from my face before I emptied the contents of my stomach.

You want it.

I didn't want it. I didn't want anything.

Ruined.

I kept my eyes closed and retched more, the whole time knowing that my life was over and it was all because of Trey.

I heard his soft murmurs but I couldn't make out the words and I didn't care.

He called my mom, now it was over.

My dad wouldn't let this go.

More stress. More worry.

My mom would be left alone. My sisters without their dad, and it would all be my fault.

Poor, stupid, naïve Adalynn.

"I hate you," I muttered and spit.

"I can live the rest of my life knowing you hate me if it means you no longer live with what's eating you up inside."

"I'll never forgive you."

"And I'd never forgive myself if I didn't love you enough to get this out of you."

"My dad will never be able to look at me again and I'll hate you for that, too."

Trey had no response to that.

And more of my dinner churned in my stomach before it came back up.

In the silence, Trey never let go of my hair, and his other hand never stopped stroking my back.

I don't know how long I was on my knees in front of the toilet. I was too far gone in my fear. But it had to be a long time. Long enough for my mom to make calls. Long enough for her to drive to Trey's. Long enough for my humiliation to be complete.

"Delaney, pull the wet blankets off my bed, yeah?" There was a pause, then he continued making demands. "Quinn, get me a wet washcloth. Emily, my tees are in the bottom right drawer."

"Great," I muttered.

"We're gonna work this out of you." He kissed the top of my head.

"I didn't want it worked out."

Then, like I was a two-year-old, Trey wiped my brow with a wet washcloth and finished with a swipe over my mouth and chin.

"Need to get you out of the bathroom."

I felt the heat from his body move away and I sat back on my heels before I twisted to get up. When I did, my mind took me back to the last time I was on my knees in a bathroom. The memory was vicious and swift. My body revolted, my mind protested, but I couldn't stop it from breaking free.

Tell me.

I could feel his breath on my neck, feel his teeth sink into my flesh.

Then pain.

"I'll never tell you."

"Fuck. Everyone out." Then I felt strong hands on my face, holding me hostage. "Open your eyes, baby."

"I can't watch."

"Watch what?"

"What he took. I can't watch him do it. I have to keep my eyes closed."

I heard noises. But nothing penetrated. I couldn't watch.

"He's not here, Addy. It's me and you. Open your eyes and look at me."

Shame.

Searing, hot, shame.

"He's always here. I beat it back and keep it locked away. I told you I had to keep it deep down or I couldn't—"

"Adalynn, open your eyes and look at me," Trey demanded.

Slowly my lids lifted and all I could see was

Trey. He was sitting on the floor, his knees bent cocked to the sides and I was between them. We were face-to-face and all I saw was him.

"He cannot hurt you."

"It hurts every day," I admitted. "Every day, I'm afraid."

"He will never hurt you again, I swear it."

"Not him. I'm afraid of my dad."

I heard my mother gasp and I closed my eyes.

"Your—"

"You don't know him, Trey. You don't know what he'll do. You don't know how it will eat him up inside until he won't be able to look at me."

"Baby, that's what you're afraid of?"

"Yes," I croaked. "You don't know. It will hurt him so bad he won't be able to love me anymore."

"I do know that you are absolutely wrong. There is not a single thing you could do that would make Jasper Walker turn his back on his daughter. There's nothing you could do that would make him love you less."

"He's right, my sweet girl," my mom said, and my heart flip-flopped hearing her voice.

Sad. So sad.

"I didn't want you to know."

"I know you didn't. My strong girl, always going

at it alone. Quiet as a mouse making her own way, but stronger than the rest."

"I'm not strong," I whispered, and Trey's hand slid from my cheek to my neck and he gave me a gentle squeeze.

My eyes lifted and I was shocked to find his eyes glossy.

"I'm sorry," I blurted out. "I'm—"

Then I wasn't speaking because I leaned forward and buried my face into his throat. He held me while I cried. He held me when the tears subsided. And he did it even longer as I tried to catch my breath.

"How about we get you out of here so you can talk to your mom?"

"Trey?"

"Yeah, baby?"

"I didn't mean what I said."

"I know you didn't." His tone was dull and his eyes were no longer glossy but they were clouded with something I didn't understand, but it scared me. "Emily, do you mind helping Addy up?"

"Trey?"

His gaze hadn't left mine and I saw him flinch.

"Yeah?"

"Nothing."

He knew.

Now everything was ruined.

Just like I knew it would be.

I didn't fight when my mom helped me stand, nor did I struggle when she led me to Trey's bed and made me get in it. And once her arms wrapped around me and Hadley got in and pressed herself to my side, my mind blanked.

I lost him.

He knew I was ruined.

I'd been the perfect Addy with the perfect life. He now knew I was flawed.

28

I gritted my teeth as pain shot up my leg. At first, I'd welcomed the numb tingling, but the longer I was on the floor, the tingling had turned into stabbing, excruciating pain. So much so, I had to ask my woman's mother to help her up because I couldn't fucking do it.

"Let me help you, and before you act like a tough guy, save it," Quinn said, and my molars ground down more.

"I got it."

"I bet you do, but you're not hiding that your leg's giving you problems. So tell me what to do."

My options were to fucking crawl to the counter like a pussy or let Quinn help me.

"Give me your hand."

She walked closer, offered me her hand, and without delay, I hoisted myself up.

"Fuck," I grunted and tried to get my balance. "Fucking hate this shit."

"Sucks, doesn't it." I caught Quinn's gaze and realized it wasn't a question but a statement from someone who understood what it meant to need help.

"'Preciate your help. I'm gonna go downstairs and see to your dad."

"Everyone's down there."

I figured that was the case but I appreciated the warning. And without another word, Quinn left the bathroom. I took a moment to get myself under control. It went against the grain to leave Addy's side while she was in pain. But after all that had transpired, I knew straight to my soul she needed her mother. Emily Walker was a healer. Addy had told me herself that her mom could perform miracles. And right then, that was what Addy needed, and I needed to talk Jasper out of committing murder while at the same time trying to convince myself that killing Keith would only cause Addy more harm.

I didn't spare a glance at the women piled on my bed. I knew if I caught sight of my Addy I wouldn't be able to leave the room. And if someone was going to contain Jasper it had to be done immediately.

I hadn't even hit the bottom step when Jasper filled my vision.

A vision of a father undone. Anguish and fury made for one hell of a look.

"Tell me."

I'll never tell you. I heard Addy's terrified demonic voice in my head.

Jesus Christ, I'd sell my soul if I never had to hear her screech like that again.

"Need a minute."

"I heard—"

"I bet you did. But for the last thirty minutes, I *saw* it. I saw it leak from her soul and when it did, I absorbed every scream, every word, and when she purged it—literally throwing up, getting it all out, I held her. So I need a goddamn minute."

I knew my voice cracked and I didn't give a fuck. I knew I limped to my back door and I didn't give a fuck about that either. And lastly, I knew I should have handled Jasper with care, but I couldn't bring myself to do it.

The cool night air did nothing to extinguish the burn that had built in my chest. I knew it was going to be bad, both what she had to say and the aftermath. But I hadn't known how bad. I hadn't fucking known that the worst was the goddamn *worst*.

She hadn't said the word and I couldn't bring myself to even think it, but I knew.

I knew what that motherfucker had done to her.

The worst.

Fucking shit, I couldn't breathe.

Sweet, shy, beautiful Addy. So fucking strong thinking she was weak.

"Fuck!"

"Brother."

Drake.

Of course it would be him. After Carter left our team, Drake had slid in to fill the role of the voice of reason. But the problem was, there was no reason that would quench my thirst for blood.

I turned to tell him I wasn't ready but stopped when I saw it wasn't only Drake. Logan, Matt, and Luke had joined him. My gaze went from my brothers to the window and I saw Carter and Brady blocking the stairs. Jasper was pacing, Levi and Clark standing close. I knew if Lenox was in town he'd be there, too.

Brothers.

Closing ranks.

I knew I had to give Jasper what he needed, but

first I had to get control. Months ago, I'd forgotten something important. Or maybe I hadn't forgotten, maybe I'd been too proud and stubborn. But now was not the time for pride. Addy needed me. Jasper had to be briefed and I absolutely had to be ready to take care of my woman when she was done speaking to her mom and sisters.

So I didn't delay and I didn't hold back. I told my brothers every last gut-wrenching detail. And when I was done, my heart was pounding in my chest. But I remembered something Addy had said, something important. Something that I couldn't ignore as badly as I wanted to.

She unequivocally did not want her father to cause bodily harm to Keith. She was terrified of it. That was what had held her back talking about it. And I knew it was going to take an act of God to convince Jasper Walker, a man who took love and protection to such a degree it was unreal, not to hunt down Keith.

I caught sight of Jasper heading toward the back door, Levi and Clark following him. Carter and Brady still at the stairs.

My brothers shifted, making room for the newcomers. I noted Levi and Clark had positioned themselves so they could make a grab for Jasper if necessary and I thought that was smart. Depending on his reaction, they might have to lock him down.

Jasper's gaze locked onto mine and I broke the silence.

"How straight do you want it?"

His jaw flexed at my question and he grunted his answer, "Straight."

"No part of this is pretty and it fucks me to say, but there's no way to cushion this for you."

"Give it." I hesitated and Jasper's already taut body strung tighter and his head dropped forward. "So I know."

Likely he did, but I still gave him the confirmation he'd requested.

"He physically, mentally, and sexually assaulted her."

I heard Levi and Clark both growl a few expletives, but I didn't take my eyes off Jasper so when his head snapped up and his eyes lit with fire, I didn't miss it.

Shattered.

Then Jasper inhaled so deeply I watched his chest expand.

"Why?" he croaked.

"This is gonna be the harder part," I told him.

"Harder than learning some fucker took his hands to my little girl and…"

Fucking hell. He couldn't say it either.

"Yep. Because the why will burn you to ash. But being the father I know you to be, you'll see your way past it and give Adalynn what she wants."

Logan and Matt moved closer to me the same way Levi and Clark had crowded Jasper.

Any other time I would've let that settle over me —the bonds of brotherhood. But right then I didn't feel anything other than Addy's pain.

"She blames herself. And she's terrified of you."

"Me?"

Jasper's torso jerked back and he looked like I'd struck him.

"You. Her fear is two-fold. She's afraid that once you found out, that it would eat at you until you wouldn't be able to look at her. But the real fear is that you'll kill him and she'll have to live with the guilt of you getting into trouble. She mentioned you going to prison. That's her fear, losing you."

"I am going to kill that son of bitch but I won't be going to prison."

"That's not what Addy wants."

"Addy doesn't—"

"Adalynn gets it all. Anything and everything she wants. This is about her and only her."

"I'm—"

"You don't think I want to beat that mother-fucker bloody the way he did my woman?" I cut Jasper off and took a step toward him. "She's your daughter but she is mine and I just relived that shit with her. She wasn't in that room with me when it came out. She was stuck in her head with that piece of shit. She begged me not to tell Emily. Then she told me she hated me for doing it. After that, she told me she'd never forgive me but I still did it because my woman needs help. She needs her mom, she needs her sisters, but most importantly, she needs her father. I took it, Jasper, I took everything she had to say, every fucking detail she gave me burned into my soul in a way I know they will be there until the day I die. I watched her shake and sob. Me. I watched her zone out and sound like a zombie. I promised you I'd dig it out and I did. So now you're gonna promise me the only thing you're gonna do is reassure her you will not be seeking revenge."

When I was done with my tirade, Jasper was silent and still.

"I'm fucking begging you. I cannot lose her, and if you don't promise me and you do something, she will be gone. *That*, she will never forgive me for. And she just won't be gone from me, she will be piled under so much guilt, she'll be lost to everyone. It happened to *her*. Not you. Not me. I told her nothing would ever hurt her again. So I'm begging you not to make me a liar."

Jasper jerked his chin in what I hoped was his promise before he stepped around Levi and made his way farther into my backyard. He stopped with his back to me and his head fell forward. Then I heard the most retched sound I'd ever heard.

Worse than Addy's demonic wails.

The worst.

The sound of a father destroyed.

And when I saw Jasper's body rock to accompany the sound, I had to turn away from his pain.

The worst.

JASPER WALKER HAD KNOWN PAIN. He'd known beauty. He was a man who had everything and every day lived with the knowledge he had everything to lose.

He was also a man who had tried to protect his children from all the ways life could fuck with them.

Yet, he'd failed at every turn. And each time one of his children stumbled, his Em reminded him he couldn't shield them from everything.

But the truth was, Jasper couldn't shield them from *anything*.

And now this.

His baby girl.

The knife twisted deeper and he started making plans. He'd wait a good long while, plan it just right. That fucker would get his and Addy would never know.

"Dad?" He felt Quinn's hand slide into his and she squeezed. "Addy wants to talk to you."

"Thanks, girl."

He pulled his daughter closer, kissed her forehead, and let her go.

He scanned the room, looking for his two other daughters, and found them right where he knew they'd be. Carter had his arms around Delaney and Brady was holding a crying Hadley. Jasper made another pass and stopped on Trey.

Fuck. He'd been wrong.

So damn wrong, it wasn't funny.

There was no better man for his daughter.

The man looked just as destroyed as Jasper felt. He'd take Addy's pain. Trey would. And he'd let it eat at him—scar him inside—and he'd take that, too, so Addy could have easy.

It was on that thought, he walked to the man. But he did not want to delay getting to his daughter so he laid it out and did it quickly.

"A man's any sort of man he admits when he's wrong and makes amends. I was wrong. I was a dick. And I'm sorry. I know you didn't ask and made it clear you didn't need my blessing but you have it all the same."

Eager to get to his daughter, Jasper moved to leave when Trey called his name.

"I did need it." Trey cleared his throat then continued. "Thank you."

Fuck, this kid was killing him.

"Then it's good you got it. But just to say, it's not me giving it as much as you proving you love my daughter more than you love yourself. You took a grave risk calling us in, knowing she needed help, knowing she didn't want that, but then fighting for her to get everything she needs. You're the type of man every father prays his daughter finds."

With that, Jasper moved through the dining room, gigantic living room, and stopped at the base of the stairs thinking he paid his employees too damn much if they could afford this. Then he was glad he did, because he wanted Addy to have this. Not the big grand house, but the big home so she could fill it with his grandchildren.

Once he made it to the second floor, he followed the murmur of voices and paused in the doorway.

His wife sat in the middle of a huge bed with her girl next to her. Their backs to the headboard, Addy's head resting on her mother's shoulder, their hands clasped together.

A sight he'd seen hundreds of times. A sight that was no less beautiful than it was any of those times.

Emily Walker loved her children. A fierce lioness and a smart woman. She'd given their children the tools to overcome any obstacle.

This would be no different.

"Hey, Dad," Addy sheepishly called, and the knife in Jasper's gut twisted.

Hell no.

His girl was no sheep.

"I'm gonna go down and give you two a minute." Emily patted Addy's knee and slid off the bed. Addy followed, and that was when Jasper noticed she was in Durum's tee.

He ground his teeth in an effort not to think about what that said.

Jasper was not dumb, his daughters were

gorgeous, Delaney had a child and one on the way, Quinn lived with Brice, and Hadley lived with Brady. But that didn't mean he wanted to admit to himself his daughters were anything but as pure as the white driven snow and his granddaughter wasn't the consequence of immaculate conception.

"I'm sorry," Addy blurted out and Jasper jerked back.

"Stop, Adalynn. You don't have a damn thing to be sorry for. Please don't ever apologize."

"I was so scared. I know it was selfish not to ask for help. But I was scared."

"I know you were and I understand why."

"You do?"

Christ, Trey was right—his daughter was terrified of him, or more terrified *for* him. How had he allowed this to happen?

"I love you. I love your sisters and your brother. The five of you are my world. Add in your mother and my grandbabies and all of you are my everything. I cannot live without you all. I'm sorry you were scared to tell me because you were afraid of what I would do. That's on me. But you need to know something—I'm so fucking proud of you I can't express how much. You went through something that would rightfully cause a woman to crumble. Yet you stayed standing. You're strong and resilient and you did it by yourself. I hope you know there's nothing in this world that would make me think less of you. There's nothing you can't tell me."

"That's what Trey said."

"Trey's a smart man."

Addy's eyes narrowed, and gone was the timid woman his daughter had been when he entered the room. In her place was the fierce lioness her mother had taught her to be.

"Are you pulling my leg?"

"No." Jasper chuckled.

"I think you are."

"I'm not, swear."

"Then why are you laughing?"

"Because you are so much like your mother it's like looking back three decades and falling in love all over again. She gave you a great many things—her beauty, her kindness—but mostly she gave you her brand of loyalty and protection. And when it comes out, it is so beautiful it's blinding."

He'd barely gotten the last word out before his daughter was in his arms.

"I messed up," she said, and wrapped her arms around her old man's middle.

God, he missed that. Missed when his kids were

little and used to hug him for no reason. So he took a moment to enjoy it before he asked, "What'd you mess up?"

"I said some really crappy things to Trey. I didn't mean them but they were awful."

"He understands."

"I don't think so."

"Trust me. When I say he understands, I mean he *understands*."

"They were bad."

He thought about how much to tell his daughter, then he remembered how strong she was and didn't hold back.

"I know why you didn't want to tell. And I know what you said. Trey didn't pull any punches when he laid it out, and part of that was he was willing to risk everything to get you help even after you told him you hated him and you'd never forgive him. What you need to take from that, Addy, is he loves you that much. God's honest truth, you really could hate him for the rest of your life and he'd feel the loss of you and not recover from it, but he'd still do it if it meant you didn't have all that ugly shit eating you up. You understand that? That's love. That's real, selfless, undying love. That's what I want for you. So when I tell you he's a smart man, what I mean to say is he's a good man. And he deserves a woman by his side that is just as loyal. He's not mad. But he is downstairs worried. Come down and put him out of his misery."

"Everyone—"

"Loves you. Period. The end. They just love you. Go down and show them you're okay and they'll be good."

"Okay."

"Okay." Jasper placed his lips on Addy's head, then pulled back and grunted, "But put some damn clothes on, would ya?"

"Yes, Daddy."

Fuck.

Daddy.

That never got old. Not one second in the last thirtyish years had Jasper Walker taken that one word for granted.

29

I knew Trey was awake because he was gently removing his hand from my bottom.

Last night while my family wandered his house, giving themselves an unguided tour, I apologized for what I'd said, he'd forgiven me, and the rest of the night he kept me close. I knew the few times I'd left his side he'd watched me and I knew why. He straight out said I'd scared him. Being as the scene had been ugly and I'd zoned out for a lot of it, I understood.

After my family left, he'd led me to bed, where we'd laid and talked. Not long, and not in depth, but he'd again assured me he held no grudges and knew I was not myself. He also made sure I understood why he'd called my mom. In his mind, it was either her or he needed to call a doctor because I was so out of it, you guessed it, I'd scared him.

But he also thanked me for sharing. He'd held me tight while his hand coasted up and down my back as he listened to me tell him about my conversation with my mom. After that I was mentally drained, Trey probably was, too, so he suggested we go to sleep.

The last thing I remembered was his warm palm resting on my hip. Obviously at some point during the night his hand had dropped to my bottom. Not only that, but it had made its way under my panties, and now Trey was doing his best not to wake me while he pulled away.

This was un-Trey behavior. If his hand was on my bottom, he left it there, then he commenced the good stuff.

But not this morning, the morning after I'd had a nervous breakdown and told him my secret.

Damn, that hurt.

"Trey?"

"Morning, baby."

His hand settled on my hip and at the same time, he pressed his lips on my forehead.

Well, at least that was something.

"I need to tell you something."

He went still.

No, not still, *steel*. The muscle under my cheek jumped, then it turned solid.

I shoved away how that made me feel and took a deep breath.

"Yeah?" he prompted but did not relax.

He'd asked me to trust him. So I was going to do that.

"I need you to know, I fully understand the difference."

"Difference?"

Crap. I hadn't thought about how I was going to explain this, but it needed to be said. Everything had to be out in the open. It would kill me if he treated me like I was broken. If he stopped touching me.

"The difference between us making love and what he did to me."

So maybe he hadn't turned into steel, because *now* he was steel and not breathing.

"I never got that part mixed up in my head. Even as it was happening I knew what he was doing was wrong and it was not my fault but his. I knew it was an act of violence."

"Baby—"

"Trey, I need you to hear this." He nodded and kissed my head. Just that small gesture gave me the courage to go on. "Yesterday was not about that, what he did, so much as it was about my fear if my secret got out what my dad would do, and what my family would think of me. And the shame I'd been harboring for not leaving him sooner. The part about that day, that I didn't want to remember, was him demanding I tell him I wanted it. Because in the end, I said what he wanted to hear. Not out of fear, but because I was helpless and I knew there was nothing I could say or do to make him stop and I just wanted it to be over. So I said it but I didn't twist that either; I knew I wasn't really asking to be violated. I just wanted it done. I don't feel shame in that but I still didn't want to remember it."

I drew in a deep breath and plucked up all the courage I had to explain what I really needed to say.

"So please don't pull away from me. I understand if you need some time before you can make love to me again. But it would—"

I didn't get out the rest of my sentence because suddenly I was on my back. Before I could figure out how that came to be—due to the fact it was done at a speed which would be considered superhuman—I was also breathless.

"Time?"

"Huh?"

"You said you'd understand if I needed some time before I made love to you. So, time?"

"Um. Yeah. Time. Last night was intense. I told you—"

"Yeah, baby, you could say last night was intense. But I still don't understand why you think I'd need time."

"Um, did you get flashed with one of those *Men in Black* thingamabobs that erases your memory?"

"Addy," he growled. "Don't be cute."

"I'm not. You're the one that pulled your hand out of my undies, yet you're asking why I'd say that I understand if you need time. What I'm trying to communicate is, I get that you might after finding out what happened to me, but *I* don't. I don't need any time."

I watched as Trey's eyes narrowed before they relaxed and he smiled.

"Adalynn. I pulled my hand out of your panties and off your sweet ass because it's nine-oh-five and you have a patient at ten. But it's good to know you don't need time, baby, because I wasn't planning on there being any."

"We slept in."

"We did. Lucky for me, I don't think my boss is gonna be too pissed I'm two hours late to work, but

I know you don't like to keep your patients waiting."

I wasn't late. I was *seriously* late. And even if we rushed, we wouldn't be to Triple Canopy by ten.

"Trey, you have to move."

"Not yet."

"Really, you have to get up. We're *really* late."

"Right, and seeing as we're already *really* late, another two minutes won't kill us."

"Trey—"

"Addy, kiss me, baby, then I'll let you up."

Oh.

That I could do.

"Okay."

In the end, I didn't kiss him, Trey kissed me. And it was the sweetest kiss he ever gave me.

———

"Thanks, Addy, you're the best," Chelsea said and smiled.

"Again, I'm so sorry I was late."

"Girl, I saw your man. I'm lucky you were ten minutes late and not ten hours."

Heat hit my cheeks and I didn't know what to say. But Chelsea did.

"He's hot, no doubt. But in my book, there is nothing sexier than a man who flaunts he's in love."

"What?"

"Addy," she drawled. "Please tell me you're not living on the banks of *de* Nile. That man is gone for you. And the way he looks at you—hot. Like he wants to gobble you up. No, like he wants to make you wear a crown and build you a castle, *then* gobble you up in your queen bed."

One could say Chelsea had a flair for drama. But she was kind of right. Trey did look at me like that and I loved it.

"Do you think I look at him the same?"

"Shoo. Are you kidding? It was a miracle you could walk across the gym with those stars sparkling in your eyes. You must've made your way on muscle memory alone because, girl, you are blinded with love and it shows."

I didn't care if she was being overdramatic; I hoped I did look like that because that's how I felt.

"Good," I muttered.

"Good," she repeated. "Next week, are we still here?"

"Yeah. If you don't mind."

"Not only don't I mind, I prefer coming here."

"Really?"

"I know your family owns this place so I don't feel bad saying it—this place is swank. The locker room alone is enough to beg you to keep all my appointments here. Top that with everything else, the brand new machines, the mats are so much better, the TVs, the sauna. And let's just say there's no shortage of hot guys walking around. So, um, yeah, really. Please keep all of my appointments here."

That was good to know. My contract was up at the center I worked at and I was going to talk to my dad, uncles, Nick, Jason, Carter, and Brady about taking over the gym. I already knew what they'd say. In part, it was built for me. The guys did work out in here but no way they needed all the room, and most of the equipment they didn't touch.

"You only have two more appointments," I reminded her.

"Well..." She trailed off then gave me a huge broad smile and asked, "I was hoping when I'm done with PT you'd still work with me. You know, so I don't get injured again. Like a personal trainer. Call it preventative measures. I'm too old for another surgery."

Chelsea was not old, she was twenty-six. She

was also only one step down from Liberty in the coolest-job-ever category.

"That sounds like a good plan. We'll set something up."

"Awesome." She pumped her fist into the air. "And please tell me you'll finally come see me ride."

"I don't know if I can handle watching you get thrown off a bull, Chels."

"Come on, please," she pleaded and smiled.

It was hard to believe Chelsea was a real life cowboy, or maybe she was a cowgirl, or maybe rodeo queen would be more apt.

"When's your next...I don't know what to call it. Your next rodeo?"

"Not for a few months. Once I'm cleared to train, it should only take me a few weeks before I'm ready for the circuit, but nothing will be in the area for a few months. If I get you and your man tickets, will you please come?"

I found I couldn't deny Chelsea's sweet smile so I agreed.

"Absolutely."

"And just to say, if tall hottie is free, I'll leave three tickets at the gate."

It was hard to imagine after the night I'd had that I was joking and smiling. The truth had come out and Trey had made sure I was still standing. My heart swelled until it was a miracle the organ didn't burst from my chest.

"Which hottie are you referring to?"

"The one that was wearing the baseball cap on backward, with the amazing ass."

No shame in her game.

"That's Matt. As far as I know, he's unattached."

"Well, bring him along."

"I'll see what I can do." I laughed.

"Awesome. I'll see you later this week." Chelsea waved and headed for the door.

She'd barely left the building when I saw my brother stomping across the gym.

Crap.

"Jason," I warned.

He didn't stop prowling, not even when he got close. He just pulled me into a bear hug and squeezed the breath out of me until I muttered, "Can't...breathe."

He loosened his arms a fraction, then in a deep guttural voice that knifed me through the heart he said, "I'm so fucking sorry I'm such a dumbass."

"Jay—"

"Please forgive me."

"Already forgiven, big brother."

"I fucking love you so much."

"I know you do."

"You're the best baby sister in the whole world. And before you give me shit, you'll always be my baby sister. I rocked you to sleep. I fed you bottles. I even changed your diapers."

"God. Can we not talk about diaper-changing?"

"Girl, you could drop a load—"

"If you don't shut up, I'm gonna knee you in the balls. Mercy might be pissed because I heard through the Walker Family Gossip Tree that she wants another after this but I'll take my chances."

"I fucking love you," he repeated, this time shaking me with every word.

"I *fucking* love you, too. Sheesh."

"Language," he snapped and I rolled my eyes.

Then I prayed to the Almighty for patience.

"Whatever."

Jason let me go but didn't move far when he said, "Mercy wants a word when you have time."

"Jay."

"Not about that. She wants to plan a baby shower for Delaney."

"Laney doesn't want one. She said you only have a shower for your first kid."

"Right. I'll let you break my wife's heart and tell

her Laney doesn't want one. Plus, she figures you women should get a jump start planning Hadley's."

So it seemed Laney was having a second shower because I was not breaking my pregnant sister-in-law's heart. No way, no how. I loved Mercy to bits. She brought my beloved brother back to life and I would be forever grateful, therefore, I'd give her anything she wanted.

"Hadley's not pregnant."

"Not yet. But you missed it the other day when she happily announced to Brady she stopped taking the pill. Dad was right behind her when she spilled the beans. Brady busted a gut. Hadley went white. And Dad looked like he was gonna puke, punch Brady, or throw Hadley over his shoulder and lock her in her bedroom."

"Seriously?" I laughed.

"Oh, yeah. It was fucking hilarious."

"There's my big brother."

"Come again?"

"My big brother. Smiling, happy, giving me the latest gossip. My Jason."

"Addy—"

"I *fucking* love you, Jason. Don't ever doubt that. Not for a single second. I remember. Every minute growing up with you. Everything you taught me. All the love you gave. I've never forgotten. I never will."

"Right." Jason's eyes darted around the gym before they found the floor. I waited for him to stop inspecting every particle of dust that collected on the very clean, gleaming wood floor. In other words, I waited for him to regain his composure. "Better get back to work."

"Okay."

"Oh, just a by the by, I'll be waiting for my invite to your new pad. I hear there's a sweet pool and a wine cellar. And make that soon, wouldya?"

"It's not my pad."

Jason's head actually tipped back as he roared with laughter. And when it didn't look like he was going to stop anytime soon, I snapped, "What's funny?"

"You are."

"I don't see how."

My brother shook his head and started walking across the gym, this time he wasn't prowling but he was walking quickly so I shouted at his back.

"What's funny?"

"I want an invite."

The door closed behind him and I was thinking that my brother had a screw loose when my phone chimed with a text. I glanced at the clock and noticed it was lunchtime, and since Trey and I missed breakfast, I was starved.

I grabbed my purse out of my desk drawer even though I wouldn't need it. Trey had yet to allow me to pay, but I'd still offer, and swiped my cell.

I was halfway across the gym when I engaged my phone and pulled up the text.

The number wasn't programmed in, so I tapped the nameless text and a picture popped up.

Oh my God.

Oh, no.

I willed my legs to work but they were rooted in place.

So I did the only thing I could do.

I screamed as loud as I could.

He'd come.

He always did.

30

"What the hell?"

I looked up from the report Nick handed me five minutes before and found he was scowling, obviously not liking the intel Dylan had dug up either.

"Cover-up. All the way to the top," Nick unnecessarily told me since I could damn well read and Dylan was good at his job. The dots were not hard to connect.

"And Belview's gone."

"Supposed to be in Wyoming with his team on a training exercise."

That information was also in the report. Belview was at the VA for a routine psych eval after a deployment. He'd passed his evaluation—his whole team had—and they were sent out on a work-up.

"Supposed? Dylan's got the flight log." I tapped the document. "His name's on it."

"Gut tells me he's not on that flight."

When Nick Clark, former FBI profiler with the Behavior Analysis Unit, says he has a gut feeling, it really means he's studied the subject well and good. Further, it means you listen to him because he's damn smart and never wrong.

"I watched the footage from the café. We got lucky and Belview's facing the camera. I was able to write a transcript of the conversation. The tone changes when Jasper's brought up."

"Yeah, Addy said Belview got pissed, said something about Jasper being a hard man to follow or some bullshit."

"Right. What he said after that was, 'Especially if he blocks the way.' Then he went on to say, 'No man will ever be as perfect as him. No man will live up to Jasper Walker. In your eyes, no man will ever love you like he does.' And in his, 'he thinks he knows what's best for everybody.' Addy said something else and Belview finished with, 'You compared me to him every day. And when you weren't, everyone else was. The great Jasper fucking Walker.' That's when you come into the frame and stop the argument. I've watched that footage a hundred times. Belview was hiding, keeping his shit together until Addy mentions her dad. Then he can't hide it. His disdain is for Jasper. Not Addy. Not you. When you entered, you cut him off from Addy—that was a hit to his ego, but he'd actually calmed himself."

Not that I would disagree with Nick, but I thought back to that day in the café. I had Belview in profile, but I hadn't missed the tightness in his frame. They looked like two people arguing. But it wasn't until I got there and saw his face did I realize how bad it was. The guy looked unhinged, and if that was calm, we had problems.

"Jasper told me Wick asked his opinion about being brought into the program and Jasper told Wick that would be a mistake."

Nick nodded. "So, Jasper blocked a significant career advancement. Belview must have found out it was Jasper. His rage goes beyond simple jealousy. I had a buddy at the BAU enhance it and slow it down. Belview's got a tell. A tic in his right eye. It's slight but there. And both his hands are relaxed on the table even though they were arguing. Once Jasper's brought up, his fists ball up and his knuckles turn white."

I missed all of that. I'd been focused on the dude's face.

"You think he's gonna fuck with Jasper?"

"Actually, after studying him, I thought he'd fuck with Emily. Belview would want the game. Fuck with Emily to get to Jasper. But now, Jasper's been poking around and going in hard, not hiding the fact he's unhappy Belview got into it with Addy. The game's changed and I think he'll go straight to Jasper."

"Fuck. We gotta warn him."

"I've called him twice this morning. When he calls me back—"

Nick's statement was cut off by the most horrific blood-curdling scream. Nick was out the door and I was around my desk following. By the time I made it to the hall, Jason was in the mix, running toward the gym as well.

Nick made it to her first, but she shoved away from him and beelined it to me.

"He has Dad."

My blood ran cold, then it ran hot.

"Here!" She shoved her phone at me but her hand was shaking so badly I had to grab her wrist to steady her so I could take the phone.

I looked down at the screen and froze. Jasper tied to a chair, head bowed, eyes closed, face fucked up, his thigh bleeding from a gunshot wound.

Tied, beat to fuck, and shot.

Belview was done.

Then I stopped looking at Jasper and read the text: *come to the cabin to pick up dear ol' dad and come alone.*

"Where's the cabin?"

"Madray Springs on Cherokee Lakes. I don't know the address."

Cold. Dead. Flat.

Christ, not again.

Never again did I want to hear her beautiful voice sound like that.

"Baby, we're gonna go get him."

Nothing.

"Adalynn, look at me."

"I am."

"No. You're off in your head. Look at me. We're gonna get him."

"Okay."

I pulled Addy's body into my arms and wrapped her close. She did not return the embrace. Her arms hung limp at her sides, her head rested on my chest, but only because I wasn't giving her another option.

Cold. Dead. Flat.

Christ.

I glanced around the gym, finding every man in

the building had heard her scream and was now waiting for orders.

I'd reflect on that later. How once again, my brothers proved themselves to be good men.

"Dylan, get us the address of Belview's cabin."

"No property in his name," he returned.

"It was his grandfather's on his mother's side," Addy muttered.

"Got it," Dylan said and dashed out of the gym.

"Where's Emily?"

"My parents' house with Quinn, going over wedding shit," Nick answered.

"Your dad there?"

"Far as I know."

"Find out. Brief your dad, then get Hadley and Delaney over there."

Nick had his phone out and stepped away from the huddle.

"Trey?"

"Yeah, baby?"

"You're...he's...don't..."

"Listen to me. We're gonna bring your dad home."

"Okay."

I gazed around the room and found the man I was looking for. He was not going to like what I had to say, and I knew because if someone asked me to stand down, I sure as fuck wouldn't.

"Brady, I need you to take Addy to the Clarks'." Just as I suspected, he squared his shoulders in preparation for battle. "Brother, please. We can't leave them unprotected."

"Clark will be there."

"He will be," I agreed. "I need you to see to Addy. Her and Hadley both. We could be walking into a trap. Belview sent the picture, could be to draw us away from Emily, Delaney, Quinn, Hadley, Addy, and Jason. If he's meaning to fuck with Jasper, then he'll go for one or all of them. We're making it easy for him by putting them all in one house. So I need you and Clark both watching."

Brady's jaw clenched and he jerked his chin in an unhappy acceptance.

"Briefed my dad. He's staying with the women but wants backup. Levi's on his way to us, Blake's going to Mom and Dad's to see to Aunt Emily. He said my mom will make the calls to get everyone to her place."

"Brady's heading there now," I told Nick and looked down at Addy. "You trust me?"

"Yes."

Strong and sure.

Thank fuck.

"Brady's gonna take you to your mom."

"Okay."

"Strong, Addy. Stay strong. Your dad is a tough son-of-a-bitch. Trust me he's gonna be fine."

"He was...I saw..."

Yeah, she saw all right. She saw her dad tied to a chair, bloody. Belview was gonna pay for that as well.

"Nothing's gonna break your dad. Believe that. By the time we get there, I wouldn't be surprised if he's waiting for us outside bitching about needing a ride."

"Okay."

Brady was standing close waiting to go, so I had to make this quick for a variety of reasons, one being I lied my ass off—Jasper wouldn't be waiting, and the gunshot to the thigh worried the fuck out of me.

"I love you, Addy."

"Love you," she mumbled.

Reluctantly, I passed a still-limp Addy to Brady and they wordlessly walked away. No one spoke until the door closed behind them. Then they waited another two beats before Jason let out a sound near as hideous as his sister's.

No one said a word and a son battled his

emotion. Once he beat it back, his gaze sliced through each man in the room, and on an angry growl, he announced:

"That motherfucker is mine."

No one argued. But we were all thinking the same thing. Belview was fair game. The objective was to get Jasper out breathing, and not a man in the room would hesitate to take out Belview.

"Gear up!" Carter shouted and prowled out of the gym. And the rest of us followed.

———————

DYLAN WASTED no time finding the address and we wasted no time driving the thirty miles to Cherokee Lakes. The south and west side of the lake was packed with waterfront houses. The north side was sparse and the east side, no houses. Belview's family owned a cabin and forty acres—no waterfront but tucked back into the forest.

It had taken us longer to trek back to the cabin than it did to drive the thirty miles.

Matt and Luke had radioed they were in position. Luke lucked out and found a tree stand a hunter had left behind that made for an excellent sniper perch. Matt didn't, and had to find a tree he could climb that gave him the vantage point he needed and a branch he could sit on. He'd done that and now they were both ready.

Logan, Carter, and Nick were coming in from northwest of the property. Drake, Jason, and I took the east. We'd fan out when we hit the cabin. Our pace was slow-moving—Belview might be a dickhead but he wasn't a stupid one and he was well-trained. Not only that, we had to watch for booby traps—which if it were me I would've set many, and they would've been the kind that goes boom. Carter had found one and he'd spotted a deer camera. Which was another issue —Belview could have eyes throughout the woods or they could be left behind by hunters. Either way, none of us wanted to be digitally captured trespassing and stalking through the thick trees and underbrush.

"I don't miss this part," Drake complained.

"Which part is that, princess?"

"The bugs. Mosquitoes are biting the fuck outta me and it's not even dusk."

"I second that," Carter said through my earpiece. "And sandfleas. Don't miss those little fuckers."

I didn't miss those fuckers either.

"They liked you, Church. You must taste sweet," Luke added.

"Yeah, that's what my wife says," Carter quipped and Jason growled.

"Jesus, can we focus?" Jason snapped.

I wasn't sure if his angry response was from hearing Carter make a joke about Delaney, or if Jason was wound too tight. Probably both.

"Easy, Jay. Everyone's focused."

His eyes came to mine, and much like his sister's, they were cold. But his were not dead, they were ablaze with fury.

"My dad—"

"No. Not your dad. Your objective. Clear that out of your head now. Jasper means something to all of us but we'll do him no favors if we let emotion take over. He's the mission. That's all."

"I can't do that."

"Then sit your ass down here and wait for us to come back for you."

"What the—"

I stopped, which meant Jason and Drake did, too.

"Ice, Jason. You have to shove everything else out. Jasper Walker is being held hostage. He has a round drilled through his thigh, he's losing blood, and he needs medical attention."

"Trey," Drake's low voice rumbled from beside me. "Have a care."

"I am. You know I'm right. We have one objective, secure the package. That doesn't happen if we need to lock down a member of the team. Everyone needs to be on point. I will *not* fail. I will not fail my woman and I will not fail Jasper. Dig deep, brother, and find it. I know it's in there. Not only were you in law enforcement, so I know you got the training, but you're a fucking Walker. Clear your mind, lock it down, and get cold. Your dad is waiting for you, brother. Flip the switch and turn to fucking ice."

"You're right," Jason grunted. "But I'm warning Carter, one more word about how my sister thinks he's sweet, I'm kicking him in the balls."

"Perfect."

I'd taken a few steps when Carter came back over the radio.

"Me? You should be more worried about Hadley walking in and seeing Trey naked."

My step faltered and I remembered Jason was behind me armed to the teeth. Then I wondered if he'd shoot me in the back. But before I could make a plan to maneuver myself out of Jason's line of sight, Carter continued to throw me under the bus. "Or maybe how Addy tried to shield Trey and Brady saw..."

Carter finally stopped speaking when Jason fumed, "Shut the fuck up."

I smiled and quickened my pace. Jason's words were heated but they held no real animosity, and Carter had done what he wanted and got Jason thinking about something other than his father tied to a chair, beaten to fuck and bleeding.

Twenty minutes later, the cabin was in sight.

Logan broke away from his team and I broke away from mine. The two of us would check the perimeter while the others covered us.

I finished my sweep and met Logan on the south side of the house.

"Too easy," he noted.

"He was expecting Addy," I reminded him.

"You told Brady it could be a trap. You think maybe that's what this is?"

"I told that to Brady because I needed him to go with Adalynn. Belview is expecting Addy to come. He knows she loves her dad and thinks she's stupid enough to come on her own. He doesn't know her. This show is for her. He hates Jasper. And he knows making Addy watch him kill her father would destroy Jasper. His last moments would be torture knowing Addy had to watch that and she'd be next."

I should've guarded my words or turned off my mic. Regrettably, I did neither and Jason heard.

"Mother—"

I pulled out my earpiece, effectively cutting off Jason's tirade. I understood his anger but I needed in the cabin. Logan flinched and his eyes got wide.

"One thing's for certain, the man's got a flair for inventing curse words," Logan mumbled. "How you wanna play this?"

"One-room cabin. Only place to hide is the bathroom and we know it's too small for two grown men. I'm going in the front door."

"Not smart going in alone."

"I won't be. You'll have my back. We got about two seconds to surprise him, we're not doing that by crawling in a window. He'll take out Jasper. Belview's got his show set up and it will be front and center. He wants Addy to open the door, walk in, and see her dad. He'll be to the side with a gun to Jasper's head, which means it won't be pointed at me."

"And if he sees you and pulls the trigger?"

"I'll be faster."

"And if you're not?"

"Then Jasper's dead."

The words left my mouth and saliva pooled. The bitter, sour truth coated my tongue.

If I fucked this up, Jasper was dead. But there was no other option. The only way in was the front door. The bathroom window was not big enough for any of us to get through, and all other windows were in the main room, therefore not a consideration.

"Hold positions," Logan radioed. There was a brief pause, then he said, "Negative. Hold." His eyes turned hard as he slipped back into the battle-hardened SEAL I'd always known him to be. "Let's move."

We moved.

The curtains on the front windows were closed. A tactical mistake on Belview's part, but then he'd thought my woman would be hightailing her ass to the cabin and barreling in the front door.

Dumb fuck.

He had no clue how smart Adalynn was. She'd never consider coming alone.

Logan's left hand was on my right shoulder as we were nearing the front door. I steadied my breathing. I had ten feet to go, Logan would break off here, step to the side of the door, and wait for me to enter. This was my last chance to tell him.

"It goes bad, tell Addy I love her."

The only confirmation Logan gave that he'd heard my whispered words were two pounding slaps to my shoulder before he moved.

Five...three...enter.

The door was unlocked and the stage was set just as I'd hoped. The only difference was I was staring down the business end of Belview's gun.

Shots rang out.

My breath left my body in a painful whoosh, white-hot pain seared through me, and my vision blurred.

Jesus Christ.

Shouts filled the room and I felt hands on my shoulders moving me back.

"We need a medic, Razor's hit."

Jesus Christ. I'd heard that before and the flashback hit hard and fast. Dust and debris raining down, hitting me on the face until I rolled and the worst of it landed on my back and it felt like I was on fire. I rolled again, looking for Luke, but my vision had been blurry then, too. I couldn't see through the smoke and the concussion of the blast had scrambled my brain. I'd closed my eyes to clear the fog and when I opened them, Liberty and Drake were there.

"I'm fine," I wheezed, blocking out the memory. "Get this thing off me."

I felt tugging, then heard the quick-detach latches go before Drake lifted the vest over my head.

"Good God, that hurts." I rubbed my chest and tried to breathe deep.

"Crazy fucker." Drake's pissed-off grunt made me smile. "You took two, asshole, maybe three."

I took three, I felt the two hit my plates. And without looking, I'd say the third went clean through my shoulder.

"Jasper?"

"Breathing."

"Awake?"

"Yep."

I shoved past Drake, ignoring the throb in my shoulder. Okay, so it was more than a throb, it actually felt like someone had taken a branding iron to my flesh, then poured battery acid into the wound.

Carter stepped to the side and I caught Jasper's gaze. A slow, bloody smile formed, upon which time I saw he was missing a tooth, his lip was torn to shit, and smiling just made the blood flow faster.

Crazy son-of-a-bitch.

"My wife's gonna be pissed," he announced.

"Likely," I agreed.

Jason finished untying his dad and I saw Jasper wince as he brought his arms in front of him.

"Forgot about this part," he groaned and rolled his shoulders. "And I'm definitely too old for this shit."

Jason, not finding his father amusing, grunted at his dad like a bear with a thorn in his ass.

"Let me help you up."

Jasper narrowed his eyes, assessed his son, then wisely allowed Jason to help him stand.

"Ambulance should be here in less than five," Nick said from the door.

"Want me to carry you out front?" I asked Jasper, and he turned his eyes back to mine.

The green so green, they still looked like emeralds even through the swelling and blood.

"You want me to shoot you?"

"No. I think one hole is enough for today."

"Yeah, my daughter's gonna be pissed about that."

"Likely. Though I'm hoping all her energy will be spent nursing you back to health so she'll forget all about it."

"Right. You keep thinking that, you'll be disappointed."

"You think maybe we can cut this short?" Jason

asked. "I'm not feeling all that happy standing in a room with a dead guy."

"Yeah, son. Help your old man to the front door."

There it was, further proof Jasper Walker was a damn good father. It was unlikely he wanted help, even if he had to drag his leg behind him, he'd still get himself to the door. But his son needed something to do, something that made him feel close to his dad after almost losing him. So being the father he was, he swallowed his pride and gave his son what he needed.

"You good?" Carter asked.

"All good, brother."

With a jerk of his chin, Carter started to the door and I pulled out my phone to call my woman and give her the good news.

31

———

"And he's dead?"

"Jeez, Mom."

My mom's gaze snapped to mine and I recoiled at what I saw.

It had been a bad day.

A very bad day, and it shone in my mother's blue eyes. The worry, devastating fear, the relief when Trey called to tell us they'd gotten Dad out and he was alive.

But that relief flew out the window when we'd made it to the hospital right before my dad was wheeled back for surgery. Jake had worked my dad over some more after he'd sent me that text.

Now we were in the surgical waiting room and

Trey—with fresh stitches in his shoulder, front and back—finished the story.

This had been delayed because after the medics had seen to his injuries, the police had shown up and needed a statement. While two detectives grilled Trey in a private hospital room, another one was interviewing each of the guys. Ethan had shown up, and being as he was a cop, I asked him if he thought Trey needed a lawyer. My cousin just pulled me into a hug and told me not to worry.

He'd been right, I didn't need to worry. One of Jake's teammates had come forward and the story he told chilled me to the bone. Jake's hatred for my dad was known far and wide. Jake had known for years that my dad had blocked some sort of career advancement. However, when Jake told them one day he was going to kill the great Jasper Walker, no one in his platoon had taken him seriously. They'd laughed it off, not wanting to believe Jake had it in him to commit murder. They'd been wrong. Jake had it in him.

It was two in the morning, my dad was out of surgery and being moved into a room, and my mom was impatiently waiting. Apparently, part of her impatience included needing confirmation that Jake was dead.

"Yes, Emily. He's dead," Trey repeated.

"Thank you."

I didn't know if my mom was thanking Trey for killing a man or rescuing my dad, being as they were one and the same I didn't think about it too hard. But I did search my feelings. There had been a time when I thought I loved Jake. Now I knew better. I didn't love him but I couldn't deny I had cared and I did give him my virginity. But I wasn't sad he was dead—or I was but only because he had parents and a sister, so I was sad they'd lost him. I also didn't have any feelings other than gratitude that Trey killed him.

It was true—I loved my father. But I loved Trey beyond reason, and in a situation where Trey had been shot three times, one leaving a hole in his body, I was grateful Trey had the wherewithal to save his life and come home to me.

"Walker family?" a handsome nurse called out.

"Yes." My mom stood and grabbed my hand to follow.

"Mr. Walker has been transferred and is ready to see you," he said.

"May my daughter and her fiancé come back with me before they leave?"

Fiancé?

Mom was laying it on thick. All day, I'd heard Trey this, Trey that. He's just like Dad. I knew she needed to talk about something to get her mind off her husband being held at gunpoint, but *fiancé*—that was a little crazy.

"Sure. Rules on the floor are three visitors at a time. Normal hours are over, so five minutes at a time. If you'll follow me."

We followed the nurse down the hall. He stopped, pointed to the door, then continued.

"I don't know if I can do this," I whispered to Trey.

"You can."

And without another word, he pulled me into the room. My mom was already at my dad's bedside, brushing his hair off his forehead.

"Em."

My dad's throat sounded dry, and instantly my mom grabbed a pitcher of water from the roller table, poured some in a cup, and held it to my dad's lips.

After he took a drink, Mom put the cup back on the table and my dad's battered face turned in my direction.

I stiffened and Trey wrapped his good arm around my shoulders and tucked me close. My dad's lips twitched and he nodded his approval.

"They get you sewn up?" Dad asked, his voice a lot stronger.

"Yep. Through and through. Didn't hit anything important."

"Good. Cops come by?"

"Taken care of and that's all good, too."

"Did—"

"Q and A later, yeah?" Trey asked.

My dad smiled then snarled, "Fucking hell, what'd they do, sew my lips together?"

"No," my mom answered. "Though I have a feeling in a few days after I've heard you complaining about being laid up, I'm gonna wish they did."

"Mom!" I giggled.

"Don't *Mom* me. You know I'm right. And since we're on the topic of complaining, I might as well get this out of the way right now. You'll be in a wheelchair—"

"Nope," Dad cut her off.

"Jasper—"

"Nope," Dad repeated. "There is zero chance I'm walking my girl down the aisle in a wheelchair."

"You're right. You'll be wheeling—"

"Nope."

"Damn stubborn," my mom announced right before she burst into tears.

"Em, darlin', come 'ere."

My dad didn't have to ask twice. Mom sat on the bed and got as close as the wires, tubes, and blood pressure cuff would allow.

My dad was murmuring softly, sometimes he'd stop to kiss her head, sometimes his hand would move gently over her back. That was love, giving his Emily everything she needed. What my mom couldn't see and what she'd never know was the whole time his face was a mask of pain.

"Take my daughter home," Dad commanded.

"We'll be by in the morning," I told him. "I'll talk to your doctor and get you sorted to start PT."

My dad scowled and Trey chuckled.

"I don't know what you're laughing about. You're back on the schedule, too, and now we're adding shoulder strengthening to your rotation."

"Right. She's like Oprah." My mom laughed. "PT for you. PT for you. PT for everybody."

My dad and Trey joined my mother. Three of the people I loved the most in the world laughing at my expense.

I could live with that.

But I still feigned irritation and snapped, "Whatever. Glad you're alive, Dad. See you tomorrow."

"Adalynn," my dad gently called my name. "I love you, my sweet girl."

"Love you, Daddy."

Trey's arm tightened, my mom smiled, and Dad gave me a wink.

"Take me home and put me to bed," I told Trey.

My father's very angry rumble filled the room.

Trey contained his laughter. But Mom and I didn't. And when the door closed behind me, Trey and I could still hear my mom laughing.

All was well.

WE'D SAID our goodbyes to my family. Which took approximately five hundred hours since everyone was there except Uncle Lenox, Aunt Lily—they were still in Texas but coming home early—and Jason, who had taken an exhausted Mercy home since he'd already spent time with Dad.

Hugs were given, more hugs, handshakes, man-slaps on the back—which I didn't appreciate since every time Trey received one he winced, but I kept my comments to myself. Uncle Levi and Uncle

Clark had pulled Trey off to the side to have a word. Whatever was said, Trey hadn't told me and I didn't ask.

Now we were finally home, and after hours of being emotionally drained, I had my second wind.

"Do you need a pain pill?" I offered Trey as he sat on the side of the bed.

"Nope, just need you."

I wasn't ready for bed, not tired, and was going to tell him I was going to go downstairs and read when his statement hit me full-force.

"You say that a lot."

"Say what?"

"When I ask what you need, your answer is *just this* or *just you*."

"Everything okay?"

"It wasn't. Everything was very, very wrong. But you made it so tonight I'm getting in bed next to you and my mom's sitting by my dad's side. So, yes, everything is okay."

"Come here, Addy."

I moved to him, and when I got close, he opened his legs so I could walk between them. When I got there, he wrapped an arm around my hips and pressed his forehead into my stomach.

"Are you okay?" I asked.

"Yep."

"That easy?" I asked skeptically.

"Yep.

"But you...I mean..." Crap. I didn't know how to say it, but thankfully, Trey understood my stuttered question.

"Addy, I pray to God that's the very last time that happens. But I think you understand it's not the first. There are things I've seen and done that have marked me. But I will not lose sleep over ending Belview and helping your dad. It is not one of the things that will leave a mark. Going into that cabin, I knew Belview wasn't coming out alive, but I was gonna try my damnedest to make sure your dad did."

"Okay."

Trey smiled so big his eyes lit.

"I love when your eyes shine," I told him.

"Baby, I'm a man, my eyes don't shine."

"They totally do. When you're happy, truly happy, they shine. I made a vow to myself to fight for that look, make you feel it so you could stop hiding it and give it to—"

"Come here, Adalynn."

"I'm here."

"Closer."

"If I come any closer, I'll be on your lap."

"That's the idea, baby."

"Oh."

That shine sparkled brighter and my belly flip-flopped.

"You're gonna have to do all the work tonight."

"Okay."

"Goddamn, I love you. Help me get these off so you can ride me, Addy," he demanded.

So I said the only thing I could say, "Okay."

Then I helped him take his pants off. Then I kissed him until he grew impatient and growled into my mouth. That turned me on so I grew impatient, and that was when I finally rode him. When I was done and he was done, he pulled me to his chest, and with my head tucked under his chin while I caught my breath, I stared at the two deep purple bruises on his chest. My hand covered them and I felt his heartbeat under my palm.

He took three bullets that day.

Two to his heart.

But it was still beating.

32

Tuesday Clark's orchard had been turned into a magical fairy tale world. Unless she always had lights strung from the trees, flower petals dusting the grass, tables with tall, wide candles lit, and lanterns set all along a white runner that led to the place where Hadley and Brady would say their vows.

I couldn't say I'd ever given much thought about getting married, and I certainly hadn't thought about the ceremony, but after looking around the large gathering—large because the Walker, Lenox, Clark, and McCoy clans were big and getting bigger—there were *a lot* of people. All of them close, all of them important, all of them family—some by blood, all by bond.

It was a far cry from how I grew up, but even I

knew this was what family meant. Arguments, disagreements, knock-down-drag-outs, good times, the best times, and the worst times, nothing broke the bond. It might shake them, but they always made amends. I supposed that was something they learned from Jasper, Lenox, Clark, and Levi. The forgiveness part of that equation I reckoned came from Emily, Reagan, Lily, and Blake.

Out of the corner of my eye, I saw Liberty hustling my way with a huge smile on her face.

"What's the deal? Is this a competition or something?" she asked when she was still five feet away.

"Come again?"

"A race?" Her unusual cat eyes danced with humor.

"Woman, I don't have the first clue what the fuck you're talking about."

"I leave on an op, I'm gone three weeks, and you've shacked up with my cousin."

"Yep."

"Yep? Just yep?"

Liberty McCoy was one of my favorite females. Not only was she the toughest chick I knew, and there was a time when I would've gladly served by her side, but she loved Drake. And just like anything Lieutenant Liberty McCoy did, she excelled at it.

And Drake now lived a life that was full of worry when his woman deployed, but so full of the good stuff it made every moment of worry worth it. She was also honest, kind, and like the rest of her family, loyal.

"Not sure there's anything else to say."

Her smile waned and she stepped closer.

"I knew," she whispered conspiratorially.

"Knew what?"

"When you were in the hospital and we were on the phone and you were telling me about the nurse who wanted to give you a sponge bath so she could see your wonker—"

"Don't call my dick a wonker."

"Well, I'm not calling your dick a dick. We're actually not even talking about your wonker, that was just a point of reference."

"My dick usually is."

"We're not talking about your dick," she growled, and I busted out laughing. I did it so hard and so long my shoulder started to ache.

"You just wanted to see how many times you could get me to say dick." She'd caught on.

"Yeah, Liberty, I wanted to see how many times I could get you to say dick while getting increasingly pissed about saying it."

"That's how I knew."

I still had no idea what she was talking about, and when my eyes landed on Adalynn in her dress, Liberty lost my attention.

Goddamn, Addy was gorgeous. She'd left her hair down, but instead of it being straight like she normally wore it, there was a sexy, messy wave to it. And while I loved Addy fresh-faced, she'd done her makeup heavy, and even from this distance, the black around her eyes made the green stand out. Perfect curves, toned but not pointy and sharp, soft and womanly. And the dress she was wearing gave only a hint at being sexy, which made it sexy as fuck. She was covered, leaving everything to the imagination, and since I'd seen and tasted every inch, I didn't have to imagine—which, again, made the dress sexier.

"Earth to Trey," Liberty called.

"Sorry, what?"

"It's awesome being the smartest in the family," she quipped.

"Still not tracking."

"You see, that day when I spoke to you, you told me that your whole life you've attracted the wrong type of women. Then you told me that you wanted a woman who had something in her other than shallow intentions. You also said you didn't like blondes or aggressive women. And I thought to myself, I know the perfect woman for Trey. She's got black hair, green eyes, she is sweet and shy, and doesn't have a shallow bone in her body. I knew I was right the first time you saw her and your eyes lit up but I figured I had to wait it out until you got settled and sorted yourself. Then I go away, hoping when I got home I could start my matchmaking mission and bam, you've hooked my cousin deep and she's living with you. So again, is this a competition?"

I loved that she knew Addy was the woman for me and she trusted me enough to want to hook me up with her cousin. But I still wasn't tracking the competition thing.

"I'm not following. What's a competition?" I asked as Addy joined our huddle.

"Hey, baby." I tagged her hand and gave her a tug until she was plastered to my side.

"Hey, Liberty, welcome home. I'd give you a hug but I've been claimed," Addy said in mock annoyance.

"Indeed you have."

"Competition?" I prompted, and Liberty's eyes danced again, this time with mischief.

"Way I hear it, you moved Addy in before the first date. She's living with you. Everyone knows

Addy and Hadley always said they'd get pregnant at the same time so their babies would be the same age. Word also has it that Hadley has already started her pursuit to over-populate the world with Walkers. Drake says he's gonna be pissed if you marry Addy before we get married, so now I'm racing to get a wedding planned. And just so you know, you're uninvited if you get married before me. Quinn's still like sevenish months out. I figured I'd go right after her. That just leaves you and Addy."

"I suggest you plan your wedding sooner than sevenish months then," I declared, and heard Addy's swift inhale. "Because I'm not waiting that long."

Liberty's smile went back to wide and she sweetly chuckled.

"You don't want to wait that long?"

I turned to look at Addy and those stunning fucking eyes were shining.

"Nope."

"But Mom wants Dad to walk one of his girls down the aisle. Big church wedding. I wanted this." She motioned around the backyard. "But I'm the last one. Mom's last chance seeing what she's always dreamed she'd see."

Damn. He'd wanted the same as Addy. Marrying her in Tuesday's orchard in a wonderland of lights.

"If you wanna give that to your mom, then we'll give it to her. But, baby, I do not want to wait seven months."

"Okay."

There she was, his Addy.

He gave her what she wanted and she gave him easy.

"We should go up. Hadley was getting impatient and asked Mom to go find Dad."

"I'm gonna find Drake. See you up there."

I didn't hide my limp when I walked Addy up the slight incline. My leg was throbbing because she was back to being the devil. Jasper and I had started PT two days ago. Addy had taken pity on her father —just having surgery, there wasn't much he could do, but she was still making him do light stretches. Me? She had me twisting into yoga poses. Something I swore I'd never do, but Addy demanded.

"You okay?"

"No. I'm sore as fuck."

"I'd say I'm sorry but I'm not." I didn't have to look at my woman to know she was smiling. "I'll give you a rub down when we get home."

It had been a week since Belview died, and in that week, Addy had been back to her place once. And that was to pick up more clothes, including her yellow bikini. She'd worn it once for about two seconds, then I took it off her and tossed it over the side of the hot tub.

"Are you happy, Adalynn?"

"Very."

I had planned on waiting until later after the ceremony when I could get her alone, but Liberty had given me a golden opportunity and I wasn't going to waste it.

I stopped us just short of where Hadley and Brady were going to say their vows. I figured if I couldn't marry her here, I could give us this memory.

I pulled the ring out of my pocket and twisted Addy's left hand so her palm was down, and gave her a tug.

"You're always—"

"Marry me, Adalynn."

Wondrous shock gleamed in her eyes, and even though it wasn't a question she still answered.

"Yes."

One word that said hundreds more—all of them I loved.

I slid her ring on and bent forward, not bothering to ask her to kiss me even though I knew she'd sweetly say *okay*.

I took my time, giving her everything she gave

me. I broke the kiss when the clapping and cheering around us got louder, and when I pulled away, Addy was smiling huge and her family was circling us.

Yeah, I'd take this memory.

Five minutes later, a stoic Jasper walked Hadley to Brady. The man looked positively pained and full of joy. I didn't understand how Jasper could feel two extreme emotions at once but his face stated plain he did.

Ten minutes later, Hadley and Brady were pronounced Mr. and Mrs. Walker.

Brady kissed his wife and he did it for a long time. Long enough that everyone nearly busted a gut when Jasper grumbled.

I glanced over at my fiancée just as she was wiping away a tear. I bent and kissed the top of her head when Jasper and Emily joined us. Emily came straight to me and kissed me on the cheek. When she stepped aside, Jasper moved in and offered me his hand.

"I see you forwent asking for my permission."

Emily sucked in a breath and Addy moved closer, readying herself to take my back.

"Thought I had," I returned.

"When was that?"

"When I was standing in a cabin with a hole in my shoulder after saving your ass."

Jasper's head dipped, he shook it, then he roared with laughter.

Emily was still not over the incident, which started with her husband getting jumped while he was out for a run. Jumped being in a literal sense—Belview had jumped out of a bush and hit Jasper in the temple with the butt of his pistol. Then he'd carried Jasper to his car and drove him to the cabin. When Jasper had woken up, he was tied to a chair.

To say Jasper was unhappy Belview—who he'd called a pussy so many times during the police interview Ethan had started to blush—had gotten the jump on him was an understatement. But that was the truth. Belview was such a pussy, he knew the only way to subdue Jasper was to jump out of a bush. Otherwise, he'd lose.

"You're right," Jasper said through his humor. "Got two more of these things, Em, then we're done."

"These things being our daughters' weddings."

"Yep."

"You know, I've been married to your dad a long time," Emily said conversationally. "And all these years later, I still don't know why he tries."

"Tries what, Momma?" Addy asked in the same serious tone, but her body was shaking.

"To bullshit me." Emily looked up at Jasper. "You love *these things*."

"No, I don't," Jasper lied.

"Whatever."

Jasper winked and tagged his wife around the waist and walked off. Or I should say limped, and he wasn't hiding it because he couldn't.

"Are you happy, Trey?"

"Never been this happy in my whole life, baby."

"Good."

Then I asked her something I hoped her answer was yes to.

"Did you and Hadley always plan on being pregnant at the same time?"

"Yep. When we were kids, we always thought it would be cool since we're twins to have our kids be the same age and grow up together like we did."

"You still want that?"

"Yeah. Maybe we'll catch 'em on round two."

"How do you feel about trying to catch 'em on round one?"

Addy's head tilted in confusion.

"What?"

"Round one, baby. Hadley and Brady are starting now."

Her eyes rounded and she started to laugh. "My mom would have a heart attack if I was big-as-a-house pregnant getting married in a church."

"Then you got what? Three, four months to get us to your big church wedding before you're showing."

"Are you serious?"

"Yeah."

"You're sure. We haven't—"

"There's nothing I want more. You as my wife, our child in your belly, you happy."

"Okay."

Then she smiled and I totally got it, that shine she talked about. It was beautiful. It had the power to heal. She'd never asked, I'd never meant to give, but she still took everything that was broken inside of me and smoothed the sharp edges. Two people with all their flaws understanding the dark, together finding the light.

33

"Luke," Lauren happily chirped my name as soon as I walked into the reception area at Triple Canopy.

I felt my eyes narrow at her happy tone. Sure, Lauren was friendly, but not overly so, and usually, she saved her cheeriness for clients. Today, she was overly so toward me. I searched my recent memories for a reason for the pretty receptionist's joyfulness and I came up empty. Not that Lauren shared. She came to work, did her job—most of the time with a smile—then left. But she'd never been overly cheery to me. Logan, sometimes, but I figured it was to mostly get under his skin. Like pulling a tiger's tail to get a reaction. Lucky for her, Logan didn't bite—ever. He simply ignored her.

"Lauren," I returned. "What's up?"

"Your one o'clock is here," she informed me.

"My one o'clock?"

"Um. Yeah," she drawled slowly like I was an idiot. "Your one o'clock with Shiloh Kent."

"I don't—" *Shit, damn, and fuck.* "I forgot I was taking over Brady's classes while he's on his honeymoon."

"We can reschedule." A feminine voice came from behind me.

A very smooth, husky voice that sounded like sex. Not empty, superficial sex that left your balls drained but your soul cold. A sweet promise to warm you from the inside out. The sound of it rich and soothing.

I felt my body grow tight and I turned, ignoring Lauren's dirty look. Then I had to look down, *way* down—the woman was no taller than five-four. A pixie face, pale blue eyes that were so light they were pastel. The stark contrast to her sun-kissed skin made them look luminescent. Blonde hair that was so shiny it looked like she'd oiled it up then brushed it smooth.

Christ.

No, Shiloh Kent was not rescheduling.

"Has Miss Kent signed in?" I asked Lauren, and held my breath waiting for a correction on her marital status.

None came and Lauren was back to smiling. The receptionist would be on the phone with Quinn before I made it to the range.

"Yeah, all her paperwork is on file and current."

"You've been here before?" I asked Shiloh, and the sexiest fucking smile tipped her lips.

Lauren snorted and I felt like I was missing a joke.

"A few times," she confirmed.

"This is *Sunny* Kent," Lauren informed me.

"I'm sorry—"

"Don't be." She waved me off. "It was nice seeing you, Lauren."

"You, too, Sunny."

I glanced down at the rifle case and that sexy-as-all-hell voice floated through the air and slammed straight into my chest.

"Fair warning, if you offer to carry my rifle, I'm gonna kick you in the shin."

"Come again?"

"Again?" Sunny tipped her head to the side and a playful smirk lit her face. "Hadn't realized I'd come at all."

It took a moment to get it. But when it hit, for the first time in a long time I roared with laughter. When I was done, I gave her another once-over. She was cute, no doubt. But that wicked dry humor did it for me.

"All right, Sunny Kent. I won't offer to carry your rifle. Do you know where we're going?"

"Yes."

"Lead the way." I swept my hand toward the hall.

"You just wanna stare at my ass, don't you?"

Who the hell was this woman, and where had she been my whole life?

"Yep."

"Well, at least you're honest."

She gave a saucy wink and started down the hall. *Damn. I think I'm in love.*

Coming up next is Luke and Shiloh. Luke's struggling to overcome his physical injuries and Sunny...well, she's struggling with *everything*. As the only female member of her SWAT team, she's just one of the guys—and she loves that. But when a hostage negotiation goes wrong she becomes acutely aware she cannot just sweep it under the rug like her teammates. Two imperfect people, two lives torn apart by tragedy—together can they make one perfect love, or are they both ready to walk away from it all?

Find out in Imperfect, Triple Canopy book 3

Get your copy here.

BE A REBEL

Riley Edwards is a USA Today and WSJ bestselling author, wife, and military mom. Riley was born and raised in Los Angeles but now resides on the east coast with her fantastic husband and children.

Riley writes heart-stopping romance with sexy alpha heroes and even stronger heroines. Riley's favorite genres to write are romantic suspense and military romance.

Don't forget to sign up for Riley's newsletter and never miss another release, sale, or exclusive bonus material. https://www.subscribepage.com/RRsignup

Facebook Fan Group

www.rileyedwardsromance.com

facebook.com/Novelist.Riley.Edwards

twitter.com/rileyedwardsrom

instagram.com/rileyedwardsromance

bookbub.com/authors/riley-edwards

amazon.com/author/rileyedwards

The Gold Team

Brooks - Susan Stoker Universe

Thaddeus - Susan Stoker Universe

Kyle - Susan Stoker Universe

Maximus - Susan Stoker Universe

Declan - Susan Stoker Universe

The 707 Freedom Series

Free

Freeing Jasper

Finally Free

Freedom

The Next Generation (707 spinoff)

Saving Meadow

Chasing Honor

Finding Mercy

Claiming Tuesday

Adoring Delaney

Keeping Quinn

Taking Liberty

Triple Canopy

Damaged

Flawed

Imperfect

The Collective

Unbroken

Trust

Standalone

Romancing Rayne - Susan Stoker Universe

ACKNOWLEDGMENTS

To all of you – the readers: Thank you for picking up this book and giving me a few hours of your time. Whether this is the first book of mine you've read or you've been with me from the beginning, thank you for your support. It is because of you I have the coolest job in the world.

Printed in Great Britain
by Amazon